ALMOST

ALMOST

ELIZABETH
BENEDICT

HOUGHTON MIFFLIN COMPANY
BOSTON • NEW YORK
2001

For information about permission to reproduce selections from
this book, write to Permissions, Houghton Mifflin Company,
215 Park Avenue South, New York, New York 10003.

Visit our Web site: www.houghtonmifflinbooks.com.

Library of Congress Cataloging-in-Publication Data
Benedict, Elizabeth.
Almost / Elizabeth Benedict.
p.   cm.
ISBN 0-618-14332-7
1. Widows — Fiction. 2. Islands — Fiction.
3. Massachusetts — Fiction. 4. Runaway wives — Fiction.
5. Childlessness — Fiction. I. Title.
PS3552E5396 A79 2001
813'.54—dc21   2001024528

Printed in the United States of America

Book design by Robert Overholtzer

QUM 10 9 8 7 6 5 4 3 2 1

Grateful acknowledgment is made to *Tin House,*
where part of this book first appeared.

For our friends and families,
then and now

Although there was in my life a man to whom I bore roughly the same relationship that Sophy bears to Will, and although I have aimed for an autobiographical tone, this is a work of fiction. Swansea Island exists only in my imagination and is populated by characters of my own invention. The details of Will's professional, personal, and family life are fiction and should in no way be read as posthumous truths.

The names of well-known individuals and those un-named in their orbits are used fictitiously throughout, and any overlapping situations are purely coincidental.

I am indebted to the many friends and colleagues who made available the quiet houses where most of this book was written.

THE CITY

Should we have stayed home and thought of here?

— Elizabeth Bishop,
"Questions of Travel"

I

A High Note

I HAVE this boyfriend who comes to visit me — it's mostly a sex thing. Unless I visit him, in which case it's mostly a babysitting thing. I'm not sure which turns me on more. You don't think of British Jews, if you happen to know any — and I didn't until Daniel Jacobs — as world-class lovers, but he must be an exception, or it could be the antidepressants he takes, which not only keep the blues at bay, but orgasms too. In Daniel's case, for, oh, forty-five minutes, give or take a few. My friend Henderson calls him the Bionic Man.

That's how I'd have begun this story if I'd sat down to write it two months ago, instead of now. I'd have put it firmly in the present tense, the intense present, a time that felt electric to me and that I know I don't want to part with yet. Two months ago, the story would have been all about the sweet madness and the math. And why not? When the numbers are in this range, you feel some obligation to history to keep a record. Remember that old Irving Wallace novel *The Seven Minutes*, about what goes through this woman's mind in the seven minutes of intercourse? Not one reviewer griped, Seven? That's it? Not one of them said, Irving, you sure this isn't autobiography?

Without my telling him, the doorman knows not to buzz me if packages, even groceries, arrive after he's seen dashing Daniel come upstairs. Phone messages on my machine pile up as thickly as pink While You Were Out slips impaled on an upright skewer. I always turn off the ringer on the phone and mute the voices on the machine, incoming and outgoing, so that we're not distracted. Or bombarded. My almost-ex sometimes calls, in tears, to say he wants me back, and my editor, practically in tears, to remind me that my novel based on the life of Lili Boulanger is budgeted for this year and I am eleven months late. And my other editor, a guy I call the Eighth Deadly Sin, who tries to tempt me to ghost another celebrity autobiography. He is a twenty-seven-year-old manic depressive with his own imprint who hired me to write the life story of a daytime TV personality, which I finished in three months and is about to be published without my name on it, thank God.

As book-writing goes, other people's autobiographies are child's play. You're handed the central character, the dramatic highs and lows, the bittersweet, inspirational ending, a deadline that leaves no room for writer's block, and money, real money. Enough to leave my husband, Will O'Rourke, and dog Henry, move back to New York, and live for a while in this studio-with-alcove furnished sublet in Greenwich Village with two walk-in closets, galley kitchen, central air, and a look of Pier One exoticism on the cheap. An abundance of wicker, batik, cotton throw rugs, and bayberry-scented candles that I often light when Daniel leaves.

The other people I don't want disturbing us are my mother, whose memory is on the fritz, and who sometimes calls to ask how old I was when my father left, and my best gay friend, Henderson, whose messages I love, except when they're broadcast into the boudoir, as this one was on an overcast afternoon: "Sophy, I trust you're not picking up the phone because you and Daniel are having one of those marathon sessions. Hi, lovebirds. Would you believe I lost the name of that guy who does interventions again? My birth father was absolutely blotto last night at *Così fan tutte,* and my wicked stepmother and I have decided it's time to send in the Eighty-second Airborne. I hope this is a quickie, because I really need to talk to you before the sun goes down."

Since I moved back to the city in March, my life often feels surreal and overloaded, like an electrical extension cord with too many attachments, on the verge of blowing a fuse. Henderson claims I'm suffering from what Jack Kerouac called "the great mad joy you feel on returning to New York City," though I think it's the generic great mad joy of jettisoning a tired old life for a shiny new one. Some days I'm Gene Kelly doing his waterlogged soft-shoe and singin' in the rain, happy again. On more difficult days, I'm Dorothy, wide-eyed at the phantasm of Oz but terrified I'll never find my way home, or never have another home to find my way to. Being able to focus completely on Daniel for several hours at a stretch keeps me from going off the deep end. Or maybe — maybe Daniel *is* the deep end, and we are a couple of ordinary junkies who don't even know we have a problem. You forget, being married, that sex can take up so many hours of the day.

A quickie in Daniel's book is half an hour, and never mind foreplay, never mind the nerves on the back of my neck, the world of whispering and slowness. Daniel's cut-to-the-chase is an acquired taste, I know, but now that I've got it, I'm not sure I want to go back to the evolved, sensitive-guy approach. When I told my best woman friend, Annabelle, that on my birthday Daniel and I were at it for forty-three minutes —

according to the digital clock on my microwave, which I can see in certain positions from the bed across the room — Annabelle said, "That's a very good birthday present, Sophy." Afterward he gave me another present, a framed gelatin print of a photo of my beautiful, sad-eyed Lili Boulanger he had an art dealer colleague in Paris track down, wrapped in wrinkled Pocahontas gift paper. Then we staggered to his house at the end of Waverly Street, stopping at Balducci's and Carvel to pick up dinner for his four Vietnamese orphans, Tran, Van, Vicki, and Cam, two boys and two girls.

Of course they're not really orphans, because Daniel is their legal father, but so far they have lost two mothers apiece, the Vietnamese women who bore them and Daniel's wife, Blair, who is, as it says on all those old tombstones, Not Dead Only Sleeping, in a nursing home on the North Fork of Long Island, with a spot-on view of a meadow, a salt marsh, and the daily sunrise, none of which she is ever likely to lay eyes on again.

Daniel explained all of this to me over coffee, days after I had moved back to the city and we met at the gay-lesbian-all-welcome AA meeting in the gay-lesbian-all-welcome neighborhood where we live. But by all welcome, they don't only mean boring straight people like Daniel and me; they mean cross-dressers, transsexuals, and a surprising number of people who haven't made up their minds. He and I ended up there separately and by accident, thinking it was nondenominational, but we stayed because, story for story, it's the best theater in New York, a darkly inspirational, Frank Capra-in-drag movie that could be called *It's a Wonderful Life One Day at a Time*. It's also a place where a man telling his life story can say, "During that period, which went on for five years, I was so busy drinking — I mean, honey, I was taking Ecstasy as a *mood stabilizer* — that I forgot to meet men and have sex, which brings us to Fire Island," and seventy-five people will howl with sympathetic laughter.

Daniel and I innocently sat next to each other, and he invited me out after for coffee at Dean & DeLuca on Eleventh Street. I was still thinking about the speaker at the meeting whose name was Robert S., and who wore a platinum pageboy wig and a chartreuse DKNY miniskirt and said to us, "Girls" — though I was the only one in the room — "I am waiting for God to work her magic," and I suppose I was waiting myself. That's what made me ask Daniel, at the start of our first date — as I began to take inventory of all the ways he appeared different from my gray-haired, salty-looking husband — where he stood on God.

"Off to the side," he answered, "quite a way. But here I am, knee-deep in drunks who talk about the Almighty as if he lives next door. It's a lot for an Englishman to sign up for. We have a long tradition of drinking ourselves to death quietly and all alone. Then again, this wasn't my idea." Daniel had the look of a youthful Tom Wolfe, long-limbed, clean-shaven, wearing a suit I didn't know then was an Armani; and there was not a strand of gray in his fine brown hair. He might have been my age, mid-forties, or a few years younger.

"Whose idea was it?"

"My physician advised me three years ago that I'd die in short order if I didn't quit. And what about you? Where do you stand on God?"

I said that for the first ten years I went to meetings, I had a difficult time overcoming my godless Unitarian upbringing, but in the last six months, I found myself leaning in another direction, dispensing with some of my skepticism. I wasn't a practicing Unitarian any longer, I told him; I considered myself lapsed. Trying that out for the first time, the "lapsed." Daniel laughed out loud. But I wanted to play it for laughs; I was flirting like crazy. I hadn't slept with anyone but my husband for the ten years of our marriage, plus the two years before, and I wasn't leaving anything to chance.

"And what's at the core of a lapsed Unitarian's belief system?" he asked.

"Nothing to speak of, so there's room for reconsideration, but not much motivation for it. What about you?"

"I'm Jewish," he said, "but in the English style, sort of half a Jew, as if it were only one of your parents, and you're not certain whether to take it or leave it."

"What's the other half, in your case?"

"Pure capitalist. I come from a long line of merchants. Fur and microchips. My great-grandfather was furrier to the czar. My father was the last furrier in London to move away from the East End when the Bangladeshis moved in. He went to Golders Green in 1962 and sold dead animals until the PETA people threw a can of fuchsia paint on my mother's full-length sable, which coincided roughly with the discovery of the microchip. He and my older brothers are computer consultants to the Queen. They have the lucrative gift of being able to endure long hours of bowing and scraping. I'm the youngest of four sons and, some say, the family rebel. Instead of software, I peddle paintings."

In AA, of course, you are not supposed to tell anyone your last name, but Daniel blithely told me his. I knew it from going to galleries during all the years I lived in New York and reading art reviews in the *Times* during all the years I didn't.

A cappuccino or two later, we were swapping infertility stories like girlfriends, by way of explaining how he ended up with four imports and I ended up with no offspring at all, except this gryphon-like dog Henry, whom I had left with my husband until I got settled. I didn't tell Daniel that night that Henry had been Will's present to me when I quit trying to get pregnant. "I still carry around a picture of him, ugly as he is."

"Your husband?" Daniel said, visibly startled.

"The dog."

And I didn't tell Daniel about the immense sadness that had made me stop trying to have a baby. It was our first date, after all, and I wanted him to think my past was safely behind me, buried like nuclear waste, in airtight containers, even though I'd walked out on it only a handful of days earlier. Instead, I entertained Daniel with stories of my test-tube encounters with Green-Blue, the code name for the nuclear physicist at the California genius sperm bank I had wanted to be the father of my child, after it became clear that Will's sperm motility wasn't what it had been when he'd fathered my two grown, soon-to-be-ex stepdaughters.

"Green-Blue is six-one, IQ of one fifty-six, and the father, as of two years ago, of thirty-one children of lesbian mothers and straight single women scattered across the fault lines of Southern California. They Fed Exed me the stuff in tanks of liquid nitrogen. But I ovulate funny. It was like waiting for three cherries to come up on a slot machine. And my husband was convinced that the only sperm donor in the joint was the skaggy-looking guy who ran the business and called me at seven in the morning — mind you, that's four A.M. in California — to say, 'Sophy, I have to know, is your temperature going up or down?'"

Daniel told me that he and Blair had done the temperature business, test tubes, and Pergonal injections. She had even made an appointment with a faith healer named Falling Rain Drop, who insisted they participate in a fertility dance in

Washington Square Park every day at dawn for a week. Daniel refused.

The years of trying piled up, and Blair, pushing forty-three, grew impatient and fearful. In one fell swoop, they adopted three siblings, two boys and a girl, ages approximately six, four, and two, who had been living in an orphanage in Hoa Binh for six months, and a fourth child, Vicki, whose sad face in a photograph Blair could not resist. They nearly emptied out the orphanage and filled every room in the narrow, turn-of-the-century brownstone Blair had inherited from her stockbroker father.

Adopting all those children, you could say she was Mia Farrow minus Woody, and now, poor lamb, poor Blair, she is Sunny von Bulow minus the millions. Not that they are destitute; Daniel's two art galleries are doing record business, despite his long afternoon absences. He was a willing partner in the international quest for children, and he is a devoted father, though he is often sleep-deprived and frequently flummoxed, as when his five-year-old said to him, "If you don't buy me a Beanie Baby, I'll say the F word all the time, starting right now."

He wants me to think and seems to believe himself — and it may be the truth — that his essential nature is now subsumed by the condition of being overwhelmed. "I used to have a personality," he will say, "and a life I rather liked. Now I run an orphanage on a street where I am the only heterosexual man for ten blocks in every blinking direction."

On the other hand, I'm not sure what that personality was, the one he claims to have had. He can predict whether a client will prefer a Miró etching to an obscure Delvaux oil painting, and he is consulted by museums and foreign governments to detect forgeries, but in matters of his heart, nuance is a rare commodity. When I asked him how his marriage had changed over the years, all he said was, "Once the children arrived, we quit having sex on Saturday afternoons."

My friends are divided over the nature and severity of Daniel's affliction. Those who have spent time in England insist that his passport is his destiny, and his answer to my question about his marriage passes in that population for soul-searching. Other friends ascribe his limitations to gender. "He sounds just like a man," Annabelle said, "but worse." It may be most accurate on any continent to say that he is what Winston Churchill said about Russia: a riddle wrapped in a mystery inside an enigma.

But there is something else you should know about Daniel: I think he is still in love with Blair. She has this embalmed, waxy, forever-thirty-nine, Dick Clark quality. Perfect, silent, stricken, enveloped in the aura of her New York Stock Exchange pedigree and a life of excruciatingly good deeds. She founded and ran a literacy-and-reading center for inner city families and was always getting plaques and certificates from the mayor, the governor, Channel 7, the *Amsterdam News, El Diario,* and the Helen Keller Foundation. Daniel sells modern masters, wears Armani underwear, and a wristwatch as thin as a quarter, but his living room walls are now crammed with three-dollar pressed-wood plaques and ersatz diplomas from local TV news anchors who think Blair should have shared the Nobel Peace Prize with Nelson Mandela.

Poor thing was hit by a UPS truck the year before while bicycling on Hilton Head Island, where she was attending her only sister's wedding. Can Daniel marry again without divorcing his brain-dead wife? The subject has not come up between us. We are efficient communicators in the sack and above-

average conversationalists on terra firma, but on the question
of our future — I mean anything beyond tomorrow — we are
neophyte speakers of English, permanently stalled in the present tense.

Blair is a tough act to follow, though I give it all I've got.
In addition to baking Christmas cookies with Daniel's children in June, I frequently do a full-dress imitation of Dorothy
in *The Wizard of Oz*, which they have seen on video twenty-
five or thirty times. I braid my hair and wear a polka-dot pin-
afore and a pair of glittery red shoes I found in a thrift store;
and I rigged up a little stuffed dog, attached to a real leather
leash, which I drag up the stairs of their brownstone and then
sling over my shoulder, squealing, "Toto! Toto! I don't think
we're in Kansas anymore!"

One night I made the mistake of imitating their father for
them. I put on one of his silk suits over my own clothes and
carted four metal lunchboxes and a handful of naked Barbie
dolls into the bedroom where they waited for me, perched on
the edge of Vicki's bed — Vicki, the oldest, Vicki, who keeps
a shelf of books about children who have no parents. This
child who first heard English spoken three years ago has read
*The Secret Garden, Anne of Green Gables, Peter Pan, Pippi Long-
stocking*, and, in a category of loss entirely its own, *The Diary
of Anne Frank.*

That night I studied each of their faces and said in the
lowest growl I could summon and my best English accent,
"What's all this blinking mess in here?" I pretended to trip and
sent the lunchboxes and Barbies flying. They landed hard and
clattered across the bare wood floor. From downstairs, Daniel
hollered, "What's all that blinking noise up there?" and we
collapsed with laughter, and I was still laughing when Tran
said to me, "Now do Mommy."

"But I don't know Mommy."

"You don't know Dorothy, either," Vicki said. I knew only that I was bound to fail in this, but four pair of beautiful, almond-shaped black eyes were on me, and I could not deprive them of another mother, even of the flimsy imposter they knew to expect.

I slipped out of Daniel's clothes and tried to organize a game of Chinese checkers with them, tried to be a funny, light-hearted, old-fashioned, TV kind of Mom, before TV moms were cops and cardiologists, but my heart wasn't in it, or maybe I mean that I didn't want them to see how much it *was* in it, so I held back, and the whole thing fell flat. "Who wants peanut butter?" I said lamely. "Who wants to take a Tarzan bubble bath? Who wants an enormous plate of asparagus for dessert?" But none of them laughed, and I was relieved when Van said, "Do Dorothy again."

At breakfast they have said to me, "Do our dad, please."

"The school bus is outside."

"Then do Toto."

"Honey, let Sophy finish her cereal."

"One little time, and we'll never ask you again."

"I will," said Cam, the youngest, always out of synch with the consensus.

"Don't get dressed up," Tran said. "Just talk funny and throw the Barbies."

Early on, when Daniel and I were in bed and it was dark and our skin was as slippery as the inside of an oyster, he whispered, "Do me."

"What?"

"Do me."

"Baby, I am doing you."

"Imitate me. The way you did today at lunch."

"Now?"

"Now."

"You pervert."

"Don't stop moving."

"You narcissist."

"I'm guilty."

"You're out of your blinking mind."

"Do me."

"'I have a little, uh, Chagall etching in the vault, uh, you might find enchanting. Once in the collection of His Majesty the Shah of Iran. Or was it the Duke of, uh, Windsor? Two-point-five.'"

"His etchings never sold for that much."

"'For you, then, two-point-three.'"

"I never bargain. Or mix up monarchs."

"You are out of your mind, Daniel."

"I know."

"I know you know."

The truth was we both were. Fourteen days before, in a howling March nor'easter, on an island called Swansea, off the coast of Massachusetts — a place as desolate as the Hebrides that time of year — I had left my husband and a hideous hybrid hound dog with pointy ears. He was not only my consolation prize for not having a baby, but a sign from God, I'm sure, that had I succeeded, the poor creature would have been Rosemary's Baby. I had driven away from a ten-year marriage with what I could fit in a rented Toyota and a promise I did not think I would keep: to reconsider my decision when I got to New York.

So much has happened since then. For one thing, the dog is gone. For another, I've just begun to write the story of my own life, at a desk in the house on Swansea that I walked out of in March, and I'm on a firm deadline. The story starts on a high note: a woman leaves her husband in search of happiness and ends up on a big-city roller-coaster ride that feels for moments at a time like sheer bliss, an urban fairy tale come true. Then, out of nowhere, her new life takes a plunge, then another, and a few dips, and before long she feels like Job. But there isn't much of a story to tell unless a few things go wrong, is there?

I'm not going to trouble you with the story of my entire life since before my birth, like David Copperfield. I think it's best to stick to what's happened lately, starting two months ago, the morning of June twenty-second, when I was still in New York, still caught up, for the next few hours, in the great, mad joy of just being there, the morning of the day the police called.

2

I'd Rather Eat Glass

THE DAY BEGAN with a proposal from my neighbor Jesús as I opened my front door to pick up the *Times* from the welcome mat that had come with the sublet. My eyes veered from the lead story to another I'd been following since the beginning, from the heat wave that had engulfed the city to my lawyer friend Evan Lambert's defense of another foreign nanny accused of killing another baby: a nineteen-year-old German girl who had allegedly shaken an infant to death in the Back Bay section of Boston. So the moniker the Back Bay Baby had entered the language. On the bottom of the front page was a story about the sleepiest presidential campaign in recent memory, festooned with the red, white, and blue banner that attempted to generate a spark of enthusiasm for ELECTION 2000. I started to back into my apartment when I heard a voice.

"Are you divorced yet?" It was Jesús, poking his head into the corridor as I skimmed Evan's strategy for defending the nanny.

"I signed the separation agreement a few days ago and sent it to my lawyer."

"Congratulations," Jesús said.

"That's one way of looking at it." He had seen me move in three months before and asked a few nosy questions, which I thought at the time would be neighborly for me to answer, not having lived in New York for the past four years, and welcoming the openness. It looked as if Evan's client was going to plead insanity, which might lead Congress to place more restrictions on all nanny visas.

"What's not to celebrate? You're free like a bird. When the divorce comes through, I know someone who wants to marry you."

I looked at him over the rim of the half-glasses I'd recently begun to need for reading. "Who might that be?" I wasn't aware we knew a soul in common, except the building's super, and he seemed an unlikely candidate.

"My Jaime."

"Your who?"

"My boyfriend. From Ecuador. He needs a green card." He went on to explain that Jaime sweeps hair from the floor at Bumble & Bumble, and that they'd pay me five thousand dollars. When I wrinkled my face, thinking not of the sum, which I could use, but of Daniel, whom I would marry tomorrow if we weren't both married to other people, Jesús said, "All right, seventy-five hundred and a perm."

"Warm, you're getting warm," I said, though of course I didn't mean it, and what I meant about marrying Daniel was not that I thought multiple orgasms could be the basis for a lifelong partnership, because even with him and his antidepressants, they don't last much longer than a bowl of chocolate mousse. What I meant was that his children were badly in need of a mother. The times I felt this most urgently, when the boys buttoned their shirts wrong and the girls forgot to put on underwear and matching socks, I often toyed with

writing a note to them from their mother — *Sugar plums,
Dumplings, my four precious Vietnamese spring rolls: When we
rescued you from the orphanage in your sad and beautiful country, this is not how I imagined the story would end* — but I did
not want to frighten them, or myself, with the depth of my
longing or the eerie projection of their mother's. Unlikely
doppelgangers, Blair and I, yearning to take proper care of
the same four orphans, if only we could.

"I'll tell Jaime you're interested," Jesús said. "By the way, I
saw your movie on video the other night. I didn't think it
would have such a happy ending. For such a sad story."

"They changed the ending of the book when they turned it
into a movie."

"What do you care, right? You must've made a mint."

"A very small mint, fifteen years ago."

"You still in touch with Whoopi?"

"No."

"So all you gotta do is write another."

"Yup, that's all. There goes my phone." It was the Eighth
Deadly calling to ask if I'd consider ghosting another autobiography. "I've got my deadline on Lili." Today was the day I'd
determined to get back to the manuscript, now that my separation papers were gone. "Actually, I've missed my deadline,
but I intend to —"

"On who?"

"Lili Boulanger."

"Is that your French publisher?"

Sometimes I thought the Eighth Deadly played the rube
only to get a rise out of me; other times I was convinced "En-
tertainment Tonight" was his principal frame of reference.
And I knew I'd explained all of this to him before. "She was
Nadia Boulanger's little sister, the first woman to win the Prix

de Rome for composing, in 1913. She died five years later, at twenty-four, and Nadia dedicated her life as a music teacher to Lili's memory. My novel is about what would have happened if Lili had lived."

"Doesn't sound right for our list."

"I didn't think so. Whose autobiography do you want me to write this time?"

"Can't tell you."

"A Republican senator with AIDS?"

"That was in our spring catalog."

"Chelsea Clinton's jilted boyfriend?"

"Can you get to him?"

"Soon-Yi?"

"No such luck."

"Bruce Springsteen's plumber? Rudy Giuliani's priest?"

"I'm not asking you to sign a contract, Sophy. I'm asking if I can put your name on a list of writers who are available." I turned to the beautiful photograph of Lili that Daniel had given me and that hangs over my desk. Lovely Lili, with her big brown, heartbreak eyes; Lili, who would disappear at the age of twenty-four, unless I finished my novel and breathed decades of new life into her. But here I was, being offered the possibility of money, and I knew mine would run out in five or six months. I couldn't afford to say no so blithely to the Eighth Deadly. And ghosting happens to be something I'm good at. A kind of ventriloquism, a species of drag, out-and-out mimicry. But how low would I sink, and how often? Lili spoke to me from her place on the wall: *Are you going to finish your novel about me, or are you going to take the easy way out again? Do you have your sights set on winning the Prix de Rome, as I did, or will you end up with your mongrel dog doing stupid pet tricks on David Letterman?*

"Sure, put my name on the list," I said, though I hoped he wouldn't call for several months, long enough for me to tangle with Lili, to see how much farther we could take our duet.

When the phone rang the instant I had replaced the receiver, I hoped it was Will. I had called him the day before and left a message on his machine, the third or fourth, about the thousand dollars he owed me, reimbursements from our health insurance that he did not want to give me. But it was Daniel; he'd be over later, and then we would go to his house for dinner to celebrate the third anniversary of the children's arrival from Vietnam. He had ordered a cake in the shape of an airplane from Jon Vie. How had my day been so far? "Uneventful," I lied, "so far." I wasn't ready to re-enact my collision with the Eighth Deadly, and mentioning the marriage proposal was out of the question. He was so skittish about matters of the heart, at least where our hearts might overlap, that I didn't know whether he'd feel relieved or threatened to learn I might soon be unavailable. "I'm about to lavish my complete attention on Lili. What time will I see you?"

"The usual."

Our *cinq à sept* usually began at four, though he frequently jumped the gun, which was fine with me. The truth was that since I'd left Will, it was difficult for me to be alone. The truth was I sometimes woke up at three in the morning with my jaw clenched and the rest of me in a panic, my brain firing flares of self-doubt in the direction of Swansea. I knew Will would have me back. But even in the midst of the panic, that never felt like the direction I should be moving; it only felt familiar and safe.

I opened the top right-hand drawer of my desk and retrieved what there was of Lili. One hundred and thirty-seven typed pages, which ended in the middle of a long sentence I had not known how to finish for the last six months — about Lili's first visit to Las Vegas, where she saw Frank Sinatra at the Sands.

Voices began to rise, like the rumble of distant thunder, and it took five or six seconds to recognize whose they were. And then the rhythm of the whole thing intensified, as if the Luftwaffe's strafing had just begun. Hearty shouting gave way to a familiar high-pitched, self-pitying shriek from the fashion model who lives on the other side of me with her on-again, off-again boyfriend. About the same time last week, she delivered a statement at a pitch so high and desperate, I suspected she was being leeched. "All I want is a relationship," she had wailed, at an operatic pace that must have taken thirty or forty seconds to deliver.

Her boyfriend's reply was so direct and sensible — though he was shouting at the top of his lungs — that I was tempted to applaud. "I'd rather eat glass than have a relationship with you."

It sounded as if they were heading toward some of those themes again today.

I poured another cup of coffee and tried to imagine what someone living next door to Will and me would have heard when we were at our worst. Nothing. Plenty of nothing. Silence, though not the silence of the monastery, not the silence Thomas Merton said can make you sense that God is right there, not only with you but in you. Not the silence of what Merton called "the quiet heart." There are no quiet hearts in states of stifled rage, in angry defeat or the black dog of depression.

I gazed at Lili in my lap and heard another species of silence: the work that no longer speaks to you. It feels like illness, like ague. I laid the manuscript aside and did something

I hadn't done since before I left my husband: put on the CD of Lili's choral music and turned up the volume to drown out the lovers' quarrel next door. I skimmed the liner notes on Lili's life and tried to revive my obsession for this woman, who had died in 1918, but who, in my novel, went on to live a long, fabulous life. Not so long ago every carat of her being had moved and inspired me: her precocious talent, her lifelong illness, her valiant, premature, unkvetchy death. Though her sister Nadia is, to this day, exalted in letters, memoirs, and musical homages, Lili is barely remembered, except by a few oddballs and cultists to whom she is angelic. I had an idea to rescue her — and myself too — from obscurity. And I wanted to take a few liberties with her memory.

In my nervy invention of a life she might have lived, had she lived, she breaks with her sister and flees to America with the real-life avant-garde composer George Antheil. When he leaves her for a chorus girl, she heads for Hollywood to write movie scores for Sam Goldwyn. To sleep with John Barrymore. To eat burgers on the Fourth of July with Thomas Mann. Christopher Isherwood. David Hockney. Steven Spielberg. Her efforts to make peace with her sister are always rebuffed.

I wanted to ransack the archives. To dynamite our ideas of worship and devotion.

You have to understand: my marriage was unraveling when I conceived of the book. I was desperate to rewrite a real woman's life, not knowing until six months into it that I really wanted to rewrite my own. Where did that leave Lili now? Was my imagination large enough to hold her only as long as she could stand in for my own stifled yearnings?

Within seconds of that thought, two things occurred that startled me, the first more profoundly than the second. I heard her music with more insight and clarity than I ever had and found it truly awful — thin, screechy, derivative. Second, the doorbell rang.

"Who is it?" I called out and crossed the room. Jesús again, making me an offer I couldn't refuse? Daniel, nearly a day early?

"It's me, darling." That disqualified Daniel. I mean the "darling." The only term of endearment in his adult-to-adult vocabulary — uttered to me about once every six weeks — was Ducks. "It's Henderson."

I swung open the door and saw not Henderson's face but an immense basket of flowers, in which two birds of paradise poked up higher than the roses and delphiniums.

"The doorman didn't announce you. Did you bribe him?"

I was so used to his drop-in calls before memorial services that I was relieved to see he was wearing khaki shorts and a shiny red tank top that said Goldman Sachs Softball Team, which I knew to be a hand-me-down from the boyfriend of a boyfriend. Sweat cascaded down his neck despite the air-conditioning. "My sunglasses are melting," he announced, "and I saw a piece on the AP wire yesterday that said sunscreen doesn't work when the ozone layer looks like your mother's fishnet stockings. Have you been watching the Weather Channel?" He deposited the flower basket on my kitchen counter and tore off a long sheet of paper towel to wick the moisture that coated his exposed skin. He was a bit sunburned, a bit overweight, almost completely bald, an aging gay man with an acquired demeanor of unflappability that comes from having lost forty or fifty of his best friends and several layers of acquaintances. He and I had also met during my first week in New York, at the gay-lesbian-all-welcome AA meeting, and I could tell right away that Henderson had what

they call in that circle "a lot of serenity." He, too, was much in
the market for new friends.

"I haven't bought my TV yet," I said. "What's the forecast?"

"Misery everywhere but Swansea Island, where it's only sev-
enty-eight degrees. You obviously didn't factor global warm-
ing into your decision to get divorced. Happy birthday, dear.
I'm sorry I'm so late."

"Just a week. I thought you were still in Provincetown.
These are beautiful, H., but you know you didn't have to."

"We all need flowers at forty-four, Sophy. It's the only thing
we actually *require* this late in life. I've got to run home and
pack for the Swiss fat farm, but I brought you a disk of
my memoir, in case my building goes up in flames. I've got
two chapters left, and if I weren't meeting Bianca at the fat
farm, I'd bail. Not that I need to pack much to spend ten days
drinking water on the side of a mountain. Where will you put
the disk for safekeeping?"

The diskette was in a clear plastic bag, sandwich size, and I
could see he'd written on the label MY FAVORITE THINGS, the
title of his memoir and of his down-at-the-heels cable TV talk
show. He aspired to be a gay Charlie Rose and hoped the
memoir, to be published next year, would give him the boost
he needed to get a better TV station, a better time slot.

"My favorite place," I said. "Inside a plastic container in the
fridge, in case *my* building goes up in flames." Henderson always began his show with a witty monologue about his favorite things, which led to his introduction of his guest for that
day. "Favorite Bach cantata? One hundred and five. Favorite
wife of Pablo Picasso? Françoise Gilot. Favorite sexually ex-
plicit classic poem? Do you have to ask? Favorite Bible story
for atheists? Abraham and Isaac. Favorite castrato? Farinelli.
Favorite suicide note? Virginia Woolf's, natch. Favorite celeb-

rity homemaker? *Please*. Welcome to the show, Martha. It's great to see you again."

"Do you have time for a cup of coffee?"

"A short one," Henderson said, "but don't make a fresh pot; give me what's left over with a splash of skim milk. How's Lili?"

"I think she's having a midlife crisis. Or maybe it's menopause."

"And how are you?"

"Somewhat the same." I stuck a mug of coffee in the microwave and told Henderson I'd Fed Exed my separation agreement to my lawyer the day before yesterday.

"How do you feel about it?"

"Sad. And Will's pissed off at me. He owes me a thousand dollars for medical reimbursements and won't send the money. Won't even answer my phone calls. I've left three or four messages."

"Still seeing the Bionic Man? Has he topped forty-three minutes yet?"

"I don't clock it every time. I've got two percent."

"Of his attention? That seems awfully low, even for a straight man in New York."

"Milk for the coffee. I've probably got ten percent of his attention. Guess what? I received a marriage proposal today."

"Not from him, I take it."

"A gay illegal alien."

"It could be worse. Though I'm not sure how."

There was the sudden blast of a bell — the doorman's intercom buzzer, which rings like an old-fashioned telephone but three times as loud.

"Yes, what is it?" I shouted into the spray of holes in the wall by the intercom.

"Mr. Jacobs on the way up."

"Oh, Jesus," I muttered and turned to Henderson, who took what I could see was a final sip of coffee, set the mug down, and began moving sideways, crablike, to the front door.

"Aren't you lucky, my dear."

"He's five hours early."

"Absence is an incredible aphrodisiac."

"He's never this early. Sometimes fifteen minutes. Half an hour."

"You underestimate your charms, Sophy. Take a good look at me, because next time you see me, I'll look the way I did on my wedding day. I'll send you a postcard from the fat farm, if I have the energy to lift a pencil. You know that's why monks fast, don't you? Because it makes you so exhausted, you can't even think about fucking. All you want is food."

"Thomas Merton never said a word about that."

"Never wrote a word, but I'm certain he said plenty, in between the vows of silence. He was too weak to write about it."

There was the faintest knock at my door. Of course. Daniel felt sheepish appearing this way, his libido raging, his libido some bucking bronco he could not control — no fasting monk, he! If I'd been alone, I might have found it more winning to be dropped in on, but with an audience, even one as open-minded as Henderson, I was embarrassed to seem so available. Did he think I was there to service him at any hour of the day? And wasn't I? I swung open the big metal door, expecting to see him in his summer suit with a lascivious half-smile, the *Times* folded under his arm, something to read in the cab coming over here, his thoughts drifting lazily between Al Gore and me, me and my absurd willingness, the almost-divorced maid of constant hunger.

But it was nothing of the sort.

It was his daughter Vicki at my door. Not Mr. Jacobs, as I'd heard on the intercom, but Miss, age ten, approximately.

"What happened?" I said. "What's wrong?" All I could imagine was that she'd come to tell me the others had perished at sea.

"Nothing, Sophy."

"Are you alone?"

"Sure." She looked like an assortment of rich sorbets — wearing peach-colored shorts and a lavender T-shirt I had seen in the Gap Kid window on Broadway, and clutching a lime-green knapsack. I stepped aside to let her in and saw her look up suspiciously at Henderson. She was small for ten, but also for nine or eleven — none of the children had birth certificates; all their ages were ball park — and had to look up a long way. When I introduced them, she said, "Is that your first name or last?"

"My last, but people started using it as my first when I was twenty-one."

"How old are you now?"

"Fifty-three."

"Do you have any kids?"

"As a matter of fact, I do. A son named Philip."

"How old is he?"

"He's thirty-one. He has a son too. His son's almost five." He wasn't camping it up when he said he was going to look as he had on his wedding day. He'd married right out of college — missing Vietnam because of a high draft number — and was so determined to prove his heterosexuality, he convinced his wife to have a child right away. When the inevitable came, she expressed her rage and revenge by taking their son to her parents' Texas home to be raised among rednecks. Though his son's name is Philip, Henderson usually refers to him as Dwight D., as in Eisenhower, because he is military-minded and homophobic. Henderson is convinced that Philip became a career army officer not only to rebel against his father but to dwell at an address — Fort Bragg, these days — that would deter Henderson from ever visiting.

"Was the little boy born, or was he adopted?" Vicki said.

"They were both born," Henderson said. "My son and my grandson. What about you?"

"I was adopted. From Vietnam. You know where that is?"

There was the slightest pause in his reply, slight in seconds, though I knew the silence went deep; that was where he had lost his first batch of friends. "I sure do."

"Did you ever go there?"

"No. I was supposed to, once, but I — it's a long story. I'll tell you sometime if you're interested. Do you remember it well?"

She nodded. "I lived on a boat on the Perfume River. When I was little I slept in a basket that hung from the ceiling of the boat. Then I slept with my parents on the floor and we rocked all night because of the waves. Then my mother died. Then we moved to Danang. I remember a lot of chickens and my father's bicycle."

"Vicki, honey, how did you get here?" I was transfixed by her appearance, the sudden intimacy with Henderson, the backward glance to Vietnam, but alarmed by the thought that Toinette, the children's Haitian nanny, would soon discover her missing and panic. And that there might be a substantial reason for her coming here — something she had to show or tell me.

"I took a taxi."

"How did you get my address?"

"My dad's address book. The one by the phone in the kitchen."

"Does Toinette know you're gone?"

She shook her head.

"You two obviously have some things to talk about," Henderson said, "and I've got to finish packing. It was a pleasure meeting you, Vicki, and I hope to see you soon."

"I'm ten," she said, looking up at Henderson. "Approximately."

"Really?"

"I mean, I'm old enough to know that I was born *and* adopted. I was just trying to trick you."

"It was a good trick." I could see he was trying not to smile. "You had me fooled."

"Excellent," she said, and her sprightly inflection assured me that she was probably not here to deliver terrible news.

When Henderson left, I invited her to sit on the couch, said I'd find something for us to snack on, and tried to affect nonchalance. It occurred to me she had read too many of those books about kids with no parents who are emboldened by their hard lives toward reckless gestures. "So what's up, kiddo?"

"Don't tell my dad I came here, please, Sophy. The other kids are pretending I'm home in case Toinette looks for me."

What did nervy ten-year-olds need these days that they had to keep from their parents? Marlboros? Glocks? RU 486? Or would this turn out to be some bit of innocence: she needed help buying a birthday present for Daniel? I filled two glasses with orange juice and a small plate with biscotti, and as I carried them to the coffee table by the couch, I saw she had taken something from her knapsack and placed it on the corner of the table. A large handmade greeting card, I thought, like something I'd helped the children make.

"What have you got there?"

"It's for you." She handed me the card, and for a moment I was too touched to speak. My name was spelled almost right, s-o-p-h-e, written in purple glittery ink and surrounded by a chain of bright blue feathers.

"It's beautiful," I said.

"Open it."

It must have something to do with my birthday the week before. The ink inside was black and looked like Vicki's fairly grown-up hand, except for the signatures, which each child had done for him- or herself, in a variety of colors and sizes, at angles all their own, and it had nothing to do with my birthday.

> We herebye want you and Toto
> to live with us
>   forevere
>   please.
> Sincerely, Vicki
>   Cam
>   Tran
>   Van

For the first time all day — an odd locution, given that it was only eleven-thirty in the morning — I was relieved to hear the doorbell ring. I turned away from all of Vicki's brave longing, and all of my own, and didn't ask who was at the door, didn't look through the peephole. My New Yorker's caution had not shielded me from any of the day's other bizarre intrusions. When I saw Jesús across from me in a dapper seersucker suit and glossy slicked-back hair, the two words that came to mind were "cognitive dissonance."

"We can do ten," he said.

"Ten what?"

"Cash. Ten thousand."

I mumbled something legalistic about my marriage and my divorce; the answer would have to be no for now, but thanks, thanks for thinking of me, as if he'd offered an extra ticket to the theater. When I turned and saw Vicki, to whom I could not mumble something so glib and final, she was ensconced on my couch, reading a book she must have had in her knapsack. She wore the glasses with tortoise-shell frames that she needed for reading, and she suddenly looked official, like a university librarian. I wondered whether she thought her invitation was one I had to reply to, like Jesús's, or one she held out to me as an expression of feeling, like an invitation to a hug.

"What are you reading?"

"*The Secret Garden.* I'm at the scene where Mary Lennox got the key to the garden where her aunt died and where no one's been for ten years. Do you know what she does after that?" I shook my head. "I know, because I read it before. She sneaks into the messy garden every day without telling anyone and makes it beautiful." Then Vicki bent her head and continued reading, as if there were no handmade greeting card on the coffee table between us.

If she were smaller or younger or mine, I could simply have gone to her and held her on my lap and played with her hair, and there would have been the illusion of security for those minutes. And then we'd have separated and she would have returned to her brothers and sister, to the life that must feel to all of them like a riddle wrapped in a mystery inside an enigma. The near-dead in this new country of theirs do not have the decency to die, and the living put on a good show, but a lot of it — Dorothy, Toto, the sight of me in their mother's place at the breakfast table — must end up feeling like make-believe.

"The card is beautiful," I said, and she looked up, with her broad brown face, her jet-black hair, teeth as white as paper. "The most beautiful card anyone ever gave me." She cracked a tight, embarrassed smile, like a shy suitor, and looked at her lap. "In my whole life." I was laying it on thick, but the kids had too, and it was true. "I would love to live with all of you." Her eyes shot up to mine, though her face was still, reluctant to smile. She must have heard the tentativeness, the dip in my voice, in the last few syllables, indicating that a "but" would follow. "I know I'd be very happy." At this she began to smile, still shyly. "But your father's life is complicated, and so's mine. It wouldn't be the best thing to do right now."

"You could stay for a while, and if my mom gets better and wakes up, you could go home and still visit us."

This was a kid's somersaulting logic. It all made perfect sense in some other universe, a fantastic, Oz-like place in which, for starters, her father and I might be able to have a serious conversation.

"You wrote the card, didn't you? I mean, you composed it?" A nod, chin at her chest. She folded her hands in her lap, interlocked her fingers obediently — a reflex, I suppose, from living in an orphanage, to show others that you're well-behaved so that maybe they'll take you home with them. "Was it your idea?"

"No. But I won't say whose."

"You don't have to, sweetheart."

"We all voted."

"That's sweet." How darling, how quickly they had made the essential democratic gesture their own. I was charmed by the theater, and touched down deep by their wanting me, but still uneasy about turning her down, and about what to tell her father about this visit. Did I need to remind him that his children's enthusiasm for me — in contrast to his own — was worthy of a splashy handmade proclamation? Did I need to rub it in his face that if his house were a democracy, they'd vote me in by a landslide?

"It was three to one," Vicki said, "but we all signed the card."

I felt the blow, this blow, in my chest and my eyes. I gaped at her in a gust of fury as she did what bookish children always do: she lowered her eyes and read. Or pretended to. How dare you! I almost said aloud. After all I've done for you! My thoughts caromed from one child to the next, swooping down on evidence of betrayal. Betrayal! Had I lost my mind? Did I think I was Richard Nixon in the White House? Hitler after the bomb in the briefcase?

She glanced up with a blistering indifference, as if she wouldn't deign to notice me. "It wasn't me," she said icily, as if the transcript of my thoughts had been projected above my head in a comic strip balloon, "in case you're wondering."

"Your father will call the police and the FBI and Scotland Yard if Toinette tells him you're missing."

"What's Scotland Yard?"

"Let's go." A bucket of cold water on my sentimentality, and a sharp fear that I had betrayed Daniel by not letting him or Toinette know right away where Vicki was. "Get your knapsack. Now." I was sure she could hear the rising anger in my voice.

"Sophy?"

"What?" I had grabbed my purse, tossed my keys into it, and was about to open the front door.

"Is Henderson gay?"

I looked at her, in her sorbet colors, the little wristwatch with the dinosaur face around her tiny wrist, the book in her knapsack about the girl with no parents. What made her mind loop back to Henderson, and how could she tell?

"Yes, he is."

"But didn't he have to get married to have a son?"

"He changed his mind after he had his son."

"Why didn't he know right away?"

"It's hard to know who you'll want to love. Some people know early on and some don't."

"But if he's gay, how come he was visiting you?"

"We're friends. He likes women as friends but men in a romantic way."

"Romantic like you and my dad?"

"Something like that." Though *romantic* wasn't the first word that came to mind. "What made you ask if he's gay?"

"Nothing. But I hoped he was."

"How come?"

"Because I didn't want him to be your boyfriend."

In the cab going west on Eleventh Street, I did what I'd wanted to do on the couch. I drew my arm around her and pulled her to me, and she came willingly. I apologized for getting angry, apologized for not being able to live with them. I said she'd made a magnificent card, and I'd spend as much time with her and her brothers and sister as I could. Her cheek lay against my bosom and my chin on the top of her head. Her scalp smelled of coconut, and the faces of everyone I saw out the window of our air-conditioned cab were shiny and slick with the unbearable heat of the day.

"Sophy?"

"Yes, sweetheart."

Her hands were curled in my lap, and I was running my fingers along her suede-soft forearm. "I lied," she said.

"About what?"

"That I remember when I slept in the basket on the boat. And that I remember when my mother died. I don't. I was only one."

"That's not such a bad lie. You must miss her a lot. And Blair too." She snuggled closer. The West Village crawled alongside us — Sammy's Noodle Shop, the Espresso Café, the Arab newsstand, Patchin Place, where E. E. Cummings had lived — and I wanted our cab ride to go on forever. Maybe Vicki and I could drive around for the rest of the day, go to a drive-in food stand and a drive-in movie. I could call Daniel from the highway and confess everything, and then we'd keep driving, like fugitives, Vicki and I, like Thelma and Louise.

"I lied about something else too."

"What was that?"

"The card for you."

"What about it?"

"I wrote the names myself."

"That's okay, to help the littler ones."

"I *didn't* help. I pretended they wrote their names, but I did."

"But you told them afterward? You showed them the card?"

"No."

It took a moment for the full meaning of this to circle back through all the psychic congestion of the last hour. "That must mean there was no voting either."

She was silent.

"No three to one?"

"No."

"Hmmmm."

"Are you angry, Sophy?"

I didn't answer right away, not because I was angry but because I was embarrassed at being so jubilant that one of the children hadn't cast a ballot against me. And silent because I wasn't sure whether to lavish on her all the praise she deserved, aesthetically speaking, for the elaborateness of her caper, or say a few words about the ethics of deception.

"No, sweetie, I'm not angry."

The voting stuff was inspired, and clearly her way of retaliating. No wonder Vietnam had won the war. My husband, who had spent many of the war years there, said the Vietnamese were both dogged and absolutely mystified as to what we were doing there, why we cared as much as we did. He spoke fluent Vietnamese, and they said things to him in their language that they wouldn't say to translators, even to reporters. *Do you think we have oil?* one man asked him. *Is that why you're here?* Will's theory was that we stayed because it was a beautiful country, because the women were beautiful and the food was French, and if you were a high-ranking military man, which he was not, you got a salary differential because it was a hardship post, and you traded money on the black market, and you ended up with enough to play the stock market on your crummy army pay, and you had a magnificent Vietnamese girlfriend and your best buddy had her sister, and your wife was far, far away. Vicki might have grown up to be one of those women, I thought. Sly, beautiful, stricken at an early age with a presentiment of loss.

"Are you going to tell my father?" she said.

The lengths to which she had gone to seize my attention bespoke more longing than I could bear to imagine existing inside her skin, and it echoed my own for her, and I wasn't sure I could speak of one to him without revealing the other, which was why I decided at that moment not to tell him, though I should have; believe me, I know I should have.

"If Toinette doesn't know you're gone, and if we can whisk you into the house as sneakily as you got out, I won't tell him. But it may be too late to promise that."

She did something then that surprised me, something else, I should say. She leaned more heavily into me and wrapped both of her arms around me and held me tight, as if she were five instead of ten. Of course I hugged her back, and I almost said something I had never said to her or the other children: *I love you.* I had wanted to say it a dozen times but always stopped myself, afraid it would confuse them, being loved and abandoned by so many people. I did not want to burden what went on between us with the weight of my love.

We held on to each other until the cab turned the corner that led to her house, and I slowly loosened my grip. In another minute, another twenty-five seconds, twenty-four, twenty-three, twenty-two, twenty-one, we'd have to say good-bye and pretend this had never happened.

3

Today, During

I DIDN'T KNOW, when I fell in love with him, that my husband was a spy. It's not like God or infertility, the sort of thing you talk about on a first date. His cover was that he was a diplomat. My cover, to use the term more loosely, was that we met as he was about to leave the Agency, that I didn't know him in the days when he was trying underhandedly to save the Free World from the Red Menace. The truth is that Will was a reluctant Cold Warrior, an ambivalent operative, someone who'd stayed at the Agency until he retired, at the age of forty-eight, because by the time he grasped how wrong our Vietnam policy was, his wife was pregnant with their son, Jesse, he had been working in Vietnam and Cambodia on and off for five years, and the skills he had acquired there didn't translate easily, or lucratively.

In those days, there was no market outside government for fluent Vietnamese speakers, and Will was neither an entrepreneur nor a man who spotted opportunities for his own advancement and seized them. He did his job, collected his government paycheck, and saw the world. By the time he told me that he was not entirely the person he had represented himself to be, I already trusted him more deeply than I had ever trusted anyone. I wouldn't say he'd tricked me into trusting him; more that he'd fooled himself all those years he'd worked for the CIA, doing things he didn't believe in. He never talked much about the details.

We had met while I was hitchhiking on Swansea, on Honeysuckle Road, the blustery north end of the island. I had my thumb out, and Will picked me up in Blueberry Parfait, the old navy blue VW Bug his kids had given that name to. I was heading back to the bed-and-breakfast in the harbor town of Cummington, where I was staying with a boyfriend, though we were a reluctant couple by then, held together by habit, inertia, and fear. Will was going in my direction, on his way to an art gallery showing the drawings he had done in art therapy in the psychiatric hospital where he'd spent a month the year before.

I knew none of this that afternoon, about the CIA or the psych ward or what led to his going there. He said only that he was a diplomat and a Sunday painter with a summer house on the island. A friend with a modest gallery on Old Settlers Road had been kind enough to hang a few drawings. I imagined seascapes, cat pictures, front porches thick with hanging plants and golden retrievers, Swansea at its cloying worst. Once we got to the gallery, I intended to hitch another ride. It's common on the island; doesn't mean you're looking for trouble. There isn't any to be had here. But there was nothing cloying about Will's drawings. They were intricate and dark and George Grosz–like, and when he offered to drive me to my destination if I could wait fifteen minutes, I said yes.

I said yes and yes and yes to him for the rest of the summer. He was gentle and loving and sad and taught me to jitterbug to Benny Goodman and Dizzy Gillespie in the living room of his charming run-down bungalow. When we danced, his aged

Labrador, Binti, thumped her tail in time to the beat. We told each other stories and secrets, the way lovers do, and, the way lovers do, we did not tell each other everything. He told me that his son, Jesse, had died the year before in a car crash, in which he, Will, had been driving, and that he had come close a month later to killing himself. But he did not tell me that he'd been a spy for the last twenty years.

I told him that my first novel, which became a movie with Whoopi Goldberg, was inspired by a true story: after my father disappeared when I was nine, my mother and I crossed the country looking for him, accompanied by my mother's friend, a wise and funny black woman named Gladys but whom we called Gigi, because she yearned to go to Paris. We never found my father, but we had a lot of adventures on the journey, some comic, some poignant, several downright pathetic. In the movie version, we find dear old Dad when we have the good sense to give up looking, when we return home defeated. There he is in the living room, with his feet on the ottoman. In the movie version, he was having a midlife crisis that dissolved, like baking soda in water, when he set eyes on my mother and me again. In real life, Mr. Warren Chase disappeared without a trace. It is possible that he will turn up yet, that he will call me, or someone else will and announce that she is my sister or my father's wife. I hoped it would happen when my book about him came out, and again when the movie with Whoopi Goldberg came out. I sometimes imagine him in Arizona or California, renting a video or turning on the TV and seeing the Hollywood version of what happened to us when he vanished.

My father's having left the way he did always made me fear that my husband would leave the same way, that I would end up abandoned and in pursuit of him, the way my mother pur-

sued my father. But I surprised Will and myself: I was the one
who disappeared.

Will's life as a spy has nothing to do with the beginning of this
next scene — a pivotal scene — but does play in an exchange
between Daniel and me toward the end of it, and it loops in
and out of much that follows.

The scene begins on a light note, with Daniel arriving
in my apartment that afternoon at the stroke of four, sweat
pouring down his forehead, a soaked handkerchief in his fist.
"Christ, have you been out today?"

"Briefly."

"It must be a hundred and bloody two. I got into a cab on
Seventh Avenue and the —"

"Do you want to shower?"

"Just a glass of water. The windows of this cab were rolled
up. I hopped in, and it was a furnace inside. The bastard was
pretending he had air-conditioning."

"Let me get you a towel."

"Jesus, what a day. A producer from the BBC rang to see if
I'd go on camera for a show about Sister Wendy and her con-
tribution to culture. 'Her what?' I said. 'She's spreading the
word,' he said, 'and she's phenomenal.' 'The word about Van
Gogh? Since when is Van Gogh a secret?' 'But you don't understand,' he said. 'She can do a twenty-minute riff on Rem-
brandt in one take, no notes.' Guess what? So can my mother.
I told him I had to take a call from the Sultan of Brunei." He
pulled at the knot of his tie to loosen it while he wandered toward my desk and the swivel chair, where we often began.
"You'll never guess who got married. For the third time. It
happened a few weeks ago, but I only now got a fax from London. What are you doing, reading Tony Bennett's autobiogra-

phy? Since when do you know him? There's a card that says Compliments of the Author."

"The editor sent it. He must have put the card in. He called me today and wants me to ghost another book. Here, drink deep. Towel down. Who got married?"

I'd been hoping for a somewhat more romantic entrance, as I always do from Daniel, but the extreme degree of his distraction that day was actually a relief: I was in thrall to my own distractions, wondering how I would delicately, discreetly, without betraying Vicki's confidence, bring up the subject of his paying more attention to his children, or a different kind of attention, to Vicki in particular.

He drank half the glass in one gulp, paused, and said, "Ginger Miles." And kept drinking.

"Are you heartbroken?"

Still guzzling water, he cocked an eyebrow at me, as if to say, You must be mad, and I was reminded that Daniel did not suffer easily from heartbreak, even the hokey-jokey kind I meant. "I haven't seen her in twenty years, for God's sake, and last time I did —"

"Who'd she marry?"

"A guy I knew at Cambridge, a barrister, a bit dodgy, I always thought. The wedding was a bash at someone's country estate. When I knew her, she was practically homeless, trying to out-Orwell Orwell. How was your day?"

"Nothing out of the ordinary," I lied. I said no more about the Eighth Deadly's semi-offer, nothing about Jesús's proposal of marriage, Vicki's visit, or my stark encounter with Lili, which ended badly: I had no idea how to breathe life into her and no clue about what to do next.

I didn't want Daniel to see me vulnerable, didn't want him to think I might be needy, truly needy, any sooner than neces-

sary. It no longer seemed odd to me that I maintained multiple versions of the truth with him; that there were so many things essential to my well-being that I didn't tell him. Where had she come from, this stranger, this woman who admitted to wanting nothing from him but sex? Had I left the rest of me on Swansea with my husband and taken an imposter to New York? I wasn't sure, but I was determined to tell Daniel that the children needed more from him, determined.

I crossed the room to turn off the ringer on the phone and to mute the voices on the answering machine, and he reached for my half-clad thigh. I was wearing running shorts and a T-shirt, and his fingers wandered to the top of my leg, and we exchanged a knowing, foreplayish laugh. "I got the fax from London an hour ago, about Ginger's wedding" — his tone low and intimate — "which got me thinking about coming over here immediately. But I restrained myself for as long as I could. Some unaccustomed impulse toward propriety."

He motioned for me to straddle him, daddy-long-legs style, on the swivel chair. I leaned forward, and he bit me lightly on my chin. I bit him back, lightly too, and felt the stubbly growth he gets in the late afternoon if he doesn't shave again. When I ran my tongue along his bottom lip, the tenderness of the flesh just inside his mouth brought to mind the feel of his daughter's forearm, and I wanted to speak about the weight of her neediness, but I did not know how to begin.

"Is it Ginger you've been wanting or me?"

"I would have to say I was at the mercy of a rather elaborate fantasy. She liked it when there was another woman."

"So you've said." Pillow talk; antique Ginger stories. By now we had swapped large chunks of our past. "But how will I know you'll be happy with only one of us?"

"I promise you'll know."

"I think I just became convinced."

His eyes closed, his tongue lightly against my lips, my front teeth, the edge of my gums. He was capable of delicacy. I wanted the delicacy of those sensations at the front of my mouth to obliterate the sour taste of this exchange. I wanted it to erase the words of another Englishman that often came to mind when Daniel touched me: *Try to love me a little more and want me a little less,* said Ursula to Rupert Birkin in *Women in Love.*

My eyes swerved from his shut lids to the clock on the microwave. I didn't want to time us; I wanted to know how long we had before we had to leave for his house, for the children's anniversary celebration. An hour. Next to the time, today's date flickered bright blue, and I was surprised it had taken until this late in the day for me to realize that it was also another anniversary: three months since we first slept together. I doubt he knew the specific date, and I'm sure he had no desire to call attention to the sentimental possibilities. Despite what I had told Henderson, I held a good bit more than ten percent of his attention, but he could not bear to be reminded of our attachment or of what it could mean. He was a deer caught in the headlights of my affection, until he bounded across the highway and disappeared into the woods. I sometimes wondered whether those days and hours and ecstasies would ever accumulate, acquire a history, a specific weight and gravity, or whether they would remain flashy ornaments on our erotic Christmas tree.

When he grabbed my thigh, I felt a spike of anger toward him for his parsimony. And at myself, for accepting it, for craving it, when I knew how slender his offering was. But what I got in exchange was this: a degree of heat and hunger that still astonished me, and concentration — submission to the act, not to each other — both focused and preoccupied. We were arm-wrestlers; we were junkies on our way to a nod.

We were still dressed, and there was about this exchange, as about all of them, what I can only describe as a mutual bluffness. I slipped my forefinger between his teeth and let it roam across his tongue and around it. Then I took the finger into my mouth and sucked off his spit. It was metonymy, and it was my finger and his spit. I did it again, this gesture that acted on both of us like a narcotic injected into the bloodstream. "Kneel on the couch," he said, and his voice made me remember what I had to tell him about his children, about caring for them, but that would have to wait. This was not the moment for that; it was the moment for this.

Crossing the living room shedding our clothes, watches, socks, as if we were clowns in an X-rated circus act crossing the ring to climb into an Austin Mini. And for our next trick. There was even, I saw as I bent my knee on the edge of the couch, an audience: ourselves. A mirror, a large rectangle with a purple plastic frame, another Third World Pier One bargain, hung in the corner, above a glass-topped end table and a kelly-green glass vase of eucalyptus cuttings, and if we turned our heads to the right, we would be able to watch ourselves.

I watched. I was not as afraid as Daniel was of looking. Not afraid to see him slip inside me, my back bent forward, like an ironing board coming down from the wall, or a Murphy bed, at a sharp right angle to his. Not afraid to study us, to steady myself, my hands gripping the back of the couch. He held my hips and drew me toward him, his head tipped back, eyes closed, and I was disappointed that he was not admiring the woman I had become. Since returning to New York, I had shrunk one and a half sizes, firmed up my thighs and buttocks at the twenty-four-hour Crunch on Lafayette Street, and found Federico of Broome Street, who can make my hair the same shade of brown it was ten years ago. I am a typical Unitarian, with grandparents from four countries between Latvia and Ireland, and from each of them I inherited a trait or a feature that makes me an ethnic patchwork quilt: a buxom, naturally curly-haired brunette, a green-eyed kibbutz-nik with a Waspy surname — Chase — courtesy of my Scottish grandfather. I straighten my Medusa curls, wax my eyebrows, pay a woman from Croatia whose father was taken away one morning to a Serb concentration camp and has not been heard from since to paint my toenails cherry red, but I could not see them that afternoon in the mirror. What I saw was a scene from a porn flick, the man's head thrown back in some anonymous ecstasy, his slim hips thrown forward, pumping fast. I was the female lead in this flick, certain that what I was doing, the unequivocal nature and specificity of it, the way it resembled nothing other than itself, would short-circuit my capacity to hold a thought. But it didn't; it doesn't. It simply concentrates the mind, as Dr. Johnson said of a hanging. By then he was moving faster than he had any right to. I swear he did not know what it meant to slow down; I feared I might never again myself. But I knew that even if I could train him to be slower, gentler, I could never teach him grace. Never teach him to kiss my neck or stroke my back and stay there. There were moments of tenderness when he touched me that way, but they were so rare and brief, and left me hungry for so much more, that they felt like punishment.

"Be slow," I told him, "be slow."

"Come to the bed and turn over on your back," he said, and I thought he must not have heard me. In the life I invented for Lili before Hollywood, she has an Algerian lover who calls her darling and holds her face when they make love and issues no commands. But after we moved to the bed in the alcove and I did what he said and he lowered his full weight onto me and held my hands gently above my head, he surprised me and did what I said, moving on top of me in gestures so small it was as if he was not moving at all, and then something happened, like a switch being tripped between my legs, and I forgot to breathe. The current surged through me and flooded my brain, and I thought, What would I give up for this? My first edition of *To the Lighthouse*? My twelve Billie Holiday CDs? A husband who used to tell me how sweet it was to see my sheepskin slippers next to his on the floor of the closet? A husband who used to say my name and my pet name and honey and baby and lover when he made love to me? All of the above, every single one of them — though I missed, I cannot tell you how much I missed, the sound of my name in my ear.

We were locked into a rhythm we had never found before and it could go on and on and on, an infinite loop of pleasure — those were the words I was thinking when I felt my eyeballs roll up in a jerky motion and a drop of his sweat fall into my open eye and sting —

The voice erupted into the room, a man at the door, interrupting the soundtrack of swallows. What we heard was him asking for me, some version of me, and I realized it was the answering machine. I'd remembered to turn off the ringer on the phone, and I'd muted my outgoing message but not the caller's voice.

"I need to leave a message for, uh, Sophy O'Rourke."

"Oh, fuck," I whisper-moaned, and Daniel and I began to laugh between gasps, but we kept going. We would not stop for a call from someone who knew me so little — so not at all — that he thought I went by my husband's last name.

Then Daniel's panting grew lower and everything else sped

up, and there was a concatenation of hard human sounds, my own rhyming with his, that made it impossible to hear every word except that this was Sergeant Burns with the Massachusetts State Police. Daniel's noises ended, and I heard a phone number, the Swansea area code, and the prefix almost everyone on the island shares. I wriggled out from under Daniel, or maybe he let go of my hands and flopped to my side, maybe we moved apart together, because he told me later he had heard the man say "State Police" and thought the call was for him, about his family, and he was about to leap to his feet when he saw me leap to mine.

I stood by the side of the bed with the phone in my hand, dazed and breathless with the effort. "This is Sophy, don't hang up," as if I had run up ten flights of stairs, and I knew in the time it took me to push the wet strands of hair from my wet forehead that there was no other reason the police would call me from there, it must be the highway patrol, though how did they get my name and number? A computer, an old insurance policy? A bolt of fear struck my knees, but for a few seconds I had my wits about me, or maybe it was that my body needed those extra seconds to prepare itself to absorb what I knew was coming.

"Do you have bad news to tell me?" was what I said, and I pictured the motorcycle he had just bought, all of him smashed to pieces. I looked down at Daniel at the edge of the bed, looking up at me, a slice of alertness, or maybe I mean terror, on top of his breathlessness, his hair blown sideways and backward, beads of sweat like quicksilver gathering at his temples. I touched his shoulder to steady myself and felt the prickly hair on the side of his thigh against my knee. On the quilted bedspread was the ghostly indentation of my body.

"I'm afraid I do," Sergeant Burns said, but I didn't wait for him to say more. I began to whimper and shake, a shuddering noisier and more feral than I can describe. Then I did all of them at once or so close together it felt like a seizure. "Is there someone there with you?" the man said, "I hope there's someone with you —"

Daniel must have taken the phone from my hand, or I must have dropped it. He was patting the night table for a pencil, and I heard myself howl, as if I were falling down a well, or someone else was.

"Officer," I heard Daniel say, "can you give me the information, tell me if there's anything we need to do immediately?"

I don't remember walking across the room and walking back to the bed, but somehow I was wearing Daniel's long-sleeved starched ice-blue shirt, which hung on me like a nightshirt, and I curled up on the bed while my entire body chattered, fueled by images of the motorcycle skidding, Will's body flung, mangled, crushed, verbs twisted into adjectives that no longer breathe. I pulled the bedsheets to me and the pillows, but I could not make myself still.

Minutes passed. I heard him say, "Uh-huh, uh-huh," and "Thank you, yes, yes, quite, of course," and then I felt him lie down at my back, curl his chest against my spine, and wrap his arms tenderly around me. I forgot after a moment how surprised I was that he knew, he actually knew, what to do. An embrace that comforted was in his repertoire, but buried so deep that you were sure it would never turn up, like the remains of the *Titanic*. "A neighbor found him in his house, a chap named Ben," he said quietly. "It seems he died in his sleep," and that was a great relief, that was nearly good news. That he did not suffer. Did not know. I bunched the pillows in a gesture I knew even at that moment had something to do with wanting to conceal my grief and shame and rage. Daniel had never seen me weep. He had been making me moan and tremble and cry out in this bed for three months, eight days a week, but if I had cried over something smaller than this, he would have fled. If I had shown half this much feeling, he would have abandoned me, and I knew even then, as deep as I was inside that wave of grief, that I despised him for that.

I was not thinking clearly, but it surprised me that I was thinking at all. I was thinking that Will could not be dead, because I'd spoken to him — when was it? — last week or the week before, about the money he owed me, but when my friend Geoff died last year, there were people who said, "He can't be dead, I just had breakfast with him"; "He can't be dead, we were supposed to go to the movies tonight"; "He can't be dead, his wife is about to have a baby." I was thinking that this state of consciousness, which must be shock, is analogous to making love, which you imagine will lead to ecstasy, and ecstasy will be so true to its meaning that you will not be capable of a clear, reliable thought, and in that too you are wrong.

I was thinking that I had to call Will's daughters and tell them. They were twenty-five-year-old twins, and their older brother was dead, and I had not had the nerve to call either of them since I left Will. Now I had to tell them this. If I could find them.

"What are you doing?" Daniel said.

"Looking for my address book. Did the police say anything to you about the medical examiner?"

"Sophy, may I give you a bit of advice? There's nothing you need to do right this moment. You're scrambling around as if there's an urgency here, whereas —" I was across the room at my desk, looking through stacks of papers and files for the address book I often misplaced. "Darling, he's dead."

I froze for an instant, uncertain whether I was more shocked by the *darling* or the *dead*. I turned to say something to him; I didn't know what it would be, but then I didn't have to, because another voice shot into the room, like a stone through the window.

"This is Joe Flanagan, Flanagan's Funeral Home, on Swansea. I'd like to leave a message for —"

I picked up the phone before he said my name and flipped the ringer switch on at the same time.

"I know this is a difficult time for you, Mrs. O'Rourke. Myself and the members of our family and staff —"

"How did you get my name?"

"The police, ma'am."

"Are they soliciting business for you? Do you intend to talk me into a five-thousand-dollar funeral? Because my husband has absolutely no interest — and no one in our family has the slightest inclination to be exploited at a time of —"

"Pardon my interrupting, Mrs. O'Rourke. I believe there must be some confusion. Your husband's body is here right now. The police instructed us to pick it up from the house. It's going to the mainland tomorrow on the first ferry, to the coroner, at no charge to you or your family. I wanted to pass on my condolences. If there's anything we can do for you, please let us know."

I was speechless, as mortified by my outburst as I was stunned by this barrage of news about Will, who was now an "it," not a "he." A piece of luggage, something attached to a bill of lading. I started to say, "Thank you, I'm sorry," but I began too late, just as he hung up the phone.

"What did he say?" Daniel asked.

"Why don't we get dressed? It seems a bit tawdry, lounging around as if we're in a Turkish bath."

"Did you find your address book?"

"Here's your shirt back."

"What did that chap say that's got you so undone?"

"His body is there. Spending the night. Off to the coroner's tomorrow. Do you suppose it's in a coffin or a refrigerator?" I found my bra in the middle of the living room floor, and as I reached down for it, remembering how it had landed there, I remembered how keenly I had wanted to tell Daniel that his children needed more from him. I still wanted to, but I knew I could find no clever way to work it into the conversation. It was a bra that hooked in the front, and as I peered down, snapping a tiny plastic rod into its plastic slot, I felt Daniel's eyes on me, the way your eyes are drawn to someone in pain, and at that instant, I understood it might not be my pain he was focused on, but its eerie resemblance to his own.

"A refrigerator, I imagine," he said, and it occurred to me, not for the first time, that I might be wrong in every one of my conjectures about what passed between us, mistaken about everything but the reality of the sparks our bodies threw off when we rubbed them together. "Particularly in this heat," he added, and for an instant I did not know to what he was referring.

"Did I already ask whether the police said anything to you about the medical examiner?"

"They didn't mention him."

"Her. She was Will's doctor on the island."

"Is she the one you're ringing?" Daniel said.

"No, his best friend, Diane. From grade school. Lives in Cambridge."

When Diane answered and I told her I was calling about Will, there was barely a pause before she said, "He's dead, isn't he?"

"You don't sound surprised."

"I'm not. The last time I spoke to him he was distraught."

"But they said he died in his sleep."

"Of what?"

"Well, I — I don't know. A heart attack, I guess. Isn't that — What else is enough to —"

"Will there be an autopsy?"

"Tomorrow. What did he say when you last spoke to him?"

"What didn't he say? He was beside himself. Kept talking about how alone he was, how terribly alone. I was afraid he might kill himself. I suppose I thought he had. I've been leaving messages for him for weeks."

"Weeks? Why didn't you call me?"

"Call you? What for?"

"We're still married. The divorce hasn't — but even if it had —"

"Sophy, this is hardly the time to —"

"If you thought he was dead, why didn't you call the police?"

I could feel Daniel's eyes on me, and I turned to see him, fully dressed, clothes freshly wrinkled from lying in heaps on the floor, his gaze as startled as my own. I could feel the stew of melodrama thickening, but I was in no way prepared for what Diane said next: "Will saw you with a man. That's why I didn't call you."

"Saw me where? When?"

"He drove his motorcycle to New York a few weeks ago, hoping to talk to you. You were on the street with a man Will said looked like Tom Wolfe, or maybe he said Thomas Wolfe; I wasn't paying the closest attention. He left the city immediately and drove here on his motorcycle."

"Tom," I said grimly. "Definitely Tom." Daniel even had a dandyish off-white, raw silk suit I'd seen him wearing not long before. Had Will seen us with the children? Seen us leaving my building, as rumpled as we were right now? "What was the date?" I asked, because I remembered Will calling me in the middle of the night a few weeks ago to say he was coming to New York so that we could talk. I'd told him not to; I said it was too soon for us to be friends. He shouldn't make the trip. But he must have, after all. He may have come the very next day.

"Let's see," Diane said, and I heard some papers rustling. "Three weeks ago this past Tuesday. It was such a dramatic event, I wrote it on my calendar."

"Dramatic for whom?"

"In one day he drove from Swansea to New York and from New York to here, on a motorcycle. He collapsed in my foyer, spent the night here, and left for Swansea first thing the next morning. I spoke to him that night. That was the last time. I've been leaving messages for weeks."

I had too, about the money he owed me, but hadn't it been only a week or ten days? Had I been leaving messages for a dead man? Angry messages? What had I said? I looked at Daniel, who put on his watch and stepped into the bathroom, closing the door behind him, retreating from the mounting mess. Could I go with him tonight and pretend all the things I'd need to pretend during dinner with the children?

"Have you talked to Will's daughters?" Diane asked.

"You're the first person I called. I'll call them next." It seemed the most graceful way to get out of this, although I knew I could not call them yet, not with the grim news that I may have precipitated his death. That his death may have been a suicide. "I'll call you back if I learn anything more."

Daniel emerged from the bathroom as soon as I hung up. "She thinks he killed himself?"

I nodded. "I was afraid he might when we split up."

"You never told me that."

"There's a lot I haven't told you. Did I ever tell you that a few months after Will's son died, a year before we met, he bought a handgun to kill himself with?"

"Actually, you did. That's how he landed in the bug house, where he did the art-therapy drawings that ended up in the gallery on Swansea, the afternoon you met."

It was more than ten percent of his attention, after all. But not so much that he would easily bear the burden of having had a role in Will's suicide, if that's what it was. "Did I tell you he's been calling me in the middle of the night to say he wants me back?"

"No."

"He thought I'd change my mind once the divorce came through. Thought I'd understand what I'd wrought, come to see the error of my ways. A few weeks ago he woke me at four in the morning and said he was coming to New York to talk to me. I convinced him not to. But it turns out I didn't." I touched Daniel's sleeve as I passed him and stepped into the walk-in closet where my dresser was, and my suitcase. "What are the seven deadly sins?"

"Hang on a minute. I have to ring Toinette and tell her I'm running late. I was supposed to pick up the cake at Jon Vie by six. Christ, I think they close early in the summer."

"Daniel, what are they?" I was dressing and packing at the same time. In a basket on my dresser I found the key to the safe deposit box at our bank on Swansea. My will was there, and his was too. Or it used to be. "There's lechery, pride, avarice, sloth —"

"You want Unitarian sins? What about missing an issue of *The Nation*? Forgive my levity. Shit, the line is busy. . . . Shit, they're both busy. Sophy, where are you?"

"In here."

He was halfway across the room, dialing and redialing, un-
aware of what I was doing in the closet. I opened my little
wooden jewelry box for a pair of earrings and was surprised to
see my wedding band. I slipped it on my finger.

"I don't imagine you're keen for a party with the kids, but
you shouldn't be alone now. Good, it's ringing."

"I'm going to Swansea."

"Toinette, hi. Sorry, terribly sorry, Sophy's had a problem.
Her husband, her ex-husband — Yes, quite serious, but she's
fine, though he's — I'll tell you when I get home. Good, you
got the cake; I was worried. How are the children? I'll be there
in fifteen or twenty minutes. Sophy will be with me, yes. I'll
tell her, but I don't know if she's up to Dorothy and the red
shoes tonight."

"Daniel, I'm going." I appeared in front of him, staidly at-
tired, clutching a small canvas suitcase, an earnest girl in a
thirties movie announcing to Mother and Father that she is
leaving home, headed for the big city.

"Going where?"

"Swansea."

"The police said there was no urgency. He's going to the
coroner tomorrow. These things often take days. Sometimes
weeks. You can plan a funeral from here."

"We're not going to have a regular funeral. Will would
never have —"

"Who's Tom?"

"What are you talking about?"

"The chap you mentioned to Will's friend on the phone
just now."

"He saw us together on the street."

"Tom *who* saw us?"

"Will saw us. He told Diane he saw me with a man who looked like Tom Wolfe, but she couldn't remember whether he'd said Tom or Thomas."

"Old CIA agents don't die," he said with a sharpness verging on vehemence. "They just tail other subjects."

For a short, shocked moment I said nothing. Then I answered him with an edge of my own. "This one just died. And he hasn't been in the CIA for ten years."

"Most of the men you know are gay, and Will knows it. Why would he assume that because you're with a man, the two of you are —"

"He must have seen something in our demeanor. He's very astute that way. He was."

"We weren't fucking, for God's sake."

"You don't need to be to look as if you are."

"You're thinking that seeing us on a street corner led him to take his life?"

"Isn't that why you're in such a snit, because you feel guilty that it could be true?"

He was quiet for a long moment, fully dressed, his hair combed, and looking me over, a visual frisk, taking inventory. I'd changed into sandals with low heels, a khaki skirt and navy linen jacket, something for a Swansea summer funeral. *Christ, she's gone starchy New England spinster on me; she's gone Emily Dickinson on me, when I had this arrangement all worked out with Fanny Hill.*

"There's quite a lot to take in," he said in a kindly, hushed voice that startled me after my accusation and my flip fantasy of what he'd been thinking. "The police said it looked awfully much as if he died in his sleep. I hope he did. Are you sure you can get to Swansea at this hour? What if you're stranded at La Guardia or Logan?"

"If I make the eight o'clock shuttle to Boston, I'll be okay. In summer the small planes run from Logan to Swansea until ten."

"Have you enough cash for a cab?"

"I'm fine. Why don't we head out?"

"Sophy, do you really need to go to Swansea tonight?"

"Of course I do."

"But you're always so cool-headed, so distant when you talk about Will and your marriage. Now that this has happened, it's as if you'd never left him. I must say, I'm rather confused."

"Cool-headed and distant?"

Daniel nodded.

I was surprised at first to hear I came off that way, that I seemed to have had so little feeling for him, when the truth was that he had been the center of my life for ten years. But I'd had to steel myself in order to leave. I'd had to harden my heart to cause the pain I know I inflicted, and I suppose I'd continued to carry some of that hardness with me, until the police called.

"I can understand your confusion," I said to Daniel. "But I'd like to go tonight. I want to be with people who knew him."

"Let me take your bag."

We were silent in the hallway, but it was an eerie silence, or maybe it was the start of everything familiar becoming eerie and surreal: a state of hyper-awareness, when you notice the weight of your eyelids blinking. I had not had much experience of this kind, but I imagined the presence of such fresh grief would smooth out rough edges, would make us embodiments of gentleness. I suppose it already had, briefly, when I cried in bed and Daniel held me and the word "darling" slipped accidentally from his lips.

In the elevator he said, "The children will miss you tonight. I'm not sure yet what to tell them about why you're not there. The truth seems rather an excessive —"

"Tell them my dog is sick," I said without thinking. "Did the police say anything to you about Henry?"

"Who?"

"The dog."

"Not a word."

"Ben must have taken him in. The neighbor who found Will."

"I suppose it's that kind of place, Swansea. Small-town America, everyone full of the milk of human kindness. Rousseau's natural man, uncorrupted by society."

"In fact, it's not, though it may look that way."

Daniel smiled and said, "That's something else you never told me."

"It's been quite a day for revelations, hasn't it?" And for withholding them. I was thinking about Vicki's visit, Jesús's marriage proposal, and my confrontation with Lili, now all fused in my mind under the heading *Today, Before*. The elevator door opened, and with the suddenness of a movie clapperboard being snapped and released, my thoughts lurched to the other heading, *Today, After*, and that was all of this. As we crossed the lobby, I said to Daniel, "He died alone, even if the dog was there."

"I'm afraid so."

The doorman opened the door, tipping his head to me. "I'll be away for the next few days, if you could hold my packages."

The thick heat of the early evening landed on us like a gigantic fishnet. The city rose and shrieked in every direction. "Jesus," Daniel muttered to all of it and began walking toward Broadway, where it was easier to catch a cab.

"He sat with two different people when they died," I said. "He was afraid of a lot of things, but he wasn't afraid of people dying. I suppose I never told you that either." I knew I had passed into some realm of neediness and self-absorption, where, rather than making conversation, I was free-associating, drifting, and there wouldn't be much to say back. So I was surprised when Daniel perched on the curb and raised his arm to flag a cab, his eyes darting between the oncoming traffic and me, and said, with a psychological acumen he had never exhibited before, "You don't know it, but you're in shock now. It will last a few days, and when it wears off, everything will be much more difficult. When you're with your stepchildren and Will's other relatives — when the shock wears off — old resentments will surface. With a vengeance."

A cab pulled up, and Daniel reached out to open the door for me, but I wasn't ready to go. I wanted what I always wanted from him: a more tender parting. "One other thing, if I may," he said.

"Yes?"

"Tomorrow morning, you must get in touch with your divorce lawyer, get a copy of your husband's will, and write his obituary. Get it to the island paper, and if you'd like me to, I'll fax it to a friend at the *Times*. Ring me later, would you, and let me know you made it?"

That was evidence of shock too, leaving New York that way, with no thought of plane or hotel reservations, of arriving on the island when everyone I knew there would be asleep. Taking off without calling Will's daughters or Ben Gibbs, who'd found Will, or Annabelle, or the medical examiner, who must have been summoned to the house to sign a piece of paper that said Will was dead.

In the commuter terminal was a bank of telephones, and after I bought my ticket, I began frantically making calls. I called my mother, whose line was busy. I called Annabelle, whose phone rang and rang, which meant she was on-line. I called the last number I had for my stepdaughter Ginny, and got a phone company message that the number had been disconnected. I knew she worked at a TV station in Maine, but I couldn't remember its call letters. I phoned Western Union, which said they did not have telegram service in the tiny California town closest to the cabin on the mountain where Ginny's sister, Susanna, lived, with no telephone and her new baby, Rose, whom Will had never gone to see.

Henderson must already have left for Switzerland, but I was so agitated by then that I called him anyway and started talking to his machine. "I'll bet you can't tell from my voice that I'm a widow. Or can you? I hadn't really thought of it that way, the W word, until this minute. I'm at La Guardia, and you're probably at Kennedy or in the air. I'm going to Swansea. I'm going to Boston on a big plane and then to the island on a little plane. You know how terrified I am of those little planes, eight-seaters with no co-pilots. Did I say already that Will is dead? The police told me it looked as if he died in his sleep, but his friend Diane thinks he killed himself. The weird thing is that I'm fine. I mean, I can walk and talk and sign my name and remember my calling-card number. Tonight I'll probably stay in the awful motel by the harbor where Will used to keep his boat. I'm sure they'll have a room; it's not the height of the season. I know you're going to be fasting, but I hope you won't be too weak to call me. I'll leave a number on your machine when I know where I'm staying. Hug, hug, kiss, kiss."

I kept talking to myself, although I wasn't sure my lips were moving. I went through the security gate, and my house keys set off the alarm. I walked to the end of Gate C in a trance and said to myself, "I'm fine, I'm fine."

But I could not sit still, could not sit down, so I circled the area, up and down the rows of chairs, past the newsstand, the bar, the clusters of commuters with their cell phones and laptops and summery seersucker jackets slung over a shoulder, the men and women both. I am not really a widow. A glance toward the window, the parking lot of planes, the giant birds with their logos, their mechanics, tiny trucks like golf carts hovering around their talons.

Call me the widow that almost was; that's what I should have said to Henderson. Then speak to me as if from a pulpit, as if I were a supplicant, a congregant, a believer. And let this grief pass over me, as the angel of death passed over the houses of the Jews and their firstborn sons one night in Egypt. But I have no blood of a lamb to sprinkle on my doorpost to let the angel know to spare me. Only this sudden wetness trickling down the inside of my thigh, and the faint bleachy scent of it. Excuse me, I would like to make an announcement here at Gate C-3, with nonstop service to Boston's Logan Airport, and lots of luck getting to Swansea at this ridiculous hour, ten days before the Fourth of July. Will you turn off your cell phones and laptops and Palm Pilots long enough to listen? I want it stamped on my boarding pass, too. That I am not really a widow. That I forgot in my shock to bathe, so you can smell it on me, what I was doing when the police rang. That's a Britishism, a Danielism. Ring me later. Ring me as soon as you get there. And call me the widow manqué, the semi, demi, quasi, ersatz, crypto, mini-widow, and tell me, if you have any idea, what it is I am supposed to do now.

THE ISLAND

"Beyond the Wild Wood comes the Wide World,"
said the Rat. "And that's something that doesn't
matter, either to you or me. I've never been there,
and I'm never going, nor you either, if you've got any
sense at all."

— Kenneth Grahame,
The Wind in the Willows

4

The Wild Wood

THE LAST PERSON to board the Island Air's eight-seat Cessna on the ten P.M. to Swansea squeezed in beside me in the back row, a large man in a short-sleeved knit shirt whose bare forearm brushed against mine as he belted himself in. It was dark and humid on the tarmac, even darker and more humid inside the cramped, shrunken cabin, but Evan Lambert and I said each other's names simultaneously. "Small world," he said.

"Small plane."

So small, it was like being in an elevator, and I didn't know how to tell Evan why I was here without announcing it to all assembled. So small, there was no easy way I could acknowledge his latest high-profile client, the German nanny baby-killer, without causing a collective stir in this almost airborne soup can. "I've been following your moves," I said softly.

"Is that so?"

"You're always on my radar."

"Same here, kiddo." We had been lovers twenty years before and friends for the last nineteen, but could go long periods without speaking. He didn't even know Will and I had separated, that I no longer lived on the island. Evan and his family were summer people; for the last four years, Will and I had been year-rounders. "You coming back from somewhere exciting?"

"New York," I said. The pilot flipped on the ignition, and the propellers flared. It was cozy and small scale, as if we were in the backseat of a car and the driver had just switched on the windshield wipers. "Are you down for a long weekend?"

"Yeah. Mavis and the kids went down last week for the season. I had a meeting late today that went on longer than I expected. I missed my reservation on the six o'clock flight. You're obviously the reason why."

"Hold my hand," I said. "I hate these take-offs and landings. And everything in between." Against the flimsy armrest between us, he turned over his forearm and opened his palm. I covered it with mine and held on tight, too tight, but he would understand soon enough. *What gives value to travel is fear. It breaks down a kind of inner structure we all have.* Was this something Evan used to quote to me in that distant summer we traveled together?

"How's Will? I think the last time we saw you guys he took the boys and me sailing. The outboard conked out, and we had to paddle into the harbor. The ferry almost ran us down. Were you there, or was it Mavis?"

The twin engines were noisy, cranking harder the faster we taxied down the runway. I got a whiff of diesel fuel and said a prayer and leaned my head against Evan's shoulder, which I had not done in twenty years, but I needed my mouth close to his ear so that I could speak into it softly, which I also had not done in twenty years. He smelled faintly of Irish Spring, and for an instant that rumbling speck of a plane about to lift off and take us on the thirty-minute trip down the penin-sula and across the sound might have been the mobbed overnight ferry we took from Athens to the coast of Turkey the summer we were twenty-five, joking about sailing to Byzantium, no country for old men, the young in one another's arms, Evan's young arms smelling of Irish Spring; he carried around a supply of it in his knapsack. I used to kid him that if we ever got separated I could get a bloodhound to go after that smell, and I wondered now if he could identify the familiar scents rising from my skin. We were off the ground, shot into the air as if from a cannon, bumping and rattling in this tin box over the suburbs south of Boston. His hand must have hurt, I was squeezing it so hard. I remembered it was Camus who said somewhere that fear gives value to travel, but I wasn't sure he meant a short hop over the water to the place where you used to live. That wasn't travel; that was just going home.

It surprised me to feel Evan's hand on my cheek, his other hand, the hand not holding mine. He had reached around as if we were lovers and pressed his palm to the side of my face, holding me tighter against his shoulder, because he could tell I was uncommonly afraid and suspected it was of something beyond the obvious. "Sophy, what is it? Is everything all right?"

I shook my head against his collarbone and explained what I could.

Once on the ground, he insisted I spend the night at his house; he would call his wife from the airport to let her know. "I don't think we have house guests until Saturday," he said, "but if I'm mistaken, the couch is extremely comfortable. Certainly better than the Harborside Motel." When the line was busy at the pay phone in the one-room terminal, Evan shrugged and said, "Let's find a cab and take our chances." Remembering these banalities a day or two later, I could see hints of what I came to learn, but that night I was not looking hard, except to notice Evan's aging. When we were young, he had a male model's raging good looks; he could have been a Kennedy. Now he had the black bags under his eyes and the modified middle-age spread of all those important men on TV news shows, but he still had a young man's energy, a full head of auburn hair barely flecked with gray, clear blue eyes, full lips I remembered kissing.

He took my bag and drew an arm around my shoulder with avuncular concern. I was grateful for his tenderness on the plane, the offer of a place to stay on the remote West End of the island, the view I knew I would wake up to if I slept on their couch, if I managed to sleep at all: the sliding glass doors overlooking the redwood deck and the ponds beyond it and the ridge of sand dunes beyond them, and the roar of the ocean from over the ridge.

But what I remember most vividly now, looking back on my arrival, stepping out of the terminal, was the shock of the island air against my skin, in my nostrils; how soft it was after the molten lava of the city, as soft as dusting powder, the coat of a puppy. The sky was sapphire blue and strewn with stars, a shower of gold dust. Across the sidewalk, to the curb and the waiting taxi, I felt myself choke at the memory of my first visit here, the summer I met Will, when I was convinced that no harm could ever come to anyone on this island, that the pristine beauty of the place was a gorgeous vaccine against death. But I had left Swansea in another season, in mid-March, when it seemed to me a metaphor for my marriage: cold, windswept, uninhabitable.

"We're going to the West End," Evan told the cab driver, "to the end of Heron Road."

It would be a long ride, fifteen miles of winding country roads, a sudden change in the landscape, opening up to mead-

ows and ponds, views of the ocean, the tip of the island, Evan's
secluded compound. I braced myself for the ride, because I
knew it would be beautiful, because I had left Will here, because I still had not told his daughters that he was dead, because it had been so much a part of Will's and my life together, even though we lived on the East End, ten miles in the
other direction. A mile down the airport road was a tiny village, Twin Oaks, with a library, a bed-and-breakfast, a bakery,
a one-room schoolhouse, a church surrounded by a white
picket fence, and across the street from it, on the lawn of the
bed-and-breakfast, the only weeping willow on the island,
which makes frequent appearances in photo books about
Swansea. Every Saturday morning, the driveway of the school
became a farmers' market, where I used to buy tomatoes, corn,
bunches of cilantro, potatoes the size of my little toe. For long
stretches, our taxi was the only car on the road. For long
stretches, I remembered how thoroughly I had forgotten that
this was once my life. I used to cook dinners, run a reading series at the public library, write the occasional article for the island newspaper, "Coping with Summer Visitors," "A City
Girl Moves to the Country," "Why I Love My Solitude," but I
did not love it nearly so well as I imagined I would.

"I haven't been back since the day I left in March," I said to
Evan.

"Why didn't you call me?"

"When?"

"Anytime. To let me know you'd left Will. You'd left the island."

"You're always busy. I'm always reading about you being
on TV. 'Evan Lambert, talking to Ted Koppel last night on
"Nightline," and the night before that, to Dan Rather, and the
night before that to Larry King — ' Don't wince, Evan. You
love the controversy that swirls around you. You're almost as

happy on TV as you are —" I noticed the cab driver, an older man with curly white hair as thick as Harpo Marx's, swerve his eyes to the rearview mirror to get a gander at this man so much in the news, but he got me instead.

"I'm wincing," Evan said, "because I don't understand why you *read* about me being on TV."

"You'll laugh."

"I could use a laugh."

"When I was packing the car to leave the island, I packed the VCR and forgot the TV, and when I did remember it, there was no room left. I actually keep the VCR plugged in to remind me to buy another TV, but so far I —"

"The settlement was so bad you can't afford it?"

"There is no settlement."

"What does that mean?"

"If you walk away with nothing, there's no settlement."

"I hope you didn't pay someone a lot of money for that legal advice."

"This is not what I want to be thinking about at the moment."

"Goddammit, you should have called me."

"So you could represent me? I can't afford you, Evan. And I didn't kill anyone."

"That's hardly what I —"

"Unless I did," I whispered. I told him what Diane thought, although I didn't mention Daniel and me, or that Will had seen us together. Evan was quiet, but not for too long. "People get divorced all the time. Most of them don't kill themselves. And you don't know if he did."

"He was bereft," I said quietly.

"You know what?" He was speaking softly, too.

"What?"

"So was I, when you left me."

"Jesus, Evan, don't flatter me."

"I was."

"You noticed that I was gone, but I left because you were so distracted by your own ambition, you barely knew I was there."

Neither of us said anything, lost in the whorls of our history. Or so I imagined, until Evan spoke again. "I find it hard to believe your lawyer let you leave the marriage with nothing."

"Before I left the island Will said to me, 'If you want out, you leave with what you came with. Otherwise you can sue me, and I promise I will be a real s.o.b.'"

"That doesn't sound like Will."

"It wasn't, usually."

"That's why the law is there, Sophy, so that a vindictive husband can't —"

"I know why it's there. And I know I didn't want to drag my life and his through the mud."

"Sophy, there's a house on Swansea. That alone . . . How much is it worth?"

Again I noticed the cabbie's gaze on me in the rearview mirror. This was not New York or Boston, where there are a few more degrees of separation between lives; there was a good chance this guy knew people who knew Will or me.

"I'm not going to talk about money tonight."

"Are you legally separated?"

"Or about legal matters."

"Just tell me whether the separation's gone through."

"I signed the agreement a few days ago and sent it back to my lawyer."

"Who's that?"

"A simple island lawyer who does wills and divorces."

"That's not like you, Sophy."

"I wanted out. That's all."

"If the papers aren't filed with the court yet, your separation agreement may be moot. You may be entitled to half of his estate."

He saw me turn away and look out the window. "The body is still warm, Evan." I was pretty sure that wasn't true, but I hoped it would tilt the conversation in another direction. Or badger him into silence for what was left of the ride. We were almost at the end of the island, almost there. The sharp scents of salt and lilac through the open windows. A smattering of weathered gray-shingled houses, a grove of tall trees hugging the road, a break in the trees and the vast pond in the clearing back-lit by the moon. The proportions of things on Swansea are different, scaled down, miniature, like the world described in *The Wind in the Willows,* a place for water rats, toads, badgers, and moles.

"Aside from all of this, Mrs. Lincoln," Evan finally said, "how do you like being single again?" It surprised me that I could laugh. "Fun, isn't it?"

"How would you know about the phenomenon of being single again?"

"I have a good imagination."

"What about you and Mavis?"

"What about us?"

"Are you happy these days?"

"Sure, we're happy. Driver, you're going to make a left immediately after the next telephone pole. She's been doing extremely well the last year or so. The dean picked her to chair the university's committee on sexual harassment. She's filled with purpose and authority and occasional righteousness that does wonders for her complexion. Her entire spirit. She leads three distinct lives: the queen of cultural studies in Harvard's English department; the hearty PTA mom and occasional Beacon Hill hostess; and now a political bulldog in bed with the PC police. She comes down here for the summer and collapses with a stack of novels by a bunch of very un-PC dead white men."

We turned onto dirt, and the cab wobbled and lurched over ruts in the narrow, woodsy road, and I was surprised at the gust of envy I felt for the fullness and certainties of Mavis's life. Or maybe surprised simply that I could feel anything besides grief. Suddenly, stupidly, I envied all those lives she got to live, with titles that could be smartly rattled off like military medals: star professor, wife, mother, hostess, member in good standing of the Swansea summer set. But how could I not envy her, living the way I was — homeless, childless, bookless, staging an elaborate show for Daniel that I was perfectly content? Even Mavis's intellectual hypocrisy struck me as a great luxury, deconstructing *Lassie Come Home* for a living and taking *Anna Karenina* to bed.

"At the fork, bear right," Evan said to the driver, reminding me of the time Will and I came here after a week of rain and took a left at the fork instead. We got stuck in a gully of mud a mile down the deserted dirt road and tromped to Evan's house to get him to rescue our car with a rope. Will was angry because I'd insisted that he bear left at the fork, his anger the public face of his humiliation at getting stuck in what he called "Evan's mud." Translation: I have the peevish right to envy your rich, famous ex-boyfriend, and the righteous right to despise him, because he defends famous killers for a living and makes millions.

I never defended what Evan did for a living — how could

I? All I could defend to Will was our history and his and Mavis's easy generosity toward us. Evan was something of a parlor game to me, a study in a kind of shameless ambition laced with enough charm to succeed in making his way into Boston society from his working-class Irish-Catholic roots. He was Jack Kennedy marrying Jacqueline Bouvier, and because the name Lambert straddled the fence between Ireland and England, he often passed for a Wasp, which is precisely what he wanted. He was abhorred by liberal, left-leaning pundits, exploited by talk-show hosts, admired by his peers — of whom there were only a handful in the entire country — and envied, grudgingly, by my husband, another poor Irishman with quite a different sense of his own destiny.

Coming down the dirt road through the dense woods, I always forgot there was a clearing, a lawn big enough for croquet, an immense Queen Anne–style shingled house with a front porch larger than my apartment in Manhattan, a circular driveway that could be a running track.

"Evan, is that you? My God, I was about to call the Coast Guard. Weren't you supposed to be on the six o'clock?" I heard Mavis's marvelous throaty voice before I saw her outline in the doorway — unless that was a house guest, a long-necked, tall young man? A large black shape low to the ground bounded down the steps, swished past me, and began to bark.

"I've got Sophy Chase with me," Evan called out. "I found her on the plane from Logan. Didn't I, Flossie? Yes, I surely did, as surely as you are a good dog." I thought of poor hideous, hybrid Henry, mangy, funny-looking, and suddenly homeless. It was much too late to call Ben Gibbs to make sure he'd been taken in. I could see now that the shadowy figure holding open the screen door was Mavis, with a close-cropped, Jean Seberg haircut.

"Sophy, welcome. You're our first visitor of the season." She leaned down to hold her cheek against mine for the briefest instant, stopping short of a kiss. When she stepped back, I saw her shorn head anew in the light and wondered if Evan might have neglected to tell me that she'd had chemo and her hair was just growing back. She had lovely green eyes, a spray of freckles across her nose, and a long neck that always reminded me of Audrey Hepburn's. "We drove past your house the other morning, and I reminded the boys of that sail we took when —"

"I'm afraid I'm not here under very festive circumstances."

"What's happened?"

"It's about Will," I heard Evan say behind me, and hoped he would explain so that I would not have to.

They had gutted the first two floors of the house, so although it looked from the outside like an enormous Queen Anne, an ornate summer house, circa 1880, its interior was bold and spacious, more like an artist's loft in SoHo than a Swansea getaway. Even in the state I was in, I was startled, as I always was, by the wide-open living and dining room, by the dramatic, comfortable splendor of their surroundings. The high, sloped ceiling, the bleached wood staircase leading up to the second-floor balcony hung with antique Amish quilts, the deep blues and greens of the couch and love seats, the pair of Rauschenberg prints over the fireplace. What I'd remembered as sliding glass doors overlooking the deck was actually an entire wall of glass, including two sets of sliding doors, the length of it now — with the darkness outside and all the light within — like a blackened mirror, like a still pond in moonlight, in which the contents of the entire room were reflected. On the long oak dining room table was a tall vase of wildflowers, fluorescent in their brightness. On end tables and a coffee table were little piles of books, scattered around the museum-like room, the way people used to set out ashtrays. Jane Austen, Vasari, C. S. Lewis for the children, Lewis Thomas for the grown-ups, Thoreau's *Cape Cod,* and an array of books about the island — picture books, histories, a cookbook — a most self-congratulatory collection.

They offered me food, drink, company, and for fifteen or twenty minutes I luxuriated in their affection, their concern, their sympathy. Mavis fixed us plates of leftovers, grilled bluefish, sliced tomatoes, cornbread. Then telephones started to ring, different lines in different rooms, and both Evan and Mavis became utterly preoccupied, separately, privately, in some complex choreography that I had stumbled into, though they returned to the living-dining room to check up on me between calls. It was, by then, well after eleven. It was also, by then, clear that I was on my own here, so I moved to a couch with a pad and pencil and was writing the obituary Daniel had told me to write when Mavis came out of the kitchen and said, "There's a phone call for you."

"Who is it? Who could it be?" There wasn't a soul who knew I was here.

"I didn't ask."

It was one of my twin stepdaughters, who began crying the instant she said, "It's me, Ginny." When she was calmer, she said, "How could his heart have given out? He was in such good shape. He sailed, he didn't smoke, he —"

"Where are you?"

"In Maine, where I always am."

"Who told you all of this?"

"Remember my friend Melanie? She called from the island. She thought she was making a condolence call. She said, 'I'm so sorry, I just heard.' I thought she meant your divorce, so I said, 'Well, it's sad but it's not the end of the world.' She said, 'Ginny, I know you had issues with your father, but this is a little cold for my taste.' 'My father? What are you talking about?' Then she told me." Ginny cried some more, and I was as comforting as I could be in this medium, at this distance, given that I was still trying to determine how she had found out where I was. It had to have been the cab driver, who must have recognized Evan and known someone who knows Ginny's friend. But we had been talking in the cab about the possibility of Will's having killed himself. How had Ginny come to the conclusion that he had suffered a heart attack — unless the cab driver passed that on, wanting, perhaps, to soften the blow?

Ginny said she would track down her sister in northern California, and we agreed to talk tomorrow about what to do next. Before I hung up, I said, "I'm sorry I haven't called you since your dad and I split up. I wanted to. I thought about you, but it was awkward."

"I understand."

Evan and Mavis were at the dining room table when I returned to the big room; it looked as if I'd interrupted them. Evan leaped up, and Flossie followed him to the bar, her claws clacking like castanets across the wood floor. She was an enormous, mostly black, Newfoundland, except for the dramatic white rings around her deep brown eyes and four white paws. She stood glued to Evan's side and nuzzled the bottle of Tanqueray at the edge of the liquor cabinet. "You know you can't mix, Flossie," he said. "'Never mix, never worry.' Isn't that a line from *Who's Afraid of Virginia Woolf?* Sophy, can I get you anything?"

"I'm fine."

"Darling, a brandy?"

"I'm happy with my wine," Mavis said, "and I just took a Klonopin. Don't want to overdo it. Do you want something to help you sleep tonight, Sophy? I've got a stash."

"Of?"

"Mood stabilizers, tranquilizers, antidepressants, the usual."

"It's part of Mavis's cultural studies program. The culture makes us mad and the culture then allows us to regulate and reinvent our madness. Isn't that the way it works, darling? R. D. Laing plus Timothy Leary? Or are they passé?" An old-fashioned seltzer spritzer, the glass cylinder a lovely aquamarine, appeared in Evan's hands, and he squirted a noisy shot into his glass of Scotch. Flossie, sitting at his feet, barked a staccato, seal-like yelp. Evan squirted another shot. Flossie barked again.

"Evan, you'll wake the boys."

"Sorry, Flossie, your mother says no nightcap tonight. But maybe she'll give you a Klonopin. Which goes very well with California Merlot." Squirt, squirt. Bark, bark. "Because you're such a good dog." Yelp, yelp.

I looked from Evan, smiling down at the dog, to Mavis and saw her eyes close and her mouth tighten in a gesture of squelched anger that I could tell went very deep. The dog barked, unprovoked, a few more times. Evan squirted seltzer a few more times. I reached for a pear from the fruit bowl in the center of the table and felt stupidly sorry for myself, piteously sorry, because all I wanted was for them to sit down and let me talk about Will and Ginny and the cab driver reporting everything he'd heard, but there were stronger currents at work in this water. Evan's allusion to *Who's Afraid of Virginia Woolf?* was turning out to be apt. The soothing, selfless company I craved had evaporated — if it had ever existed.

"Sophy." I looked up to see Mavis gazing at me with a glimmer of the care I needed. "What a nightmare for you. You must be devastated."

"I'm not sure what I am."

"It's shock. Thank God for it. And for Klonopin. Are you sure you don't want half a milligram? I don't suppose you know yet about the funeral. Did you talk to your stepdaughter about it?"

"No, but Will told me last summer he wanted to be cremated. We had one of those conversations that feels unnecessarily morbid, but turns out not to be after all."

"Speaking of people dying," Mavis said, "did you ever finish that novel about Nadia Boulanger's sister?"

"As a matter of fact, I was working on it today. But it's not going too well." I remembered that I hadn't called Daniel, and now it was too late.

"A toast to Will," Evan said and held up his glass. "To our memories of Will, Sophy's memories of Will. He was a good man."

Our glasses clinked. Mavis said, "He was indeed," and her voice cracked. A quick torrent of tears slid down my face, though I didn't sob or convulse; only this water over my cheeks and chin like a sudden summer shower. I brushed it away and saw Evan and Mavis with their eyes on me in exactly the kindly way I needed. Mavis reached over and covered my hand with hers. I was sure that what I was identifying as pain in their eyes was aching empathy with me.

It was later that I learned both of them had received devastating news in the past few hours, reiterated in the phone calls they had been taking since my arrival. My itinerant pain, I would soon discover, was only one cause of the stricken looks on their elegant, affluent faces.

But all I knew at that moment was that I needed to talk and

felt the need fiercely, like a great hunger, like lust. I told them the story of the day I met Will when I was hitchhiking on Honeysuckle Road. They told gracious stories about Will too, and I knew what good hosts they were, despite what happened later, because the truth was that they were both as lost in their own secret suffering — secret not only from me but, for the time being, from each other — as I was lost in mine.

I stayed up until four in the morning, writing Will's obituary on a computer in Evan's study. When I woke up, I faxed it to the island newspaper and to Daniel's office, with Evan's phone number and a brief note — *Found an old friend en route to island. With him until further notice* — which I wanted to be as ambiguous as possible.

5

Island Marxism

I felt the road curve and dip sharply as it ran alongside the Lawson's sheep farm, and then began to climb the hill that passed the old cemetery, studded with headstones from the island's earliest European settlers. A moment later the landscape changed, as it does on the island so suddenly, and we were on the same sweet two-lane road now swathed in leafy trees, dense as a rain forest, the trees seeming to bow across the road to one another, like fingertips touching. None of the sweet narrow roads on Swansea leads anywhere except to other narrow roads or to the ocean or one of the harbors. When you come to the edge of the land here — but wherever you are, really, on the island — you feel you are in a place quite apart from every other you know: the colors, the light, the proportions of things, a sense that this was the world before the world was made.

I FOUND THIS the other day in an old issue of the *Swansea Sentinel;* it's from an essay I wrote four years ago, soon after Will and I moved here to live year round. We had left New York after a series of violent crimes that came too close to our lives: a friend was murdered when a man followed her into her building, several blocks from ours, forced her into the elevator, and onto the roof. You would know her name if I mentioned it; it was news for weeks. She was the third friend in six months who'd had a gun pointed at her, though the others came to no harm.

And there was also my wanting a child. In the city, we had a cramped, expensive one-bedroom apartment, and on Swansea, a rundown Cape Cod bungalow Will had inherited from an eccentric relative twenty-five years before. It had no heat, the original windows, an ancient kitchen, "a lot of potential," as realtors say, and "needs TLC." We were not the first people to flee the perils of the city for Arcadia, but that accounts, you understand, for the idealized view of the place I expressed in my essay. We winterized the house and tried to settle into the pastoral life the island seemed to promise. I tried to become a mother, a gardener, a short-story writer, because I was always just about to get pregnant and didn't want to start something I wouldn't be able to finish before the kid came. The short stories turned out to be the only soufflés in the bunch that rose. Motherhood eluded me. So did a green thumb. And, of course, I had to revise my dreamy picture of the island.

Among year-rounders, one of the quips about Swansea is that half the people here are in AA and the other half ought to be. Another is that in winter it is a floating mental hospital. My first winter, I became good friends with a woman photographer, until I found out that her boyfriend had a collection of automatic weapons and a restraining order against him from the mother of his children, and that what he and my friend did for kicks was break into locked summer houses and videotape themselves in strange beds. The guns made me nervous.

But mostly what I discovered in the years I lived here is that winter people keep to themselves. They are not summer people — organizing dinner parties and power picnics and whale watchings — transported to another season. They keep appointments, as Thoreau did, with beech trees and yellow birches; they live on the island because, like Bartleby, they would prefer not to. Not to hustle and hassle with life on the other side of the sound. Quite a few of them call the mainland "America." Small is still beautiful, and the world is too much with them late and soon. I don't know; maybe they're shy, or maybe they're more clear-headed than the rest of us about what's important: natural beauty, safe streets, clean air, the wild wood, not the wide world beyond it.

I called my lawyer, the morning after I arrived on Swansea, to find out what my marital status was. A machine answered. I called my stepdaughter. A machine answered. When I called to get the messages on my machine in New York, my mother had called to ask when I was coming to visit her, and I realized I had to tell her about Will. Then Evan and I took a ride to the other side of the island, to the village of Cummington, the house where I used to live, to look for Henry and for my husband's will.

I thought of going to the house as I did of getting on the eight-seater airplane the night before: if there were any other way to do what I had to do, I would have done it. Evan insisted I not do it myself.

The street we lived on was modest, its shingled houses an assortment of saltboxes, old Cape Cod bungalows with dormer sheds and front porches, and a few hodgepodge two- and three-bedroom places of no precise architectural nomenclature, almost all of the shingles unpainted and in various stages of weathering. These were not beach-front properties, and most of us were year-round residents, which meant we had more in common with the cab driver from the night before than we did with Evan. The street and its surroundings were quaint, well-tended, and probably looked the way they had forty years before. Everyone, except Will and me, had a garden. And because I failed so miserably at making things grow in the ground, I had bought an assortment of colorful nylon flags to hang on the front porch. I don't mean countries; I mean long windsock-style decorations. A rainbow, an engorged tulip, a puffy bright yellow sun with four-foot streamers that twirled wildly in the wind but hung like a wet sock on a clothesline when the air was still.

As Evan turned the corner, I dreaded seeing the flags as much as anything else. Evidence of my folly, my sentimentality, my walking out on Will. Evan must have seen something on my face — a darkness, a twitch — because he reached across the gear shift, squeezed my hand, and said, "How are you doing?"

"Let's talk about something else." I kept my eyes down, afraid to look at the house, like a kid trying not to step on cracks in the sidewalk, but when I glanced up, it wasn't my house I saw, but Ben in his driveway, about to get into a car. "Slow down," I said to Evan and called out the window to Ben. He was startled to see me; he looked pale, not well. Evan pulled into his driveway and I got out of the car. It was difficult for both of us, because Ben was Will's friend, because Ben had found him, because Ben and his wife, Emily, had been witnesses to the last four years of our marriage, to the quotidian reality of it, the easy affection, Will's pain when I left. They had never puttered in their driveway and heard us shriek at each other. They had never gone out to empty their trash and heard Will holler, "I'd rather eat glass than have a relationship with you." We did not often quarrel. Our style was to withdraw, suffer silently; and to the neighbors, Ben and Emily right next door, I suppose everything looked fine. We had a sunburst flag on our front porch. Of course we were happy.

One day last summer, when I caught a glimpse of Ben coming home from work in his greasy mechanic's jumpsuit, I was startled to realize that this man who owned a service station and had never lived anywhere but Swansea was a much happier man than my husband would ever be.

He and I had never so much as brushed pinkies, but standing now on the pea gravel of his driveway, we threw our arms around each other and cried together.

A minute later, when we disengaged and I told him I was going into the house to look for Will's will, he shook his head and reached for my hand. "You can't."

"What do you mean, I can't?"

"I'll show you what I mean." He walked to his car, opened the door, took something from the seat, and showed me two black video-cassette boxes. "Here."

While I looked at the labels, two movies I'd never heard of, Evan introduced himself to Ben. "I don't get it," I said.

"He rented them on May thirty-first. You know he was obsessed with getting them back the next day, because he hated paying extra. I found them in his bedroom. June twenty-second."

"Did you take them before the police came or after?" Evan said.

"I came back here and called the police."

"Do the police know you have them?"

"I knew that the date he took them out would tell me —"

"Why don't you walk me through what you did, step by step?" Evan said.

"I don't need to walk through it; I lived through it, eighteen hours ago."

"What you did might turn out to be tampering with evidence at the scene of a crime. It's removing evidence that could —"

"No one's thinking it was a crime."

"I haven't spoken to the police myself."

"You don't understand what I'm saying, do you?"

"Unfortunately, I think I do," Evan said.

"He's a lawyer," I said to Ben. "That's why he's —"

"I know who Evan Lambert is, for Christ's sake. I see him on TV all the time defending the Nazi baby-killer. I've changed the oil in your cars a few times, but I wouldn't expect you to remember that." Then Ben turned to me. "I called a cleaning company to come in."

"That was sweet, to think of a maid at a time like —"

"It's not a maid, Sophy."

"What he's saying —" Evan began, before Ben interrupted.

"You think I have trouble expressing myself? Is that it? And who the hell's been talking to you? What was I about to tell her, since you're so goddam smart?"

"It's a restoration company," Evan said, uncannily, "not a maid service. Am I close?"

"I think it would be easier if Ben and I could have a few minutes to ourselves," I managed to say, and Evan, visibly relieved, went back to his car.

"I'm sorry," I said softly. "I had no idea this would become —"

"I found him on the floor," Ben said as softly, "next to the bed."

"But the police said he died in his sleep."

"If you have a heart attack, they say you can get jolted out of the bed. I don't know what happened. He was naked, not far from the bed. They're going to replace part of the floor. And fumigate. They should be here soon."

"Didn't you realize when you opened the front door, from the odor —"

"Emily and I hadn't seen him for weeks. We were starting to get worried. He always let us know when he was leaving on a trip and when he came back. Yeah, I guess I knew when I opened the door. I went upstairs anyway."

"Was the dog there? Is he with you?"

"I thought you had him. Will kept talking about taking him to you. When I didn't see Will for a few days — must've been the first week of June — I thought he'd either gone sailing, one of those yacht deliveries he did with Craig down at the shipyards, or that he'd taken Henry to New York."

When I got into Evan's car a few minutes later, I was too stunned by the details of the death to say anything, and too angry with Evan to want his sympathy. He started the ignition, backed out into the street, and headed down Longfellow Lane toward the village. "Sophy, I'm not looking to be an accomplice in an investigation of tampering with evidence on my summer vacation. He could have called the video store and asked when Will took them out. He didn't have to remove them from the house."

"It wasn't fair of you to pull rank."

"That was not pulling rank."

"You'd never talk down to that Patrick guy I met at your house last summer."

"He'd never do something so stupid."

"Because he's a Harvard professor, right? Ben happens to make an honest living. Which is more than I can say for either of us."

"Sophy, don't get started with island Marxism. People talked like that around here in the seventies, but there isn't much of an audience for it anymore, except for what's-her-name who grows biodynamic turnips out at Lavender Point and thinks she's Che Guevara. Do you need anything in Cummington, or should we —"

"That's three weeks. May thirty-first to June twenty-second. I kept calling and leaving messages about money he owed me. I thought it was odd that he didn't call back. I knew he was pissed off, but I never imagined —"

"Of course you didn't."

"Poor baby. Poor darling. I hope he didn't kill himself."

"I do too."

"Because I hate to think he was so unhappy that he'd given up every hope of being happier. It hurts me to think of him in that much pain."

"I know it does."

"He used to say, 'When the time comes, put me on a rickety old sailboat with a carton of Scotch and a case of cigarettes and push.' It always made me cry. About a year ago it stopped making me cry. He knew. That I wasn't devastated anymore by the idea of losing him. He hated that everyone thought he was such a nice guy. Hated it. It would have done him good to be more of an s.o.b. now and then. Like you."

"Thanks. Thanks a lot."

"I hope he didn't know he was going to die. I hope he didn't have time to be afraid." Tears had been rolling down my face and into my mouth, and Evan handed me his handkerchief. His hand had slid over into my lap, and he was squeezing my fingers and stroking my wrists, and I was trying to take deep breaths because no air was moving through my nose. "Evan?"

"Yes, dear?"

"We have to go to the post office, because there's three weeks of mail that hasn't been picked up. Then we have to go to the video store and read the descriptions of the movies Will took out, on the chance that he meant them as suicide notes."

"What are you talking about?"

"He was a spy. He was clever."

"Sophy, you'll drive yourself nuts with amateur sleuthing."

"I lived with this man for ten years. I know the way he thinks."

"Aren't you speaking to the coroner later? He may have the results of the autopsy."

"I still want to look at the videos. Then we have to find Henry."

"Henry who?"

"The dog. Nobody knows this yet, but Henry's the one with the answers, because if Will planned for some time to kill himself, he might have given the dog away, to protect him, and whoever he gave him to, they could tell us what he'd said and when it happened and —"

"Of course, Sophy, of course."

Evan told me, some time later, that he thought I'd gone off half-cocked, between my pursuit of the missing dog and the secret messages in the videos, but he indulged me that day without further commentary. I was the grieving widow after all, and entitled to a touch of madness.

When we returned to Evan's house, with three tall bundles of mail, there was a message for me from Ginny. She would be arriving on a four o'clock plane from Portland, Maine. Evan, Mavis, and their two young sons invited me sailing for the rest of the afternoon, but I declined, because I'd have to go to the airport in a few hours. They gave me the keys to the Saab Evan had driven earlier, invited Ginny and me to stay at their house until Sunday, and said we were welcome to join them that evening at a clambake down the beach with their friends the Winstons.

"You know Sue and Bob Winston, don't you?" Mavis said. "She's been writing a biography of Louisa May Alcott for a zillion years that's finally being published, and he's a colleague of mine at Harvard."

I did not remember meeting them before, but my appearance that night at their clambake would linger long in all of our memories.

6

Clare's Funeral

THE NEXT SCENE could have passed for an ordinary summer afternoon at the Swansea Island Airport. The sky bluer than robins' eggs. The praying mantis–like private planes and sleek corporate jets all parked in a row down the side of the tarmac. A cluster of us in khakis and T's and jeans — this was Swansea wealth, after all, not Palm Beach — behind a chain-link fence that defined one edge of the outdoor waiting pen, some of us waving even before the tiny Cessna came to a stop on the runway and made its sharp right turn and parked in a spot beside three or four other Island Air runabouts. I wasn't one of the ones waving. Otherwise, Ginny and I could have passed for ordinary summer people, which is to say monied and carefree, accustomed to coming and going in high style. Ordinary summer people, and even what looked like tears as she crossed the tarmac, shoulder slung with a colorful Guatemalan bag, could have been explained away. She is a high-strung, emotional type who weeps almost as an affectation on arrivals and departures. How touching; that must be it. Or: she is suffering from a broken heart and has come to Swansea, to Mom and Dad, to mend.

I had not seen Ginny in more than a year, this young woman I had known since she was thirteen, when I could not tell her apart from her twin sister, except for their noses: Ginny's more aquiline than Susanna's. Even their voices were identical. She was lean and sportive in that row of travelers, like the pictures I'd seen of her mother when she was Ginny's age, but wearing a pair of awful jeans with gashes in the knees, and a flimsy tank top, and, so it seemed from the distance, a row of small silver hoops that rimmed her ears. She was squinting against the bright sunlight and smiling a contorted, bittersweet smile, unsure of what was called for. I must have been, too.

She was the third or fourth one through the gate into the waiting area, and I could see that it was difficult for her to look at me the closer she got, a sort of adolescent nervousness — lowering her eyes, letting them dart everywhere but in my direction. But when we were finally face to face, she flung her arms around my neck with a force and neediness I had not expected and began, suddenly, violently, to sob against me. We were blocking the exit, but people squeezed around us. I held one hand against the back of her head and the other on her shoulder; I held her that way for a long, long time.

It is a peculiar thing to be, a stepmother, and, stranger still, an almost ex-stepmother, and I don't know if we were happy to see each other, but we were relieved. Or maybe the relief was all mine; I had so dreaded telling her the news that comforting her now was effortless. But how could it not be? She and her sister were the closest thing to children in my life, and comforting one's children, even those not born of your flesh, is easy, so bred in the bone that even Daniel was good at it.

At first it was a cakewalk. For half an hour, the edges of our personalities, the burden of our history and of the present, were blurred by grief and good will. We were relief workers at the aftermath of a tornado; one of us would switch to being a survivor, and then we'd dive backward into the opposite role. We were as close as we had ever been. There was no courtesy not indulged, no tenderness denied. We were so finely attuned to each other's needs, the whole thing could have been choreographed by George Balanchine.

"I came right away because I wanted to say goodbye to him," she said, holding my arm as we approached the luggage carried off the plane.

"Of course," I said, kindly, lying, lying. I would tell her the truth in the car, dispense it in small bites the way I had learned it; no point having it land on her all at once like an avalanche.

"Susanna's trying to get here tomorrow. I had her neighbors drive up the mountain to the cabin last night and tell her. She and Daddy hadn't spoken for months."

"I was afraid of that." Actually, I had pushed that fear to the back of my mind until this moment; that's how much distance there was between this family and me. Now I carried Ginny's bag to the car with a new fear: that all of our gentleness would evaporate before the hour was up. I still was not used to the island breeze, the lightness of the air, the terrible closeness I felt to her, terrible because it had taken this death to bring it on, because I knew how fragile it was. Then we were off, on the long road to Evan's.

"Susanna was furious that Daddy didn't come to California to see her when little Rose was born."

"I was too. I did everything I could to get him there." Rose had arrived six weeks before I left. Will's refusal to go to see her — and his daughter and son-in-law — helped push me out the door, allowed me to see that Will was so tangled up in his fears that he could not make the most basic parental gesture. If he could cut himself off that thoroughly from his beloved children, who was he? If what he wanted in this world — or if all he could handle — were retreat and isolation, why had it fallen to me to stay and be his lifeline? "He was afraid," I said to Ginny.

"Of a two-day-old baby?"

"Of his feelings. All his guilt about Jesse" — his son who had died many years before — "and his sadness that Susanna lived so far away. He never let go of the idea that she lived out there in order to avoid him. Maybe he thought that seeing Rose would bring back his grief over Jesse."

"Susanna sort of gave up, after he wouldn't come. When he called and left messages with her neighbors, she wouldn't call him back. He wanted to buy her a cell phone, but she said the reception was terrible on the mountain. He wanted to buy her a computer so that he could send her e-mail. But she needed a phone for that too. He wanted to be in touch with her but only from a distance."

"How did she take the news that he'd died?"

"She asked if he'd killed himself, first thing. That's what our mom asked too." Why didn't I tell her right then that it was a possibility? It would have been easier than what we went through later, but I was still raw from everything Ben had told me, and from reading three weeks of Will's mail. According to the phone bill, the last call he made was at 10:05 the night of May thirty-first, a Wednesday, to his friend Diane in Cambridge. They had talked for fifteen minutes. His last ATM withdrawal was that afternoon: $200. The last charge on his credit card was a week before, for a CD from Amazon.com. There was also a curious letter he had written to someone named Crystal Sparrow; it was stamped RETURN TO SENDER: NO FORWARDING ADDRESS. The address was a rural delivery route on the West End of the island, about halfway between the airport and Evan's house. In the handwritten letter, he asked her out on a date. I'd stuck it in my purse, intending to track her down. And there was a postcard from the video store: the movies he rented 5/31/00 were overdue.

I did not know where to put the fact that he had been dead for three weeks while I had romped around in bed with Daniel, playing mother to his children, playing the carefree divorcée. All the great mad joy I'd felt on returning to New York had gone to dust, ashes, rot.

"How come you didn't call me right away?" Ginny said in the gentlest tone, almost as an afterthought, like someone genially tying up loose ends, someone other than my perennially angry stepdaughter.

"I tried. The number I had for you was disconnected, and I couldn't remember the call letters of your TV station. I was going to look for your father's address book in the house. I'm sorry you found out the way you did. And sorry it's been so long since we've talked."

"It's all right." This in the same understanding, unfamiliar voice. "I thought about calling you once or twice, but, I don't know, it seemed disloyal to Daddy."

"I understand."

The island's great beauty rolled alongside the car, a ticklish distraction not only from the shock of Will's death but from the high wire on which Ginny and I teetered. It was always that way with her, things going along fine, then a flare-up, spontaneous combustion. Would we make it to Evan's house in one piece?

"I know you feel guilty, Soph. I do too."

"About what?" Might she know about Daniel? Had she spoken to Will's friend Diane?

"Not being with Daddy when he died. When I was little

and he traveled, I was always afraid the State Department would call and say he was dead in a country I'd never heard of and couldn't pronounce. When I was seven I learned the name of every country and capital in Europe, Africa, and Asia. Some weird, like, self-defense. When I was fourteen and Daddy retired from his job, when you and he were first together, he confessed he'd never worked for the State Department and he'd hardly ever gone to the places he told us he'd been. He and Mommy would say he was in London, and he would be in, like, Cambodia. Then I had to rethink the geography of my whole childhood. That's how I feel right now, like Daddy said he'd be in a particular place, and I was counting on it, but he's not."

I reached across the gear shift and took her hand, and she let me hold it.

"I don't remember a funeral parlor on this end of the island," Ginny said. We were more than halfway to Evan's place, heading into island farmland, rolling meadows, the ancient cemetery I had written about when I first arrived.

"There isn't one."

"Then where are we going?"

"To Evan and Mavis's house. Where did you think?"

"I thought you were taking me to say goodbye to Daddy. That's why I came so soon."

"There's an autopsy. Off-island. The medical examiner ordered it."

"Why didn't you tell me? When will he be back here?" The questions had sharper edges, arrowheads, say, but not steak knives. Not yet.

"I had no idea you thought we were going there now. I'll call the coroner as soon as we get to Evan's and find out when they'll be through with the body." I should have said everything at that moment, instead of storing it up, but I was trying to spare her, give her a few more hours before she had to endure another round of horrors. "You remember Evan and Mavis, don't you?"

"I just saw him on Ted Koppel. My boyfriend has to watch it every night, like that disease where you have to wash your hands every five minutes. I said to him, 'My almost-ex-stepmother used to be his girlfriend.' 'Ted Koppel's girlfriend?' He was, like, wow. So I said, 'Don't you think I'd have told you that when you first made me watch this? The *lawyer's* girlfriend, the guy who's sticking up for the German girl who killed the baby.' He was, like, 'Your stepmother dated that guy? He would defend Slobodan Milosevic if it would get him network TV time."

"I hope you told him it was when Evan was in law school, and that he didn't defend any celebrity murderers before he passed the bar."

"Whatever."

"I meant to ask you about the dog."

"Horrible Henry?"

"Did you ever talk to your dad about taking him?"

"No. I thought you were going to get him once you were settled, and I figured it had already happened."

"He's missing. And speaking of missing, do you know if your father has a will?"

"It's in my suitcase. He sent it to me a few months ago in a sealed envelope that said, 'To be opened only in event of death.' It gave me the creeps. He sent Susanna a copy, too."

"How many months ago?"

"I don't know, a few."

We had just turned onto the dirt road, and the car was wobbling over the ruts. "Did you open it?"

"This morning. I'll give it to you when I unpack. I think Daddy mentioned you in it."

"Really?"

"Yeah, but I can't remember how it went."

I am still not sure whether she was telling me the truth. Did she really not remember what her father had said about me in that document, or was she doing exactly what I was doing to her: withholding unpleasant information until it was impossible not to?

"The only thing we can rule out now is a stroke," the coroner said while Ginny took a shower upstairs. "We can't determine if it was a coronary. Too much decomposition. Next, we test for substances in the system." Flossie was sleeping under the dining room table, her furry chin on my bare foot. "But to tell you the truth, it doesn't look good."

"Good for what?" It was an unexpected word, under the circumstances.

"A conclusive answer."

"Because?"

I heard an unprofessional sigh. "We normally test the blood, and there's not much of it to test."

I understood this was a euphemism for "none," but something made me ask the next question; my stubbornness, my refusal to believe that every inquiry would lead to darkness and more darkness. "I think I know the answer, but if my husband's daughters want to see him, you know, to say good-bye —"

He did not let me finish. "There's nothing much left to say goodbye to."

I have since parsed that sentence clean. I have had dreams about it, have thought, in lighter moments, that it would make a decent refrain in a country-and-western song, but I have no idea precisely what it means. It is not in the least descriptive; it simply deters intruders by not inviting a single clarifying question: *What exactly do you mean by "nothing much"? A skeleton picked clean, like a Thanksgiving turkey two days later? And if not that* —

"I'll tell them," I said to the coroner. "Or maybe I won't. One other thing; I'm not sure what happens next."

"We'll call you with the results. Sometime next week."

"No, I mean, the body. Are you finished with it?"

"Yes. The funeral home will pick it up."

"But we're not having a funeral home service, and he's going to be cremated." I saw Ginny come down the stairs in fresh shorts and a white T-shirt, her long blond hair wet and ruler-straight. I watched her gaze around the sunlit showpiece room as if she were visiting a Moroccan bazaar.

"You'll have to talk to the funeral home about all that, Mrs. O'Rourke. I assume you have the number."

As Ginny crossed the room, I saw she held an envelope, and when I hung up the phone, I was surprised to see her glare at me. "That's not going to happen," she said sharply.

"What's not?"

"He's not going to be cremated."

"He told me last summer that's what he wanted. Did he tell you something else? Is it in his will?"

"That's not what *we* want. Where's the phone book?" She found the slim island directory on one of the end tables and began flipping through it, biting the inside of her cheek, right at the V of her mouth where her upper and lower lips met. The instant I realized she would do that until her anger abated, and that she'd been angry for all the years I had known her, I got up and walked across the vast space into the kitchen, which was connected to the big room by a cut-out in the wall. I tried not to storm off or bang around angrily. It was too soon for that, and it was not my style. In a calmer moment, I would tell her again what Will's wishes were. In the meantime, I would do my best to take care of her.

"Are you hungry?" I called out. "Mavis left us chicken salad and peach pie from Sharon Asher's farm stand. Can I fix you a plate?"

"I don't eat meat," she mumbled. "Or chicken. Or fish."

"I thought you'd started again."

"Then I stopped." On and off the wagon. It sounded as if she had a speech impediment, still chewing on her cheek.

"What about peach pie with vanilla ice cream? That's what Jack Kerouac and his buddies ate at truck stops in *On the Road.* Cheapest way to get all that protein; in the ice cream, I guess. Though it may have been apple, not peach."

"I don't eat dairy either."

"It doesn't hurt the cows when you milk them, Ginny. They actually kind of like it."

Silence, then more silence from the other room. I guess I had sounded sarcastic, when I only meant to sound playful. "There are also some grilled vegetables, let's see, and a loaf of homemade bread."

"Anything's fine, Sophy."

But of course nothing was fine, not what I'd said about cows or cremation or probably peach pie. This kid and I had a history or maybe it was only the future we wanted to steer clear of, the upcoming forty-eight hours spiraling across the prairie like a tornado. Disasters. Disaster metaphors. The Christmas she was nineteen, in a blazing non sequitur, she accused me of wishing that it had been she who died in the car accident, instead of her brother, whom I had never known.

I carried food and plates into the dining room, expecting that she would dislodge herself from the armchair, where she was still studying the phone directory. She did not budge.

"Who you looking for?"

"Father Kelly."

Not a name I knew. "Are you thinking of having a Catholic funeral?" I asked this with as little inflection, and astonishment, as I could.

"Of course."

"Your father hadn't been to church in thirty years. Maybe forty."

"Except when Jesse died."

Here's what you don't know about shock until its insulating effects fall away like chunks of plaster from a wall: it acts not only as a painkiller, a mega-Klonopin, but it deadens years of long-term memory, your history, and perhaps your spouse's, which you have come to know so thoroughly, it has become your own, the way property does in marriage.

Until that moment I had not remembered Will's accounts of the civil war that had erupted over Jesse's funeral.

Will's history. He had wanted his son to be cremated, the ashes scattered in the sea, and a secular service to be run by a Berrigan-type former priest who would have let the college kids speak about their friend and classmate. Jesse's mother, Clare, no longer Will's wife, had wanted the Roman Catholic ritual, the coffin with white-satin lining, the procession of limos to the cemetery. "Haven't you done enough damage?" she was unkind enough to say when Will described the ceremony he wanted. That cruelty and his guilt were enough to make him submit to Clare's funeral arrangements. That's what he used to call it: Clare's funeral.

Will's funeral. Across this vast room, the late-afternoon light slanting in against the couches and kilims in trapezoidal shapes, Ginny looked up from the phone book and said, "I forgot to tell you. My mother's coming tomorrow afternoon from Chicago. She's trying to rent a house for a week so that Susanna and I have a place to stay. Hotels are all booked. Do you know if Saint Anne's by the Sea is the church with the Gothic fretwork near the saltwater taffy place, or is that the one by the elementary school that looks like a bank?"

"Can't say that I know."

Those were the only words I could utter right then, and just barely. I closed my eyes and must have sighed in self-defense, as I do now, remembering the cumulative force of this news. Clare's Funeral Redux? Clare the real estate agent, Clare of the deep pockets and the religious right, Clare the mother of his children who had endured the sufferings of the Virgin Mary. Was this going to be Clare, who worshipped money and property and God with a capital G, versus me, who had spent the last three weeks in bed with another man? This was not a competition I could win.

Will's will. When I opened my eyes I saw at Ginny's bare feet the white envelope she had brought from upstairs. "Is that your father's will?"

"This? Yeah." She plucked it from the floor while the phone book slid off her lap. "Here." Holding it out to me with the most studied indifference, as if she were passing me a newsletter from her congressman or a Coke can to be recycled.

It was a slender wad of papers I began to read as I moved to take refuge in the kitchen. The page on top was not his will but a life insurance policy he had had since his children were small. The last time I'd seen it, my name was listed beneath the girls', and I had been entitled to a third of the $300,000 payout. It did not surprise me that my name was no longer there, but I was surprised to find it replaced by Diane Schaefer Berg, Cambridge, Mass., who was to receive my entire share. The papers were dated a month after Will and I had separated.

When I flipped to the next page, I was looking at the will. My eyes fell to my name, in the fourth line — "I am married to Sophy Chase" — and to my name in the next line: "I give one dollar to Sophy Chase, who, in anticipation of a divorce that she requested, entered into an agreement with me to define our respective financial and property rights and all other rights, remedies, privileges, and obligations which arose out of our marriage."

"Who were you talking to when I came downstairs before, that you told you wanted to cremate Daddy?"

I had not made it to the kitchen, only to the dining room table, and when I turned to look at Ginny, she was still studying the phone book, backlit by the sun. I was startled by the glare, the way you are as you come out of a movie theater in the middle of the day. I don't think my hands were shaking, but my voice was. I must have sounded scared or flustered, or maybe the word I mean is "humiliated." "The coroner," I said, but the *c* caught in my throat, and I had to start over.

"When will he have the results?"

"Why don't you put down the phone book for a minute." She did, reluctantly, and I got my voice back; it had been a touch of stage fright. "Come and sit down at the table. There are a few things you need to know." She complied. She took an orange from the fruit bowl and rolled it between her palms and then against the table, like a ball of dough she was trying to smooth. Sitting at the head of the table, I laid out what I thought she needed to know, one, two, three. I spoke more softly than I usually do, and more slowly, because I knew the restraint would help me control my rage. Part of my anger was at myself, over the unfairness of taking any of this out on Ginny, but there it was.

Yesterday, Ben Gibbs found him naked on the floor beside his bed, but according to the phone bill in the stack of mail, the last phone call he made was on May 31.

Diane Schaefer Berg, Daddy's friend since grade school, married to a physicist at MIT, suspects suicide.

The coroner said it was not a stroke and that he'd been dead too long for them to detect a heart attack. He wasn't sure how much he'd be able to learn, given the length of time Daddy had been dead. My version of "no blood left."

And if you were thinking about a viewing and an open casket, the coroner told me that there is nothing much left to say goodbye to.

She closed her eyes as the tears poured over her face every which way, as much at the news as at my bluntness. But I don't know whether she understood what had motivated it: the wallop of the will, the specter of her mother's arrival, the sudden ascendancy of the Father, the Son, and the Holy Ghost into the funeral of my atheist husband. Ginny's hair was mostly dry, but her face was sopping wet and swollen, and she pressed her palms to her cheeks and let her head drop into them. I did not get up and comfort her, my stepchild whose father had died. I was, genuinely, for the first time, the wicked stepmother she used to accuse me of being. But I knew I was just angry at all of them, including Clare, whom I barely knew, and Will, who was dead, and I was about to apologize, to explain myself, when I heard the front door open and Evan call my name. At the sound of his voice, Flossie woke up from her nap under the dining room table, where I had forgotten she lay, and hurled herself to the door, barking to the salsa beat of her unclipped claws clicking against the floor.

"We're in here," I called back.

Ginny pushed away some of her tears and blew her nose in a napkin. I expected to hear a clatter of feet and gear and children's voices, but Evan was alone, red-faced from an afternoon on the water, still wearing a canvas sailing cap, which he removed as he came to the table to shake Ginny's hand.

"I'm sorry about your father. What a terrible shock. I'm afraid we can't put you up for longer. My brother and his wife and kids arrive the day after tomorrow, and every room is —"

"My mother's coming and renting us a place for the week."

"Lucky she could find anything so close to the Fourth of July weekend." He turned to me, and I noticed that his knees were sunburned. The hair on his forearms had blond highlights. There seemed to be more gray at his temples than there had been in the morning, and deeper lines on his forehead. I wondered whether I looked as old as he did. "How was the rest of your day?"

"As good as can be expected."

"I'm here to pick up Seth's asthma medicine and feed Flossie, but if you want to join us at the clambake, Mavis and the kids are already there. It's a few miles down the beach. If you take our Saab, you can leave early."

"Only on Swansea," Ginny said, and you could see her face lose its darkest scrim. "You come for a funeral and end up at a clambake. Daddy would have liked that, wouldn't he?"

I had to smile, but I could feel the tightness in it, and the fury. I wanted to remind her that ten minutes ago she would not eat anything that moved in salt water except seaweed.

"Did you get the message that your mother called?" Evan asked me. "Mavis said she left it on your bed."

"I haven't been up there. Did you tell her?"

"No. We thought you'd prefer to."

When I'd called her first thing that morning, I left a vague message. On Swansea for a few days; give me a call. I did not want her rushing to the island, thinking I needed her help or her comfort, when I knew that I would end up helping her, comforting her, chauffeuring her, this woman who had hauled me and her friend Gladys — Whoopi Goldberg in the movie — across the country thirty-five years before in pursuit of a man whose leave-takings she chose to read as a series of hints that he wanted to be found. Now she was frail and forgetful — too forgetful to be properly quixotic and keep track of her delusions — but I still had to tell her that Will was dead, just as I had to inform the bank and Visa and the pension department of the Central Intelligence Agency.

On the short drive to the Winstons' — Ginny and I followed Evan in his car — there was a woman hitchhiking, thumb pointing in our direction, but we weren't going far enough down the road to do her much good. I didn't stop, but I drove slowly enough to see that she bore some resemblance to me — to me twelve years earlier, thumb out on this same road, her hair in wiry curls because of the sea water, the salt air; a pair of cutoffs, an embroidered Indian blouse; a can of beer. Dumb girl, I thought. I'd never have hitched holding a beer can, even back when I drank the stuff. I didn't drink like that anyway, the slow, steady infusion, the morphine drip, my best friend the bottle. I binged. I could go for weeks with nothing. Then I'd have fourteen beers or seven gin-and-tonics or four giant happy-hour margaritas, whatever it took to render me speechless and horizontal. I knew Will for three weeks before he saw me take a drink. Then he saw me take six.

This is not a subject that is easy for me to talk about, not only because under the influence I have behaved abominably, but because giving it up was at the heart of the transaction I made with Will. In exchange for my abstinence, he would give me the closest thing to a normal family I'd had since my early childhood, the years before I understood that there was something freaky going on in our house; not everyone's father vanished for months on end. By the time Mom, Gladys, and I drove through Death Valley with a pair of binoculars, as if he might be hiding behind a creosote bush — by then I knew that our trip was not five days and four nights in Fort Lauderdale, not the spring vacation other kids in Mrs. McGrath's third-grade class at Carteret Elementary School went on. One of the things that made my father's leaving puzzling was that when he was with us, he seemed to be enjoying himself. He was not quarrelsome or short-tempered; the mood around the house was not storm, whoosh, bang, I'm outa here. The worst thing you could say about him was that he was remote. The best was that his remoteness was excellent preparation for life without him when he was gone for good.

It was not a long ride down the asphalt to the Winstons' dirt road, but it was long enough for me to feel the sudden weight of these memories, the intricate ways in which they led to one another and made a mockery of all the work I had done to keep them in the very back of my mind. Now they were front row, center, and my head was swimming

"I guess I thought he was over that," Ginny said, and it took me a moment to realize that we had not exchanged a word since leaving the house, and that she was talking about her father.

"Over what?"

"Suicide. After Jesse died and Daddy was in the loony bin, whenever the phone rang, I was sure it was someone calling to tell me he was dead. But then he met you, and he was so happy."

I waited for her to say something more, to acknowledge that that was a long time ago, all that happiness, and there is only so much we can do to make unhappy people happy, and it is not much, after all. But she was only twenty-five, and it takes a few more decades to come to that, if we ever do. In any case, Ginny was way past comforting me. She was doing to me what I was doing to myself, what I had been trying to contain in the back of my mind, a place as crowded with unpleasantness as Pandora's box. Quietly, in only a few words, with all the years between the great happiness and the present disappeared into ellipses, my stepdaughter was blaming me for her father's death, as I was blaming myself.

7

Slipping

LOW TIDE.

Piping plovers.

Sanderlings with their toothpick legs, skittering over the shoreline like wind-up toys on speed.

A light canopy of clouds far out over the ocean, which I knew would tint pink when the sun began to drop in a few hours.

The bustle and buzz of a cocktail party, a catered clambake for forty. Voices coasting on the wind, wholesome early evening laughter, a parade of small children chasing a beach ball. The sassafras fire in a sand pit, lobsters, clams, corn, all cooking beneath a canvas tarp, the guy cooking, whom they kept calling the Bake Master, in a butcher's apron and corny chef's cap, telling stories of getting his eyebrows singed and his forearms blackened. The name of the catering company across the apron, something about lobster tails or sea legs. I don't remember anymore.

I remember the oddness of the wild setting and the precious dinner decorations, Martha Stewart fetched up on the shores of Swansea. Bales of hay covered with blue-and-white-checked tablecloths and baskets of baguettes and trays of miniature carrots and zucchini. Galvanized tin pails of wildflowers and sunflowers, cloth napkins that matched the flowers, a wicker basket of lobster bibs. A high school girl, maybe the Winstons' daughter, going around with a petition on a clipboard to build a series of airborne nests on the public beach to save the plovers from certain extinction. This was not public beach. And the dogs. I remember the dogs.

I remember that I kept looking low to the ground for hideous Henry, but these dogs were fleet, pure goldens and Labs, made to run, made to be cuddled and kept close by, not abandoned, as Will must have abandoned Henry, because I could imagine no other fate for him.

I remember wondering what I was doing there, waiting on the drink line to get a glass of club soda from a kid who could be a Kennedy, a young man with lopsided Irish good looks and a toothy, bright smile. I was half-listening to the hostess, Sue Winston, tell a woman with an English accent about her forthcoming biography of Louisa May Alcott. Behind me another woman was talking about the celebrity auction always held in the middle of the summer, to which celebrities in years past had donated lunch or dinner with themselves to raise money for the social service agency that provides help for winter people impoverished by the departure of summer people at Labor Day. And then Hunter Abbott's voice began to come in clearly, a bit upwind, the familiar stories of the aging newspaperman, a cranky widower who still smoked Lucky Strikes, whose favorite subject was still the Old Days in Saigon. He and Will could work up a routine, even though they had been there on opposing teams, Hunter in the press and Will in the CIA. Will's distinction was that he was one of the few CIA people deeply opposed to the war, which made his life there another kind of hell from the hell of the war itself. After I got my club soda, I would stroll over to the circle where he stood and tell him Will was dead.

The surprise of a hand on my shoulder made me jump. It was Evan. "How're you doing?" he said quietly.

I did not know where to begin. I was not sure I wanted to begin. I noticed Ginny at the foot of the sand dunes talking intently to Mavis, Mavis nodding and then reaching to pat and hold Ginny's arm. It hurt me to think of my awfulness toward her; it made me want to flee from myself and from here, and once I felt that, or named it, everything I heard and saw encouraged flight, especially the silly sight of the beach done up as a Pottery Barn display window.

"Did Ginny have a copy of the will?" Evan asked.

"Did she ever."

"Surprises?"

"He left me a dollar."

"Ouch."

"Made his grade school friend one of the beneficiaries on his life insurance policy. She got the share that used to have my name on it, but it was only a hundred thousand. I know in your crowd that's chopped liver."

"Hardly, my dear."

"Evan, this looks like a wonderful party, but I — "

"I'm not sure what the law is, but I think that in the middle of a divorce —"

"I'm not quite in the mood for this — the lobster or the law. You won't be offended if I take a powder, will you?"

"Don't run off to be by yourself. After my father died . . . You're not going to look for the dog, are you? I know you're tough as nails, but —"

"Nails? Me?" Crying with Ben today? At the airport with Ginny sobbing in my arms?

"I meant that you're strong and you don't seem to need a lot of —"

"Maybe Styrofoam, Evan, but not steel."

"Will was angry, Sophy. That's all the dollar was about. But whether the whole package will stand up in court . . ."

"That makes two of us who are angry. And you know what?" This had just come to me, this nugget of justice or wisdom, though I am no longer sure it was either. "Now we're even. He got back at me for leaving him, so I don't have to feel guilty anymore."

"I'm a lawyer, not a psychiatrist," Evan said, "but this line of thinking could impair your judgment about suing his estate, which I believe you have every reason to pursue."

"Evan, may I have a word with you?" It was a man who looked silvery, distinguished, already tanned, a man who went around saying, May I have a word with you, and got all the words he wanted.

"Sophy, would you excuse me for a moment?"

I nodded and walked a few steps to the drinks table and asked for a club soda. "How's it going?" said the bartender.

"Swell."

"You look familiar. Did you ever wait tables at Bradey's? Lemon or lime?"

"Yes lime. No Bradey's."

"Were you the receptionist in Dr. Crane's office?"

"No, sorry."

I was not in the mood to play Where Do I Know You From. I took my drink and scanned the nearby conversation circles, looking for Hunter, looking for the plume of cigarette smoke that was always rising from him. I didn't know anyone else here, but what I understood, as I crossed the beach with my club soda, weaving through the clusters of beautiful people and their beautiful children, was that none of them would be at a clambake among strangers the night after a father or a spouse died, the way Ginny and I were. These people did not have to reinvent their lives every day. All they had to do was show up for the ones they'd been born into or signed onto. And when one of them died, an elaborate protocol system fell into place and operated with a balletic grace and precision of the sort used to get children into the best schools and then the best law firms. Though all these people had servants and secretaries, the calls around death, even to the florist, were made by principals, by Mr. or Mrs. And there were always two or three in a circle who knew exactly whom to call about obits in the *Times,* the *Globe,* the *Washington Post.*

"Could that be Sophy Chase?"

It was Betsy Schmidt, who, with her flirtatious husband, Terry, owned the only bookstore on the island, in a refurbished old barn out by the airport, with its own café and art gallery to lure people out there. She was conspicuous in this *Town and Country* crowd, her dyed, rust-colored hair, her permanent winter pallor, the cigarette always at her side, springing up to her mouth between conversations so that she wouldn't blow smoke in anyone's face. What was she doing here? Of course. Sue Winston had her Louisa May Alcott book coming out and wanted to ingratiate herself with Betsy and Terry in the hope that they would bestow on her the honor of a reading at their store.

"I didn't know *you* knew the Winstons," Betsy said.

"I didn't know you knew them either." I was surprised by her invitation to do the island minuet: jockeying for position. It hadn't gone out of fashion in my absence.

"Any interesting plans for the summer?"

"I don't live here anymore. I'm back briefly under difficult circumstances. My husband — we just separated — he died."

"Oh," she said brightly. "Is that good news or bad news?"

The statement hung in the air, and hangs still in my memory, like an enormous red flag. It stunned me. It stung me. It provoked me. Then it enraged me. It revisited the accumulated shocks and humiliations of the previous twenty-four hours and added another, the suggestion that I might be having a good time. I can articulate this now, but in that moment I was so rattled that this woman's pitiful attempt at levity, or sisterhood or whatever it was, shot through me like a seismic tremor, the earth violently rearranging itself, and all I could do was gape at her and try to remain standing. I lost the capacity to speak. And the will to speak. And the energy to say one more civilized thing to one more person who saw me as a bystander at the scene of my husband's death. I had not uttered a syllable, but the venom in my gaze had penetrated Betsy's skin, and it was she who spoke, or tried to, next.

"I just meant . . ." she sputtered. "You know, in terms of resolving the separation, because sometimes the friction in a marriage carries over into a divorce, and you get so angry you think it would be easier —"

"You must know a lot about that."

"We do have books on divorce in the store."

"And you've read those, have you?"

"Not all of them, but maybe more than your average —"

I interrupted. "Your average happily married woman? And what about love? Do you read books about that too?" I stared at her until she raised her cigarette and took a deep drag. She forced herself to nod, like a child who has misbehaved; smoke poured from between her lips. "It's one of my favorite subjects. Maybe next time I'm in the store you can point out the ones you like best."

I saw confusion and a touch of fear in her eyes. She had no idea how to get away from me or how far my hostility might go. I had no idea myself. I could imagine her wishing that I had just told her to fuck off, instead of being so perverse and unrelenting.

"I'd be happy to, next time you're in the store," she lied, and turned stiffly in the sand, like a penguin, and waddled off toward the cooking pit, to join the huddle of spectators upwind of it, waiting for the canvas to be ceremonially lifted and the steaming feast uncovered, disrobed. I continued to stare, but instead of seeing what was there, a bunch of summer vacationers about to clap for a pile of steaming lobsters and clams, I saw this semicircle of people gaping at the pit, the way I was gaping at them, as spectators in an old operating theater, and the Bake Master, in his butcher's apron, as the surgeon about to saw off someone's limb without anesthesia. I remembered the play Will and I had seen the year before at Island Rep about the history of medicine. In a scene nearly impossible to watch, the writer Fanny Burney had her cancerous breast cut off and described it in a famous missive of 1812. The actress recited bits while the staged operation took place, and I found the text later in a collection of famous letters: *When the dreadful steel was plunged into the breast — cutting through veins — arteries — flesh — nerves — I needed no injunctions not to restrain my cries. I began a scream that lasted unintermittingly during the whole time of the incision — & I almost marvel that it rings not in my Ears still, so excruciating was the agony.*

I drank down the club soda in my plastic cup and went again — did I march, did I saunter? I don't know, I found myself there, that's all — to the drinks table. "What kind of beer do you have in a can?"

He listed a few names. I chose Heineken. I said, "Why don't you give me two of them?" I could feel the tempo of everything speed up and the notes shorten. Like marimba music but sinister. I had lost my balance. I was losing my way.

He bent over a trash basket filled with crushed ice and

drinks in cans. The amount of alcohol in twelve ounces of beer is the same as in a shot of whiskey. Two cans, two shots. I shook with fury. I wanted the alcohol to take the edge off my rage and my rage to fill the well of my grief, and my life — which seemed a distant foreign country — to return to the messy, tattered, serio-comic routine it had been the day before.

"I know who you are. You're Sophy," the bartender said, and held out two icy, dripping cans of beer.

"Yeah, that's me." I wiped them on my sleeve and slipped them into my shoulder bag. I was about to say thank you and walk away — I did not want to know he remembered me from the vet's office or the post office or a clambake I'd never been to; all I wanted was to get away from there and drink — when he said something that caused me to shudder.

"I used to see you at meetings." This was not chipper bartender banter. It was pointed, it had a lot of subtext, we both knew exactly how much. "But I haven't seen you for a while."

"I don't live here anymore. I'm visiting." I did not say why. I did not want to admit that I was doing the pitifully predictable thing: succumbing to drink in a crisis. They call it "picking up," and if I had not been half mad with Betsy Schmidt and grief, I would have said to myself, "Don't pick up," and would have listened. Instead, I did what he had just done to me: put him on the spot, called him on his behavior. "I thought it was kind of a no-no for people like us to work as bartenders. All that temptation."

"I don't usually. I'm helping out a friend who had to go to Boston."

"You really ought to be careful," I said. *Ciao.*

As I turned, he said the one thing I dreaded he would say — the slogan offered to someone who's recalcitrant or slip-

ping or doesn't quite get how the whole thing works: Keep
coming back. It means, come to enough meetings, and you'll
like your sobriety. You'll find God in the morning sun and in
your breakfast cereal. You'll deal with crisis by reaching for a
meeting instead of a drink. You'll mutter slogans to yourself
without irony, without cynicism, without muttering.

"Keep coming back," he said as I pressed my way through
the sand.

"Stupid little prick," I said, way under my breath.

I had not had a drop, but I could already feel I was in danger. I was not sure where I was headed, but I knew I had
to stop myself from getting there too fast. I slogged over
the dunes and along the dirt road that wound around the
Winstons' property, looking for Evan's car. I was nearly trem-
bling with desire for the beer I took out of my bag and popped
open, desire not for the taste but for the numbness it would
give me, numbness against the dreadful steel plunged into the
breast and the dreadful death of my husband, which I felt in
the same place and felt as hard.

I was astonished by how yeasty it was, after all these years
away from it. Dumb, dumb girl. Amazing how fast it made
my tongue tingle. My tongue, the only part of me that wasn't
in pain, that didn't need anesthetizing. I didn't know where I
was going, but when I got into the car and maneuvered along
the badly pocked road, I told myself I was not going to drink
the other beer in my bag. I would throw it into the Dump-
ster in the lot of Nelson's Supermarket. I took South Road
toward Cummington and drove the speed limit, because I
knew how easy it would be to go above it. The road was narrow and loopy and passed rolling farmland, meadows, a hand-
painted sign nailed to an oak tree that said SWEET SWEET
CORN. Not thinking about it, I took the left fork where the

road divided, and when the landscape changed, the sudden forest, the back woods, when I found myself beneath a canopy of thick green leaves, I remembered that the turn-off for Cynthia Knox's was somewhere around here.

But I was wrong. There was no turn-off. Her house was the gray-shingled gambrel up ahead. KNOX was painted on mailbox number eight.

I saw her old Volvo sedan, with a nicked Harvard decal in the rear window, in the driveway. Her office door was around back, but this was nowhere near an office hour, so I walked along the flagstones and onto the porch and rang the bell.

A moment later, she opened the door and peered at me through the screen. "Yes?"

"It's Sophy Chase, Will O'Rourke's wife."

"Oh, my God —" She pushed open the screen and came out. "I heard this afternoon. I'm so sorry. The receptionist in Nancy Goldsmith's office told me when I ran into her at Nelson's." She took my hand firmly in hers, and her smile oozed sympathy. I was struck as always by her aquamarine eyes, her city attire. She was fifty-something, lovely in a natural way, wearing the sort of women's clothes you find in Cambridge, what academics wear when they dress up: the baggy batik vest over the knit cotton top, handmade silver jewelry, silk scarf. She took a lot of trouble with her appearance for a year-rounder. I used to kid Will about his having a crush on her. "Maybe a little one," he'd say sweetly.

"I was wondering when you last saw Will."

"You know, I was thinking about that today, after I heard. A month ago? Island Hardware? I was buying a trellis for the garden, and he —"

"I mean, as a patient."

"I don't have my book here."

"Roughly?"

"Three months ago?"

"What did he say about the divorce?"

"You know, I really can't say, Sophy."

"Did he talk about killing himself?"

"I can't discuss that, even if —"

"You mean he did, and you didn't do anything?"

"Sophy, I know this is upsetting, but I can't talk about these matters with you. It wouldn't be ethical to —"

"Do you know that he may have killed himself?"

"I was told there's going to be an autopsy, so I'm withholding —"

"Were you prescribing medication for him?"

"That's a confidential matter."

"I was hoping you might tell me something I don't already know, but obviously that's not —"

"It might be helpful for you to talk to someone on the island. If you need a referral, I'd be happy —"

"What are you hiding from me?"

"Only the usual confidences of the doctor-patient relationship."

"Were you sleeping with him? Is that it?"

"This line of questioning is not appropriate." She turned and slipped into the house, giving me the back of her subdued and politically correct Cambridge vest, whose red tendrils no doubt came from organic raspberries and cotton from politically correct cotton pickers. She glared at me through the screen and added, "I'm sorry about Will, sorry you're left alone. But I'm in the middle of dinner. Excuse me." After she closed the door in my face, I kicked the flimsy wood frame of the screen and remembered Daniel asking me last night if Swansea wasn't a pastoral playground where everyone was filled with the milk of human kindness. Everyone except me.

I did not throw away the second can of beer. I drank half of it as I drove through the tunnel of trees on my way to the main road and decided I would return to the awful Winstons' awful party. I could keep drinking there and not worry about driving, the hell with the pious bartender. I bloody well *will* keep coming back. I didn't know what made me think she'd been sleeping with my husband. I'm not even sure I thought so; maybe it was the bluntest weapon I could find, an attack on her prissy reticence. All I wanted from her was a solid piece of information, anything other than a phone bill or an overdue video or a missing dog. Or was there something twitchy and suspect in her reluctance to speak to me?

I didn't know, but when I came to the intersection, I did not turn right, toward Evan's house and the Winstons' and the setting sun. I turned left, toward Cummington, toward Will's place. He had a diary, I remembered, and in it might be the answers to all my questions. Unless I got it out of the house tonight, I would lose it tomorrow to Ginny and Susanna and Clare.

8

Diving into the Wreck

THE LIGHTS were on in Will's house. All the windows were open. There was a van parked in the driveway, black with white letters stenciled on the side, but when I saw the words, I could not put my foot to the brake, could not bring myself to stop.

AAA Disaster & Restoration Specialists
EMERGENCY CLEANING REPAIRS CONSTRUCTION
WATER FIRE SMOKE WIND
24-HOUR SERVICE

But I drove only to the end of the block, where I made a wide U and turned back, because I knew the men working in the house could do what I had come to do, and what I dreaded. I would not even have to go in. I could tell them where it was, where it might be.

I thought they might object, since I was asking them to give me not a composition book but a laptop computer, bright orange, what the company called tangerine. It made a trilly, musical sound when you lifted the top. But I guess they felt sorry for me, because I said I was the wife, because they didn't know the whole story. All I know is that they ended up replacing a section of the floor beside the bed, four feet by eight feet, the floorboards, the insulation, everything.

Five minutes later, I drove away with Will's diary on the seat next to me.

Five minutes after that, I stopped at a place I had not seen inside for many years, Oysterman's Package Store, and bought a half pint of Jack Daniels, because it fit easily into my purse, and because I could not face reading Will's diary without it. Those were the excuses I recited to myself instead of the slogans I could have recited, without irony, cynicism, or muttering. And now, what I tell myself about that night is that it could not have happened any differently, though of course I wish it had.

I wish, for instance, that I had had the patience to drive out to Evan's house, about forty minutes from Oysterman's, and retreat to his study with the computer before anyone came back from the clambake. Or I wish I had taken it to my friends Sally and Tim Baylor's house, outside Cummington, and plugged it in at their kitchen table, instead of going where I went. I wish, I wish — wishes as pretty and insubstantial as soap bubbles. The truth is that I wanted to do what I did all alone, without having to explain to anyone what I had just done. The computer was not mine to take or borrow — I knew that — and I had no idea what I would do with it once I finished the diary. There was also the small matter of the Tennessee sour mash, which I did not know what I would do with either, once I was done reading. And the notion, the probability, that the bottle might be empty by then — I did not know where in my gallery of terrors that stood. Or maybe I knew exactly.

It was dark when I turned onto the back road that led to Bell's Cove. I was heading for the secluded grove of old trees near the entrance to the sound, where people parked and then hiked a short distance to the beach. Dark, when I got there, but not pitch dark. There were lights from the occasional passing car, a house across the road, a sliver of the moon. Mine was the only car in the dirt lot at the edge of the grove. I moved into the passenger seat, where there would be room on my lap for the computer, and flipped up the top, hoping it had been plugged in, the battery being charged, until I had removed it from the house. It emitted a cheery twang, and the screen got bright and busy, as if a video game was beginning, and, in a way, it was. Then it surprised me and spoke. A woman's voice said, "Welcome." I reached down to twist the top off the Jack Daniels.

In a corner of the screen was the folder icon I dreaded: JOURNAL. I took a long swallow and double-clicked on it. A window flashed onto the screen: THIS FILE IS ENCRYPTED. ENTER PASSWORD.

I typed "Ginny."

INVALID.

"Susanna."

INVALID.

"Jesse."

INVALID.

"Henry." Though I knew this was unlikely.

INVALID.

"Sophy." This even more so.

REPEATED INVALID ATTEMPTS DENY ACCESS TO FILE.

I took another swig of the stuff, calling it "stuff" in my mind because I did not want to call it what it was and call what I was doing what *it* was. That little bit, the second swallow, surged through me in two directions, north and south, my head and the vast vicinity of my heart, which felt as if it were clenching and expanding in a parody of its normal function. I took another mouthful, because I liked the exaggeration of my heart and the numbing of everything else — my tongue, my lips, the tips of my fingers. And another, which traveled down my throat and to the back of my brain in a great burst of color, Jackson Pollock's paint or the splatter of blood on a wall from a gunshot wound. I mean to impress upon you the drama of the sensation, because it made what happened next, first the one thing, then the other, that much more intense.

The first was finding, in the right-hand corner of the screen, a folder called CORRESPONDENCE. I clicked on it, and a listing of letters appeared, organized by date, the most recent May 27, five days before the last phone call and the video rentals.

> Dear Svelte, Sophisticated Sailor:
> I noticed the ad you ran in the back of *Sailing* and thought that if you didn't mind an ace sailor still a little rocky from a divorce (that I didn't want), we might find our way to smooth seas without becoming becalmed. I am a 59-year-old retired diplomat living on Swansea, for the time being anyway, in possession of a somewhat rickety but seaworthy Valient 28′ (which my wife had no patience for, though I don't think that had anything to do with the divorce). My friend who urged me to write this letter insists the protocol is to send a photo, so I'm going through a shoe box I have that —

The letter ended there. The next one was dated the same day, also addressed to the Classified Department of *Sailing:*

> Please run the following ad for my boat in the next possible issue.
> Valient 28′. Windwave, 32V130, 1977, $14,000.

The next letter was dated the day before the classified ad.

Dear Sophy:

Here's the $873 from the insurance company, as per our conversation/fight. I know you think I have been a bastard about the money, and maybe I have been. But that's what comes of all my goddam niceness, bottled up until it explodes. I never did figure out how to be more like Evan Lambert, who is too ambitious to waste time being nice, and less like myself, afraid so often, except in situations where everyone else is scared out of their wits: Vietnam in 1968; crossing the Atlantic in a 30' sailboat; at the funeral of my son. I cannot describe my condition at those times, except to say that I lose my self-consciousness, I lose the crushing fear, with me so much of the time, that I am about to fuck up. Was I born like that — poor Mick who seems to have done pretty well, but it's a house of cards, a guy who lives on Swansea, which sounds like the top of the heap, except we're not summer people, and I'm alone again? Ever since Jesse died I have tried to live with less fear, because with his death, I know I faced the most frightening thing a parent possibly could. But I don't . . .

The letter did not end here, but my concentration was suddenly severed by what happened next, the second thing in this series, though when I tell you, it may be hard to believe that I didn't see it coming. The truth is that this letter Will had never sent took more than all of my attention, and I didn't notice the car until it was directly beside mine. But it took only a tenth of a second, once I did, to remember the bottle, which I'd had the good sense to keep returning to the purse on the floor between my feet, not to conceal it from anyone except myself. I'd wanted to add another few steps to the process, slow it down, and thank God for that, thank God I was not sitting there swilling it like Diet Sprite, dumb, dumb girl, Jesus H. Christ. It was the State Police.

"There's no parking here after sunset." The red and yellow lights on his roof were twirling as if this were a crime scene. He had leaned into the driver's window, seen me on the other seat, and come around to my side, a large guy with a modified gut and a twangy, slightly nasal Boston accent at odds with his girth: *No pahking heah, my deah.*

"I didn't know that."

"Says so on the sign."

"I'm sorry. I'll —"

"What are you doing here?" *Heah.*

"Nothing illegal. Fooling around with my computer." I was trying to close the file and shut the thing down and sober up, with his circus lights bathing everything in surreal colors. My hand was shaky against the tracking pad, and I was trying to keep my eyes from darting down suspiciously to the purse between my feet.

"We don't see too much of this *heah.* In the *pahking* lot. On a Friday night. Computers, I mean." More wonder than condemnation in his voice. For an oversized cop, it sounded almost friendly.

When I said what I said next, I meant to sound friendly, too. "Who knows? Maybe I'll start a trend."

The screen went black and I shut the tangerine lid and moved to put it on the backseat when he asked the question that made me wish I had kept my mouth shut: "Can I see your driver's license and registration?"

I carefully fished my wallet from the purse, handed him my license, and tried not to look as if I had no idea where to find the registration. I checked the ashtray, the glove compartment. There was nothing in the stacks of papers and maps and brochures, nothing.

"Problem?"

"I borrowed this car from a friend. I'm not sure where the papers are. The circumstances are somewhat . . . The car belongs to Evan Lambert. You know, the lawyer? The guy who's always on TV defending the girl who —"

"It's a hundred-and-fifty-dollar ticket and three points on your record for driving with no registration, I don't care who the car belongs to."

I went through the glove compartment again and looked up at him through the window, wondering how much more it would cost if he found the bottle. Could he throw me in jail? Could I convince him that I wasn't driving while intoxicated — I was just sitting? He had jet-black hair slicked back with something shiny and a slightly squashed nose that may once have been broken. I knew that the awful truth might be my best defense. "It must have been someone in your office who called me yesterday."

"What about?"

"My husband's death. William O'Rourke, in Cummington."

There was a pause of two or three seconds while he squinted at me, very unpolice-like, and I could tell he was connecting the dots: the dead man, the wife off-island, the Englishman who grabs the phone when she collapses, and now she's in a parking lot in the dark playing with a laptop? "So you're the wife in New York?"

"I am," I said, more solemnly than I had ever said anything, including "I do." I wasn't faking the solemnity, but I was aware of the effect I hoped it would have.

"I'll be right back."

He returned a long moment later and handed me my license and something that looked like a ticket, which I could see was called FORMAL NOTICE OF WARNING, as if they had to

add a few extra words to "warning" to flesh it out, make it less
naked, less flimsy as a punishment on the page.
  "Thanks," I said. "Thanks very much."
  "I'd get your friend's registration into the car" — the *ka* —
"as soon as possible."
  "I will."

It did not take me long to decide that the FORMAL NOTICE OF
WARNING was a message I would be wise to read as broadly as
possible. On my way back to the Winstons' end of the island,
I did what I should have done earlier in the day. I drove to
the Congregational church in the village of Twin Oaks, where
I knew there were meetings three or four nights a week. It is a
quaint little village, as perfect as something you'd see in miniature, in Lord & Taylor's Christmas window. An austere white
clapboard church and a one-room schoolhouse, weathered
shingles with lovely baby-blue shutters that often match the
sky, both buildings set back from the sidewalk, their lawns
framed with freshly painted white picket fences. Across the
street, a one-pump filling station with a white clapboard cash-
ier's booth. After dark, there is rarely anyone about, and driving through it, the place always seems — though this cannot
be the case — bathed in moonlight, frozen in a time long
before now.
  There were no signs of life in the church or the parish hall;
just this perfect tableau and my imperfect self.
  My exact state of mind as I drove west, not sure of my destination? The word that comes up repeatedly is "beyond." I was
beyond anger, fear, disappointment, humiliation, somewhere
close to feeling beyond feeling, which resembles numbness
but also craves it. By which I mean that I felt enough to know
that I wanted to feel even less.

That's the closest I can come to a reason for doing what I did next, though a countervailing theory says that neither psychology nor free will has anything to do with it: if this is your affliction, once you begin, your body chemistry does not permit you to stop. You are in the thrall of something akin, say, to the force of gravity. You are, say, a brick sitting on the table. If the table disappears from under you, or you're pushed off the edge, you — the brick — have no choice but to fall.

So I went back to the Winstons' party and had a few more. I'd had only the two beers and a few swills of the Jack Daniels, but because I was out of practice, I stumbled in the dark going from the Winstons' dirt road to the Winstons' beach for what remained of the clambake.

The catering company had left; there were a dozen people milling around, some sitting on blankets, and a help-yourself cooler stocked with beer and a few open magnums of wine. I helped myself. I drank fast. It was easy to do in the dark. I guess I had two or three like that, glug glug by the cooler, and by the time I went looking for the people I'd come with, I was a lot worse off than when I had parked Evan's car. There was no way I could drive.

I wobbled over the sand, stopping deliberately at each clump of people, looking from one face to the other, staring as if I were painfully near-sighted and had lost my glasses. I could have asked whether anyone had seen Evan or Mavis, but I was feeling rude and combative, and I wanted these people to know how much I didn't like them, so I drifted from one group of strangers to another, as if the beach were a giant aquarium and I a spectator on the other side of the glass. Conversations floated past me, or I floated past them, and the wind picked up. I bent down to take off my sandals, and when I stood up, I was face to face with a shark. "If it isn't Betsy

Schmidt," I said, and I must have said it too loudly, because she lurched backward, and another familiar face swam toward me. "And Hunter S. Thompson. Swansea's Gonzo journalist. How are things in Hanoi these days, or do you call it Ho Chi Minh City?"

"I think you've got your geography a little screwed up tonight, my dear," Hunter Abbott said. "And your cast of characters. I heard about your husband only an hour ago. I'm sincerely sorry. Good man, Will was, despite that business with the CIA."

"You mean his career?"

"Approximately."

"So you don't think it's good news that he's dead? Because that was Betsy's first question, wasn't it, Bets? From now on we'll call you Good News or Bad News Betsy. Maybe you should rename the bookstore, Good News or Bad News Books. What would be the good news books? Maybe all the ones about massacres and cancer and suicide. And the bad news books would be, um, gardening. Cookbooks. Natural childbirth in your own home. What to name your pet. Hunter, do you know anything about what Will did with our dog? We had the sorriest little mutt. Will gave him to me as a consolation prize because I couldn't have a baby, and after he died —"

I stopped talking because a large arm clamped around my back and its fingers gripped my upper arm so hard it hurt. "For Christ's sake, Sophy," Evan said softly, but not kindly, in my ear.

"Let go, will you?"

Again in my ear, and not kindly: "I'm taking you home." The arm tighter around my shoulder, pushing me across the sand. "Come on."

"Don't push. Where were you? I was looking everywhere.

Don't hold my arm like that, it hurts. What happened to Ginny?"

"Mavis and I were watching you make a spectacle of yourself. Our kids had fallen asleep on our quilt, and we were packing up, when your voice rang out across the beach. Sue Winston heard every word. It was quite a display."

He maneuvered me to the dunes, and we sank into sand with every step. "It was quite a clambake. I can't remember. Did you tell me where Ginny is?"

"She ran into a family she used to babysit for, and they invited her to their house. Any idea where you parked the car? Or if you parked the car?"

We were on solid ground by then, the dirt cul-de-sac at the Winstons' house. "Right behind that SUV. And though it may be hard to believe, I was not driving around the island in your car sloshed like this. This is of very recent vintage. I know I seem extremely potted, but I'm not."

"Good thing, because I'd have been worried."

"See? Just as I said. Here we are."

We got in and I handed Evan his key, though I can't recall now how much I was aware of hiding from him; how much I remembered at that moment about the rest of the evening. What I was acutely aware of as we turned around in the cul-de-sac and bumped along the rocky road was Evan's anger, which he expressed as silence punctuated with an occasional deep sigh. He glanced over at me. "Put your seatbelt on," he said gruffly, and I fumbled for a bunch of seconds until I got it on. I didn't know what to say to make him less angry, so I didn't say anything for as long as I could stand it. Then I said, "It's hard, being with all of you and your perfect lives. Your perfect houses and your perfect children and your perfect marriages and your perfect dogs."

A minute later we were on blacktop, on the two-lane road

that led back to Evan's house and to the lighthouse at the end
of the island, and I was not so drunk that I couldn't hear the
self-pity in my voice. But Evan's answer pulled me in another
direction, and the shock may have been what sobered me up
enough to take part in the conversation that followed. "I have
two perfect children and a perfect dog and two beautiful
houses, but the rest, I'm afraid, leaves something to be de-
sired."

"You look awfully picturesque on each other's arms. That's
a good start."

"Or a good finish."

"Evan, am I slurring?"

"A little."

"I'm sorry. Jesus."

"I'm used to it. Being unhappily married isn't the most
original tragedy. Or the most serious."

"No, I mean, the mess on the beach. Betsy Schmidt."

"I shouldn't reward you for such bad behavior, but it *was*
funny."

"Sorry about your marriage, too. Is it *blanc?*"

"Is it what?"

"*Marriage blanc.* White. Virginal. No sex. I think the
French specialize in that."

"Very *blanc.*"

"How long?"

"Two years."

"So you must have someone else."

"Until last night. That's why I missed the six o'clock flight
and ended up on the ten with you. She told me she was getting married. When I got to the island last night, she called
again."

"So that was all the chaos last night?"

"That was some of it."

"And Mavis has a friend too?"

"She has a number of them. Or did. We don't swap stories like girlfriends."

"Good sports, the two of you. Will and I didn't do that."

"It's not something I recommend."

As he turned onto the dirt road leading to his house, I thought of how often I'd banged over this pocked road in the last twenty-four hours and of all I'd learned between rides. "Was it Heraclitus who said you never drive over the same dirt road twice?"

"I think so," Evan said.

"How old is she, the woman who's getting married?"

"Twenty-five."

I turned to him in the darkness of the wooded road, the greenish glow of the dash a kind of intimacy between us, as if we were under a blanket with a flashlight. "I am not exactly speaking from the highest moral ground at the moment, but I was hoping you'd be more original than that."

"That wasn't my intention, Sophy — originality. The heart wants what it wants."

"Isn't that what Woody Allen said about Soon-Yi?"

"I'm sorry you disapprove."

He drove onto the shrubbed path that led to the gardens and the circular drive. It was like coming on a boarding school or a country inn, an impersonal place with a sinister sound-track, the rhythmic roar and crash of the ocean, the wind rustling acres of leafy trees as hard as the tides drove the water. And this fresh chill between Evan and me. What was I thinking, to criticize his girlfriend's age?

I started to apologize as we entered the foyer, but Flossie barked and prodded. Evan brushed his hand against a bank of light switches as he slipped away in the direction of his study, and lights all over the first floor came on with the flair of a Broadway musical. Flossie galumphed behind him, and I drifted into the kitchen, wondering — no, it was more acute, more desperate than wondering — if I'd seen an open bottle of white wine in the fridge. You see, when you're in the vortex of it, there is no reason involved or etiquette, and certainly no common sense. It's closer to the tides or the course of a fever or the brick, with nothing under it. I opened the refrigerator, pretending that I wanted juice, in order to see what was there, and as I gripped the handle of a glass pitcher filled with something purple, I heard Evan's voice behind me. "There's a message for you from Daniel Jacobs. Call him even if it's late."

He was out of the kitchen by the time I turned around, holding the pitcher aloft, and said — to myself, it turned out — "Thought I'd just pour myself a glass of grape juice."

"Do you realize you're the only person in the world who knows what was really going on when the police called yesterday?" I lay on the bed in the guest room in the back of the second floor, and by the time I called Daniel, I'd had a little more to drink, even brought a glass with me upstairs. I was angry at myself and didn't want to tell him what a mess I'd made of everything; what a mess everything was. So I opened with a distraction, a *divertimento*.

"I'm sure I am the only person, but there's something I need to —"

"You know, yesterday, before that phone call, it was so intense that I don't know what would have become of me if —"

"You sound rather in your cups, Sophy, though I'm inferring, never having witnessed you that way."

"A little."

"I don't bloody believe it," he said. "You're not supposed to —"

"Of course I'm not, but —"

"No, I mean *you*. You're such a good little scout; you're such an advertisement for the whole bloody thing. The slogans and the meetings and the God business; you're such a noble soldier. But Sophy, listen, there's something I must —"

"I've had a bad day, Daniel. A wretched day. All day. So I had a little something to drink. Are you going to report me to the AA police? Are you going to send me to a rehab?" I'd opened a window, and there was a breeze and the hokey, movie-soundtrack crashing of the ocean, which made me feel sorry for myself. *From Here to Eternity,* I must have been thinking, or something even cornier. "I just got back from this clambake on the beach. The blinking beach with the blinking aristocracy of Swansea. Everyone is furious with me because —"

"Sophy, listen to me. My daughter is gone."

"What?"

"My daughter is missing. I called you hours ago, right after I spoke to the police. Vicki. No one has seen her since one o'clock this afternoon. She was in her room and then she wasn't."

I was silent, saying to myself, *Concentrate, remember, sit up, what day is it?* "But that was yesterday and I took her home. I saw her go in the front door. She was fine."

"What are you talking about?"

"She came to see me yesterday, I think it was yesterday. To my apartment. Before you came over. I took her home in a cab. I watched her go through the door."

"Why didn't you tell me?"

"I was going to." Why hadn't I? There was a reason, but I

couldn't make it come back to me, and that was such a long time ago. "But then the police called when we were — and then everything got so —"

"What was she doing there?"

"She wanted to talk to me."

"About?"

I remembered this part. The card. The message. I even remembered the message. The vote. Jesus, the vote. The elaborate story she'd made up. "Her mother," I said. "In Vietnam." Did I have to tell him the truth, the whole truth? *Concentrate, Sophy, put the drink down.*

"That's all she said?"

"That was one of the things. What did the police do?"

"They've been over every inch of the house. They've issued alerts at every — I don't know where. They're not supposed to do anything until someone's been gone for two days, but I rang the mayor's office. He's a great admirer of Blair's work, and his wife is her friend from college, so he got the police to make an exception, and they've begun a —"

"If she'd gone back to my apartment to look for me, the doorman would have told her that I'm away. How much money did she have?"

"Thirty-seven dollars. It's gone."

"She was reading *The Secret Garden* yesterday. I wonder if it influenced her. There's a girl about her age —"

"For God's sake, Sophy, don't read things into every little —"

"Does she know I'm on Swansea?"

"I told her the name of the place, though I doubt she knows where it is on the map."

"Does she know why I'm here?"

"I told them your husband was sick."

"She has enough money to take the train to Blair's nursing home on Long Island. Tell the police to check the nursing home and all the transportation that leads to it. And tell them there's a Greyhound bus that leaves the Port Authority twice a day for the ferry that comes to Swansea. If she had enough money, she might have got on that bus."

"If I don't know about the bloody bus, how would she know?"

"She's clever."

"There's something you're not telling me, Sophy."

There was so much I hadn't told him that I didn't know where to begin or which of my omissions may have led to this moment. "She talked about her mother in Vietnam, and her father. I took her home. I watched her go in the door."

"Why didn't you call me when she was there? Or afterwards?"

"She asked me not to."

"That's the shabbiest reason —"

"I mean, I didn't tell you straightaway when you got to my apartment, but I was going to, and I would have, if the police hadn't called. How are the other children?"

"I can imagine Vicki going to find her mother, but why would she go to such lengths to find *you?* Why would she run away? If she wanted to speak to you, I'd have rung you up for her. Don't you think she knew that?"

"The heart wants what it wants," I said softly.

"What did you say?"

"When she came to my apartment yesterday, she brought me a card she'd made. It said she wanted me to live with all of you."

"Why didn't you tell me that?"

"I just told you."

"What else haven't you told me?"

"Let's see. My husband was dead for three weeks before anyone found him. He left me a dollar in his will. The woman he was married to twenty years ago is arriving tomorrow to plan his funeral in a Catholic church, though he stopped believing forty years ago. Should I go on?"

"I'm sorry."

"Call the police now. Maybe she's around the corner. I'll call you in the morning."

I drank down what was left of the wine, but that wasn't the only reason the room spun when I lay down to sleep.

I drew the extra down pillow to my side, listening to the sea whoosh and boom like Beethoven's Ninth, imagining my dear Vicki on a bus traveling up I–95 to find me, imagining the other kids in all their terror and confusion in their little beds on Waverly Street. I gathered them around me and assured them that everything was going to be all right. The trick, my precious dumplings, I said, is to keep our eyes on the sky, not on the ground, and I described the endless blue sky over Swansea, how on a clear day you can see nearly forever, farther than Kansas and Oz and even Vietnam, and Vicki will be back home so soon, they would hardly remember she had been away. After that, I must have passed out. When I woke up the next morning, I was wasted, good for absolutely nothing, and Mavis wanted me to leave.

9

The Morning After

SOPHY, there's someone here to see you."
This was Swansea, that was Evan's voice outside the guest room door, and I was in agony. "Am I dead? Is it a condolence call?" I could barely speak, but even the phlegmy croak of my voice was deafening.

"It's Henderson."

"Henderson?" Was it possible that my eyelids hurt? There was thumping with a hammer in the place where my brain matter had been. Henderson was in New York. No, Switzerland. With his friend Bianca. So maybe all of this was a dream. That Will was dead, Vicki was gone, and I was hung over. "Is there coffee?"

"Open your eyes."

"I can't. It hurts."

"Open your hands."

"Can you hook up an IV with a caffeine drip?" I was whispering, I was stiff. It hurt to think. Words hurt. Sentences hurt more. Light, even the idea of light, was excruciating. A body sat down on the bed beside me. "Evan?"

"Yeah."

"Henderson's here?"

"Downstairs. See if you can tip your head up a little. The mug is hot."

With my eyes still closed, I pushed some pillows under my head and opened my hands, holding them out as if to cradle a cantaloupe, then an orange. The sensation of Evan trying to fit the mug into my fingers, and my fingers trying to grip it without burning myself, plus the thudding in my brain, made me think of the famous movie scene. "Wa wa wa wa," I croaked and finally took a sip. "What's that from?"

"What's what from?"

"I'm Helen Keller. You're Annie. This is water. I can speak."

He let out a tight, miniature chortle. "Not so loud," I whispered. "I'm the opposite of deaf. Every noise is fingernails against a blackboard. The ocean is too loud. Please turn it off." I felt Evan stand up and heard his rubber soles squeak across the bare wood floor. My hangover registered every beat of every breath, and what I heard in Evan's inhalation was annoyance. I opened my eyes a crack and saw him about to walk out the door, and maybe I detected or maybe I imagined a spike in his annoyance. "I fucked up, Evan. I know I did." I was still whispering. "I could hear you sigh as you walked across the room. I'm sorry. A thousand times. Flowers. Candy. Handwritten apologies on monogramed note cards." Silence. And more of it. "You have no idea how bad it is."

"I can see."

"It's worse than that. A friend's child —" I said, but stopped. Vicki's disappearance was too awful to mention to someone already burdened by the grimness of my last two days. "She's having trouble. Serious trouble. I found out late last night." I, who rarely expect anyone to hold open a door for me, had become a bad luck charm, an alchemist in reverse, Sheridan Whiteside in *The Man Who Came to Dinner,* the difficult house guest who won't leave. "Thank you for the coffee. Tell Henderson I'll be down in a minute." Henderson, I thought, thank God. This is his territory, life at the pitch he's used to. He'll put up with my hangover jokes and know where to look for Vicki.

"Sophy?"

"She's in here," Evan said. He pushed open the door to let himself out and Henderson in. I could see him through my squinting and raised my hand for him to take as he leaned down and kissed my cheek. He sat at the edge of my bed as if this were a hospital and I was dying.

"You're looking very J. Crew," I whispered, "very Swansea in your khaki togs," and swallowed as much coffee as I could, trying to remember how many cups it takes for a headache like this one to run its miserable course. "Don't look at me that way."

"What way?"

"As if you feel sorry for me."

"Of course I feel sorry for you. Do you think I came here for the fishing?"

"What happened to your trip? Switzerland, the fat farm?"

"We taxied down the runway, and at the moment the plane was about to lift off, there was a massive noise that sounded like the George Washington Bridge breaking in two. I'll spare you the details, though there were no fatalities. I didn't get on the next plane they rolled out."

"For me?"

"Because I was scared to death."

"But what about Bianca and losing twenty-five pounds?"

"Twenty minutes before I left for the airport, I got a fax from her. Her doctor forbade her to lose another ounce. She proposed meeting me afterward in Milan. Frankly, Sophy, I wasn't looking forward to starving to death by myself. So I'll have to diet. You know, not eat too much. I can't bear it, it's such an ordeal. Jesus, look at you."

"How do I look?"

"Hung over. And very much the widow without portfolio. She's a popular archetype in homosexual circles. I just this second realized that I am trying stupidly to entertain you, being the magnanimous homo impresario funeral director that I am, but I haven't said a word about poor Will. And poor you. How ghastly the whole thing is. Evan filled me in. I'm sure you're still in shock. It lasts for days, months, if you're lucky."

"H., I fell off the wagon."

"I know, dear. It was in the *Times* this morning."

"It may as well have been. I made a scene at the clambake last night. It would have been obnoxious in New York, but here it was obnoxious *and* unforgivable."

"It happens to the worst of us. And the best."

I closed my eyes and was surprised to feel tears leak from below my lashes. "Daniel's daughter disappeared."

"I know that too."

"How do you —"

"She was on the eleven o'clock news last night." My aching eyes opened wide against their will. "If I hadn't met her at your apartment, I'd never have known there was a connection."

"TV? I spoke to Daniel last night and he didn't say anything about that." It must have been before eleven when we spoke, and he may not have known it was coming. But all of this meant that she was officially missing — and that my life was awash with missing creatures. I noticed Henderson squinting at me, the sympathy squint I'd seen directed at me a dozen times in the last twenty-four hours. "That's why you came today, isn't it? Because you figured that might push me over the edge, and I was already close enough?"

"Yeah."

"Thank you, Henderson." I reached for his hand. "But how did you find me? When I left a message for you last night, I didn't know I'd end up here."

"I took a cab to Will's place from the airport and —"

"How did you know where he lived?"

"The phone book, darling. And if there was no one at his house, I intended to perch on the front porch looking as out of place as I possibly could. Attract a crowd and ask everyone where I'd find you. But the instant I got out of the cab at his house, a nice fellow accosted me. Said he lives next door. He knew exactly where you were."

"Sophy?" It was Evan's voice again, but it sounded distant, as if it were coming from the bottom of the stairs. Far away and businesslike. "Can I have a word alone with you down here?" A little too much emphasis on the word "alone." Henderson did not dare follow me out of the room.

Evan, sitting at the dining room table in a Red Sox T-shirt and lavender shorts, half-reading the *Globe,* gestured to me to sit down at the place setting. A mug of coffee, a bowl of fruit salad, and an English muffin. "For me?" He nodded. "Thank you." I had brushed my teeth and changed my shirt but still felt my brain was encased in porcupine quills.

"I have to talk to you before Mavis and the kids come back. She was upset about last night."

"Do you think the best thing would be for me to write a note and leave it here or —"

"She was mortified by the attack on Betsy Schmidt. As was Sue Winston and everyone else who —"

"I can certainly understand that."

"And furious about this." He reached into the back pocket of his shorts and brandished my FORMAL NOTICE OF WARNING at me, holding it out between his forefinger and middle finger, a jaunty, cocksure gesture that I did not appreciate. I must have left the notice in the car.

"It looks worse than it is," I said.

"Of course, it's not a ticket, but —"

"I couldn't find your registration. He almost gave me —"

"But to be stopped for a DWI —"

"I wasn't. I was parked in the lot by Bell's Cove. It was a lovers' lane search. That's all." But where, I wondered for the first time since last night, was Will's tangerine computer? And where was my stepdaughter?

"Sit down and eat, for God's sake." Evan studied the fine print on the warning, not certain what new verdict to pass on me. I glanced around the room and saw the laptop on one of the coffee tables, next to a splashy book of photographs called *Swansea Summers: Island Dreams and Dreamers.*

"Where's Ginny?"

"She took a cab an hour ago to the house her mother rented in Cummington. How'd you get out of the ticket?"

"Sympathy. I reminded him the State Police had called the day before to tell me Will was dead. I had him practically in tears. Do you think if I explained all this to Mavis that she'd —"

"Even without the ticket, I'm afraid it's beyond that. Sue Winston was so keen to win Betsy over that I'm not sure —"

"You want me to leave?"

"Mavis does. I hate to do this, Sophy; you know that. I abhor it. She actually —" Evan twisted up his mouth, a prelude to saying something even more difficult. But one of the advantages of my condition was that I was in such physical pain, using so much energy just to keep my eyes open, it would have been hard for anyone to hurt my feelings. Though this came close. "It would be best if you weren't here when she got home. In about an hour." Very close. "But I have somewhere you and Henderson can stay. It's a converted chicken coop on Jimmy and Edna Baxter's property near the cove."

"You own it?"

"I rent."

"For house guests?"

"No."

We were doing Twenty Questions, and I was getting warm. "You rent it on the sly?"

"Since you ask."

"Use it a lot?"

"Not right now."

"You're full of surprises."

"So are you, Soph."

"There must be a bed."

"There are two. One in each room."

"There must have been a lot of chickens in that coop."

"And a good architect. You'd never know who the previous tenants were."

I smiled, a tight, shallow smile, all lips. I was beginning to feel this was an Escher print or an old-fashioned amusement park funhouse, where the stairways lead nowhere and the corridors are mazes lined with distorting mirrors. "If I stay there, where will you tell Mavis I've gone?"

"I'm not sure she'll ask." Evan was gazing at the editorial page as he said this, Everyman at the breakfast table, having an important conversation with a woman. Did he and Mavis speak to each other only to issue edicts? And did he believe his secret hideaway was really a secret on this island, where gossip travels like chicken pox?

"How long have you had it?"

"A few years."

"Since you stopped sleeping with her?" His head swiveled to me in an exaggerated jerk, as if I'd said something shocking. "You told me that last night."

"I didn't think you'd remember much of last night."

"Unfortunately, I remember every word. Maybe every other word."

A phone was ringing somewhere, a series of high-pitched electronic blasts. "Excuse me," Evan said and headed across the great room to disappear once again into his study. It may have been the twenty-five-year-old. Or Ted Turner. Or Ted Koppel. Or Ted Kennedy. I heard Henderson coming down the stairs and Flossie on the deck, scratching at the screen door and sending out her short, sharp barks, like a smoke detector trying to tell you its battery is dead. I let her into the living room and ran my hands over her great swath of fur warmed by the sun. She crossed the room and stood with her nose to the closed door of Evan's study. When that brought no response, she plopped down with a calm, canine display of resignation and promptly fell asleep. Something in the directness of her longing and her certainty of her place in the world made clear to me that I did not belong in the chicken coop, even for a night or two. Nor did I want another favor from Evan, certainly not one that would draw me into his illicit love life.

"Trouble in Denmark?" Henderson said as he lingered at the bottom of the stairs.

I saw him gaze around the sun-drenched space, as every visitor does, especially those of us who live in one or two rooms, in walk-ups, on air shafts, yearning for the light and color in this room, for the abundant peace it promises.

"This house reminds me of the summer I spent on Swansea

ten years ago," Henderson said, moving to a shadowy corner of the room. "I was at a party in a house that looked like this, being chatted up by a lawyer from Boston who asked where I was from. New York. *New York* — long, pregnant pause. He had to ponder that one, as if I'd said the Mississippi Delta or Azerbaijan. Too many avid people in New York, he said. Well, it *is* chaotic, I agreed. They're everywhere, he said, starting to sound paranoid, and I knew we weren't talking about the same thing. 'Especially the universities. Especially Columbia.' He was talking about Jews. The avid people. It may even have been this house. I decided not to tell him I was avidly queer. What's our next move?"

Three cups of coffee and the proverbial glass of cold water in my face — Evan's telling me I had to leave — had enabled me to work through some of the choreography. "How long can you stay on the island?"

"For the duration. My show's in reruns, since I'm supposed to be away, getting photogenic."

"Thanks, H. But you know, there'll be a sharp decline in the accommodations. A motel room and a Rent-A-Wreck. Let's find the phone book and start calling around."

"I'll make some calls while you pack up."

"You're game."

"You forget I could be drinking water three meals a day at a Swiss fat farm. By myself."

"I did forget that." I was going over what I needed to do, a list taking shape in my addled brain. *Find Vicki. Find Henry. Be kind to my stepdaughters. Quit putting myself and my suppurating wounds at the center of every encounter. Ask Henderson for help. Do whatever he says.*

"Sophy, are you all right? I mean, I know you're miserable, but at this moment is there something newly awful that —"

"The great mad joy is over."

"It always ends, you know. You think maybe this time it won't, but it always surprises you and goes up in a puff of smoke."

Take Will's computer with me. Dream his dreams. His night-mares. His passwords. Ghost-write the last days of his life. Now that he is a ghost himself. I crossed the room to pick up the laptop when I heard a loud knock at the front door. Evan was still sequestered in the study, so I went into the foyer and swung open the door. It was Swansea, and you never hesitate. But I didn't expect what I saw.

"We're looking for Sophy Chase."

"I'm Sophy."

They were two large men wearing dark gray suits and white shirts, like funeral directors, and for a moment, until they simultaneously flicked open their wallets and flashed gold badges at me and said, "New York Police Department," I thought they were.

Do you invite them in? Do they take you somewhere? It didn't occur to me to ask how they'd found me, but I was about to tell them that I needed to leave here, needed to be gone before Mavis returned, when I heard Evan say, "Who is it? Who's there?" and felt him come up beside me. One fright-ening thought tripped another, and I got it into my head that Vicki was dead and they were here because I was guilty of I-knew-not-what in connection with it, which prompted me to say something I never imagined I would have to say. I said it in case it became necessary, said it without even knowing why the cops were there, said it in the event they intended to whisk me off and rough me up — and yes, I was overreacting, but only because I was terrified. I held out my arm to Evan and said to these men, with their gold badges and their pasty, pockmarked, "Dragnet" faces, "This is Evan Lambert. My at-torney."

"You won't need a lawyer," one said. "We just need to ask you a few questions."

"I don't think we've been introduced," Evan said to him, "formally."

They took out their wallets and badges again and said, "NYPD" — only the letters this time — and Evan, in his lavender shorts and Boston Red Sox T-shirt, underwent a split-second transformation. "Why don't you gentlemen come in?" He extended his arm and led them through the foyer and into the big room. "Will you be comfortable here?" Upturned palm to the armchairs that overlooked the deck, the pond, the sky still bluer than robins' eggs.

"This is fine," one of them said.

"Yeah, fine," said the other, trying to pretend nonchalance.

"Flossie, lie down. Right there." Master to dog, another minor power play, keeping her from their big feet, their highly polished black shoes.

I looked around for Henderson and saw him through the open door in Evan's study, head down, talking on the phone with the island phone directory in front of him. He must have known to make himself scarce. As Evan knew to make himself into the maitre d', even though he had no idea why these men were here.

"Can I get you a cup of coffee?" he said.

"We don't want to take up much of your time. Why don't we just get started?"

Evan held out his arm to me and pointed gracefully toward a third chair. I sat down and understood his ballet as a series of gestures to disarm the police, and understood that when confronted with loyalty to lawyering versus loyalty to his wife's desire that I leave — I had my eye on the clock, expecting to see an angry Mavis any minute — there was no contest as to which would prevail. Evan stood back with his arms crossed, affecting the most casual demeanor, as if he were waiting for a tennis court to free up. Every so often he'd scratch the side of his chin or use the fleshy part of his thumb to brush an imaginary crumb from his lower lip, something left over from breakfast. One of the cops — they were detectives, hence the suits — ran through the facts of Vicki's disappearance, and Evan pretended it was not the first time he had heard them.

"Mr. Jacobs called us late last night and said he'd just learned the girl had visited you the day before in your apartment. Is that correct?"

"Yes."

"Had she ever done that before?"

"No."

"What was the reason for her visit?"

"I don't think it's fair to ask Ms. Chase to interpret the motives of a child," Evan said. "Or anyone else's, for that matter."

"Why did she say she was there?"

It took me a moment to know how to answer, and in that silence the police must have imagined I was inventing or choosing among inventions or trying to conceal a truth that implicated me in her disappearance. "She invited me —" I started over: "She presented me with a card she had made expressing her desire that I live with her and her family."

"What was your answer?"

Again, I paused. I had no choice: the disparity between what I had felt and what was permissible for me to say to her was so vast, it made me nearly dizzy, then and now. "I said that her father's life and my life were too complicated for that right now."

"Then what happened?"

"I talked to her for a little while and took her back to her house in a cab."

"We understand you saw her father later that day?"

"Yes."

"But you didn't tell him she'd come to your apartment."

"I intended to."

"But?"

"The police called — the police here — and told me my husband was dead. We're separated. I came almost immediately, so I never had the chance to —"

"Mr. Jacobs said that you didn't tell him because she'd asked you not to. Suggesting that you didn't intend to tell him."

"She did ask me not to, because she was embarrassed."

"About what?"

"She was telling me — through this card she'd made — how much she cared about me, and I guess she was embarrassed that —"

"I'm uncomfortable discussing what any of us guesses this child's feelings were at the time," Evan said with more delicacy than I'd have imagined.

"All we want to do is find the child. Did you make any plans with her?"

"No."

"Did you promise her anything?"

"No."

"Did she tell you anything that would suggest where she might have run away to?"

"She came to my apartment to see me. It occurred to me that after she found out I was here, she might also try to come to Swansea. But I imagine people's inner lives all the time — something of an occupational hazard — and I don't always get them right."

"You are Mr. Jacobs's girlfriend?"

Was I required to tell them that I was and that I wasn't, that

I wanted to be and that I knew well enough not to want to be, but that I would marry him in a minute to have the children in my life? Was I required to tell the NYPD that I had never told Vicki that I loved her and now I wished I had? "I guess you'd say I'm his girlfriend."

"You are having a sexual relationship with him, aren't you?"

"I don't believe the details of Ms. Chase's private life are relevant to this matter," Evan said.

"I am," I said. I wasn't sure the details were relevant either, but it was a relief, finally, to give a straightforward answer, one that was more true than any of the others. And answering it seemed a good-faith gesture, to let them know I was not evasive out of a desire to conceal; that all I wanted to hide was my vulnerability. "It is most definitely a sexual relationship."

None of us said anything for ten or fifteen seconds. Then one of the detectives said, "So we have to assume the girl has some understanding of this surrogate-mother-type situation."

Henderson suddenly appeared at the study door. "Excuse me, Sophy, you have a phone call. It's your mother."

"Is it all right if I take this?" I asked as I raised myself from the chair. "I've been trying to reach her since I learned my husband was dead."

"Of course," the men said in unison, "of course." I could hear the deference in their voices, even though my widow's weeds had a decidedly off-the-shoulder look. I closed the study door behind me and picked up the phone.

"Sweetheart, there must be something wrong if you're back on Swansea in someone else's house and calling me this way," my mother said. "It's Will, isn't it?"

She knew little of the life that the police knew all about, and had forgotten a lot of what I'd told her about the end of my marriage, so when I said, "Yes, he's dead," she felt my pain and her own without interference, without qualification or hesitation. She did not think of me as the widow manqué, as I thought of myself, and she did not ask if that was good news or bad news, and did not try to entertain and distract me, as Henderson had done. She cried.

I wish I could say that the purity of her response buoyed me or comforted me or touched me, but she was my mother, and those tears, echoing other tears I had heard her shed, flung me back to a time when there was no distance between us, just a porous membrane, and her pain flowed everywhere, coated me as if it were paint, body paint, although there was nothing light or playful about it. It had been house paint in my pores, and it had taken me years to remove.

"It's difficult to get to Swansea," she said now, collecting herself, "and I'm just not sure I can —"

"Mom, don't even think about it. It *is* too much of an ordeal."

"But I don't want you to be alone at a time like this."

"There are lots of people around. And Ginny and Susanna are here."

"Who?"

"Will's daughters. We're planning the funeral together."

"Good. What was he?"

"Catholic."

"I thought so."

"But lapsed."

"It's coming back to me. I assume he was generous to you in his will. Was he, honey?"

"We were in the middle of a divorce, so things are — a bit up in the air."

"But you'll get the house, won't you?"

"No, Mom. I told you before, I won't. His children have —"

"What kind of divorce lawyer did you have? I don't think it's too much to expect that, after how many years of marriage?"

"Someone here needs to use the phone. I'm at my friend Evan's."

"Which one is Evan?"

"He's on TV a lot. Defending the German girl who killed the baby in Boston."

"A friend of yours is defending *her?* How did he get hooked up with *her?* Can't he choose the people he —"

"Mom, I really need to go. I'll call you later today."

As I set down this conversation, I see that it wasn't my mother directly who caused me to make the next connection, but my mother indirectly. The connection between what she did with my father when I was a child and what I was doing now with Will: chasing a phantom, someone who wasn't there; someone, in the case of my father, who had chosen to leave; someone, maybe, in the case of my husband, who had chosen to leave. It was the first time since all of this began that I understood I did not have to be doing what I was doing — sleuthing. And that sleuthing might be a substitute for what I should have been doing, and the same might have been true for my mother, when my father disappeared. Sleuthing instead of mourning.

When I returned to the living room, the landscape had changed. Evan was gone, and Henderson was in my seat, but leaning forward, talking animatedly to the detectives, who had loosened up enough to look as if they were enjoying the sunshine, the island breeze, the good life of a defense lawyer whose work it is to unravel their own. "'They're all over New York,'" Henderson was repeating to the cops. "'Especially the universities. Especially Columbia.' But I don't think there's much support for that on the island, even among the summer people. Would you say there is, Sophy?"

"Is what?"

"A lot of anti-Semitism on the island?"

"Only among the Jews. Where's Evan?"

"On the phone in the kitchen. How did your mother take the news?"

I didn't want to say any more than I had to in front of the police, but I did want to counteract the impression of myself as a not entirely sympathetic character. "She was devastated," I said quietly, turning to the two men, uncertain whether I should go on without Evan. They were not exactly Laurel and Hardy, though one was appreciably thinner than the other, one was dark and one was fair, and the dark one had coarse, wiry hair and the fair one was nearly bald. Both wore gold wedding bands and sports watches with a lot of buttons and options. "If there's anything I can do to find Vicki, I'll do it. I'll leave the island if there's somewhere you think I —"

"You've got plenty to do right here, with your husband's —"

"He has grown daughters who can handle everything." Of course what I had told my mother was a lie, that I was planning the funeral with them.

"Excuse me," Evan said, coming to stand beside me. "I had to take that call. Is there anything more you need to go over with Ms. Chase?" For some reason, he was holding a purple plastic beach pail and shovel. Because Evan never did anything casually where legal matters were involved, I knew they were props.

Dutifully, exactly as scripted, the detectives stood up. The dark-haired one said to me, "I think we're done. If we need to get a-hold of you —"

Henderson interrupted. "She'll be at the Lighthouse Motel

in Cummington for the next few days. Let me get you the number." He went back to Evan's study.

"And if you need to reach us," the taller one said, handing me a card, "there's always someone at these numbers. Obviously, if you hear from her or if you have any ideas —"

"Just out of curiosity," Evan said, "if she disappeared only — when was it, twenty-four hours ago? — how did you get involved so quickly? Isn't there a forty-eight-hour rule before you'll —"

"The girl's mother has some connection to the mayor. And naturally, the girl's father . . . We were asked to expedite it. Unusual set of circumstances."

"Of course," Evan said knowingly, nodding, the purple pail pressed against his hip and no idea who the parents were.

When they left, I headed to the kitchen for more caffeine before going upstairs to pack. Evan followed me. "Who the hell are you dating, Donald Trump?"

"Daniel Jacobs." I found a jar of instant coffee in the cabinet, next to a prescription bottle of Mavis's Klonopin. *Take one as needed for anxiety.* One way to start the day: coffee and a tranquilizer.

"Refresh my memory."

"He's an art dealer."

"Divorced, I trust?"

"She's hospitalized."

"I hope for more than a day or two."

"She's in a nursing home, in a coma. Before that, she ran a literacy program for poor kids. I guess that's her connection to the mayor." Forty-eight hours ago, before the bottom dropped out of the great mad joy market, Blair was a comedy routine in my exotic new life. Now her story was leached of whatever ghoulish hilarity I had invested in it; now it was as sad to me as it must always, always have been to Daniel.

I turned on the gas under the kettle and looked at Evan across the counter, Evan on his summer vacation, getting sunburned on his extremities, wheeling and dealing in his living room with his son's purple pail. "Thank you for helping me out with the cops. With everything. I'm not usually the man who came to dinner. And thanks for the offer of the chicken coop, but we've made other plans." I tapped a teaspoonful of coffee into a beautiful glazed mug, a palette of rich, complicated blues that bled into and out of each other like pieces of the Swansea sky. "There are already enough secrets to go around. More than enough."

"If you had nowhere else to go, that's all."

"Thanks."

The kettle whistled. Things inside me thumped and rattled and hurt. I was still hung over, and people and animals were dead, missing, unaccounted for. I seemed to have had the effect of a tornado, a twister, strewing wreckage everywhere in my path, in all the places I had visited and lived and left. Or was I simply choosing to organize events this way, placing myself at the center of them, conferring on myself a power I did not have?

When the phone on the kitchen wall rang, Evan answered and was engrossed in seconds. Had the twenty-five-year-old changed her mind again? But wouldn't she have used the phone number for the study? How many lines did they have and which belonged to whom? I didn't need to wonder anymore. I needed to make my exit. I went upstairs with the instant coffee in the beautiful mug and began to pack. Henderson stuck his head in and said he had called a cab; it should be here any minute. Then he was gone.

As I packed, I remembered a ride in a car with Will years ago — remembered it in the present tense, as I would a dream a few moments after dreaming it, pieces drifting back out of sequence, rearranging themselves, like a skein of geese flying into formation. It is the fifth or sixth month of our romance, and we're driving from his apartment in Georgetown to mine in Manhattan. As we cross the Delaware Memorial Bridge, he says he has something to tell me: he doesn't work for the State Department. Just ahead is a station wagon, a German shepherd in the back looking out at us; something both comic and menacing about this sudden surveillance. I even think that word, "surveillance," about the dog, because as soon as Will says this, I know what he'll say next. The State Department is his cover. He works for the CIA. He isn't supposed to tell me and he doesn't want me to tell anyone else, but he thinks I should know, given the intensity of the feeling between us. In any case, he's leaving the Agency soon, early retirement, the instant he can, next month, and it will all be behind him, though it must still be kept secret.

"I have to lie too?" I ask. "I have to tell people you worked one place, though the truth is something else?"

"That's what people do. That's the way it works. It's only for another month. After that —"

I hear him stop in the middle of the sentence and see him, although my eyes are still on the dog, swivel his head toward me for a few seconds. "I don't have to tell you any of this," he says. "And maybe I'm making a mistake doing it. But I think it's fair, because I love you, to tell you the truth."

He can feel my dismay, the amplification in my silence. It has a lot of bass and treble and prompts him to say, "Do you mean your love is contingent on where I work? You fell in love with me because of my job?"

I shake my head and say, "Of course not," but that's not what I'm thinking. I'm thinking: *I fell in love with you because of your grief. Because it is so thick and complicated, it makes me forget my own.*

Now, at Evan's, I zipped the canvas bag that I'd packed two days earlier in New York, that distant evening as Daniel dressed and Vicki and her siblings waited for us in the house on Waverly Street that had since become a police stake-out. Where do you look for a missing child? Who do you call? Where do you begin to begin? At the bottom of the stairs, I stepped over sleeping Flossie, whose shiny black coat brought to mind a seal prostrate on a rock. She emitted a brief, high-pitched squeal, and her front paws clenched, then fluttered — dreams of chasing squirrels. Sweet dreams.

"Sophy —" It was Evan at the kitchen door, at the other end of the great sunny room; I felt as if I were looking down a lane in a bowling alley. "Your stepdaughter's on the phone. Why don't you take it in here?"

10

Later the Same Day

I HAD NO IDEA how much Ginny knew about my behavior the night before. News on the island traveled at lightning speed, but there were different laws of physics and etiquette at work in that family. My uncertainty made my *hello* a bit wobbly, as if this were a call from a collection agency, and that made her hesitate. "Soph, is that you?"

"Yeah, how are you this morning?"

"Oh, God, I went to our house, it was awful, I was so —"

"Are you there now?"

"No, I couldn't stand it. I came over to talk to Ben and Emily — that's where I am now — and Ginny said I should call you about —"

"Isn't this Ginny?"

"It's Susanna."

"Oh, Boo-kins," I said without thinking, using one of Will's childhood names for her, before I remembered that she didn't like it, "it's you."

Have I mentioned that Susanna was my favorite? Of course not. I've always worked to push it out of my thoughts, my vocabulary, such an uncharitable formulation, even for a stepmother who arrived late in their lives. Instead, I've stuck to the facts. Susanna's looks and voice, identical with her sister's, though not her temperament. When Ginny was hurt or angry, she snarled and sometimes pounced. Susanna grew silent; she withdrew, did not return phone calls, moved to the side of a mountain beyond the grid, outside the reach of Pacific Bell. But now, no doubt at my "Boo-kins," and its reminder of her father, Susanna came undone, as Ginny had a day ago at the airport. I winced and said what I could in the way of comfort. I, too, felt the blow of Will's death again, but through the filter of Vicki's disappearance, it felt less urgent. So when Susanna said what she said next — "Will you come over now?" — I did not feel, as I would have earlier, that I had to go right away.

"I have an errand or two, and I'm on the West End, so it may take me a few hours to —"

"Ginny told me everything," she said softly, "and I want you to know I don't blame you."

The change in tempo caught me up short, as did the backdoor accusation. "Blame me for what?"

Henderson appeared at the kitchen door, tapping his index finger against his watch face, mouthing the words, "The cab's here."

"For what happened to Daddy. Oh, God, I just saw the time. I need to nurse the baby. Mommy rented us the yellow gambrel next to the library on Ames Street. Come as soon as you can."

When I hung up and went to say goodbye to Evan, I was effusive in my thanks and my apologies.

"Mavis will survive, and so will Betsy Schmidt," he said, "though Sue Winston may need to be hospitalized." We laughed a little and did not have to mention the real casualty of the evening. "She'll turn up," he said, to be kind, and I nodded, to be kind to myself. "Let me know what happens. And when the funeral is."

It's a long drive to the other end of the island, and I settled into the taxi and closed my eyes against the sun, against all that remained of my hangover, my shame. If I'd known where to begin looking for Vicki, I would have. But the only missing creature I had a shot at finding — or a clue as to where to begin looking — was the dog Henry. "Let's check into the motel," I said to Henderson, "and go to the newspaper office. I want to take out a big ad to say Henry's missing, run it with the picture I have in my wallet. Then I need to see my step-daughters."

"Sounds like a good plan." But Henderson had another stop in mind before those on my agenda, although he didn't tell me until he absolutely had to, until the taxi driver slowed down as we came to the village of Twin Oaks and pulled over to the curb right across from the church. Of course Henderson had told him to do this, and of course I understood why, as soon as I noticed the parked cars lining the side street.

"Obedience school," I said.

"It's entirely voluntary, Sophy."

"I wish you'd said something at Evan's house, instead of —"

"There were a few too many conversations going on there to conduct an intervention. I intended to, but . . ." His voice trailed off. The driver kept the engine on but was silent, like a chauffeur who knows to wait for instructions. He must have waited here, or outside some other church on the island, a time or two before now.

"You think I don't know how badly I fucked up?" Soon the entire island would know, as soon as the driver let us off, here or at the Lighthouse Motel.

"I'm not sure that's the most useful way to think of it, Soph."

"Oh, all right, for Christ's sake, don't look so triumphant."

"I'm not at all —"

"I know, I'm just pretending to be combative, to conceal my —" But I stopped speaking and started to gather my belongings. My shame, my embarrassment, my headache without end. Henderson paid the driver and we filed out of the cab.

"I'll meet you inside," he said, and he let me go across the street through the gate of the white picket fence, down the brick path, and around back to the door of the parish house. The church lawn was bright green, shaved as close as a golf course, the sky swept blue in every direction, and fear collected across my forehead in the space not occupied by my hangover. I pushed on a pair of dark glasses as I climbed the four steps to the closed door; the meeting had started five minutes earlier.

There must have been forty or fifty people in the room, seated on metal folding chairs, or about to be. The room had always reminded me of a suburban 1950s rec room: cheap wood paneling, lights recessed into the acoustic ceiling panels, the ceiling so low that tall men reflexively slumped. The only empty seat was close to where I'd entered, in the back row against the wall. Best seat in the house for hiding, for being nearly not there. Once I was seated, I looked over the crowd, at partial profiles, and didn't recognize anyone.

The speaker was being introduced, and I gazed at my lap, concentrating on the cuticle of my index finger.

"Please join me in welcoming someone I first met when she came into the program three months ago. How she's coped with the early days and weeks and months has really been an inspiration to me and, I know, several people who've come in since." A round of applause, and the speaker, who I guess was already sitting at the table in the front, out of my sight, cleared her throat and said, "Hi, my name is Betsy, and I'm an alcoholic."

"Hi, Betsy," said everyone in the room, in something like unison. Everyone except me. I was speechless.

"It still makes me pretty nervous to tell my story," said a disembodied Betsy Schmidt, "even though the nervousness ends once I get going, and I always feel a whole lot better when it's over. My sponsor says that's pretty normal. I guess I took my first drink at boarding school when I was fourteen. I had a lot of resentment, because my parents were divorced, which was rare back then, and my mother sent me to boarding school because she was very determined to find herself another rich husband. It was a night the second semester of tenth grade. My roommate, a bright, delicate flower of a thing, had come back from a swell family reunion in Bermuda, and I was green with envy. That was my excuse, anyway, for ending up on the fire escape with two juniors, who were eventually expelled, and a bottle of Thunderbird. I'll never forget the look on my . . ."

As quietly as I could, I slid back the metal chair so that I could slip through and slink out of the building. My head was low, my dark glasses still on, and I had momentarily forgotten about Henderson. When I saw him across the street, sitting on the park bench under the weeping willow and reading a newspaper, he looked like a bored husband whose wife is trying on dresses in a fancy shop. It was a dreamy shot, one that shows up in a lot of island photo books: the weeping willow on the lawn of a Gothic Revival bed-and-breakfast, with a quaint park bench beneath it, on which a tourist is invariably sitting and reading, as Henderson was that day. Our few flimsy pieces of luggage were at his feet, and my bad humor had evaporated like cigarette smoke in the pure island air.

"Why didn't you come in?" I called out.

"I thought you might want to confess in private. So to speak."

"You look very Southern under this tree."

"It's like sitting under a waterfall."

"Rumor has it it's the only weeping willow on the island. Swansea's the sort of place where people spread gossip even about the flora and fauna." I smiled down at him. "I came out here to escape my past."

"Someone you'd slept with?"

Lightness as real as rain washed over me, and I laughed; something funny for the first time in days, laughing not at Henderson's line but at the lines and circles of connection that had led all of us to that meeting room and to this picture-perfect spot by the weeping willow. "Better than that."

"What could be better than that? He sure seems to have improved your mood."

"She."

"All that in five minutes? Miracles don't usually happen so fast. I'll call us another cab. And then you can tell me what happened." Henderson started to reach into his bag for his cell phone.

"Let's hitch to Cummington. It'll take twenty minutes for a cab to get all the way out here. Did you know that's how Will and I met? I was on Honeysuckle Road with my thumb out, and he picked me up." We each grabbed a piece of luggage and wandered toward the curb, glancing at the traffic heading east. "It was a perfect Swansea summer day, like today, when you know there'll be one of those electric-blue sunsets you see in all the posters. We were young, optimistic, and, as you know, we lived happily ever after."

Seeing Betsy at the meeting had had a strangely soothing effect on me. It had knocked out some of the venom, made me laugh at my self-righteousness, at the island social scene, the irony of the two of us ending up at the same meeting the morning after we had both behaved badly — Betsy newly sober, and me newly drunk.

When I stepped into the street and extended my hand to the road and the oncoming cars, I remembered the acute poignance of that distant day with my thumb out and Will stopping to pick me up — same thumb, same island, a woman who resembled me, a man who resembled the corpse on the floor of our house. I felt panicked then about getting to the *Sentinel* office and placing my ad in the paper — as if it would appear instantaneously and incite the townsfolk to search the beaches and woods for Henry. And when they found him, he would speak and reveal the mystery of Will's death. Which of my chimerical fantasies would I be disabused of first? That Henry held the secret of Will's death, or that Vicki would turn up unharmed?

An old forest-green Volvo station wagon stopped for us, and I leaned down to the passenger window to see the driver. "Dave Robbins," I said. He had spent three weeks in our kitchen a few years back, building new cabinets and counters and giving impromptu lectures on Beethoven's break with classical structure in the Ninth Symphony and the late string quartets. He and Will would talk about Oriana Fallaci's interviews with Henry Kissinger, General Giap, and Nguyen Van Thieu. In more ways than one, time stands very still on Swansea.

"Jesus. Sophy. What timing. I just heard about Will. From Ben. Not half an hour ago. I'm sorry. Where you headed?"

"The *Sentinel* office."

"We're going right past it. Hop in. Girls" — there were two teenagers in the back seat — "squeeze over." Dave was a single dad whose wife had left the island years before with his business partner. Henderson slid in with the girls; I took the front seat.

"Starting Monday," Dave said, "we're renting out Toad Hall for the summer and living in the cabin. It's a little tight, but there's no other way to pay the damn property taxes. We just finished cleaning the place up for the renters and stopped at Ben's filling station. Poor guy looked as white as a sheet. I thought he'd been sick. Then he told me."

We drove across the island discussing Will, although Dave had spoken to him only a few times since I'd left, and about nothing personal. Then it occurred to me that he and his girls might know one of the missing on my list, the woman with the funny name Will had written to, asking for a date. "Crystal Sparrow," I said. "Does that name mean anything to you?"

"Her name used to be Brenda," said a voice in the backseat. "It was Brenda when she babysat for us. Brenda Barnes. That was ages ago. We were like maybe five."

"How old was she?"

"Eighteen, twenty?" Dave said.

"Is she still around?"

"I haven't seen her," one girl said.

"Me neither," said the other.

"Dave?"

"Crazy Crystal," he said softly, a little too knowingly. It was a tone that made me understand that I shouldn't ask more in front of his daughters; that Crystal was someone known to men on the island whose wives had left them. And then I didn't have to say anything, because we were at the top end of Cummington, at an intersection of three busy streets. A ferry had just come in, and traffic was stalled. Cars from faraway places were filled with children and golden retrievers and Boogie Boards and all the bright promise of summer on the island.

"Henderson, it'll be quicker if we walk. It's only two blocks down Main."

I managed, in the next forty minutes, to place an ad in the paper for Henry, check into the Lighthouse Motel, which was miles from the nearest lighthouse, and get an old VW Bug from the Rent-A-Wreck office down between the shipyard and Swansea Bagels & Buns, and did it all without running into anyone I knew.

Ginny was on her way out the door when we arrived at the yellow gambrel on Ames Street, its freshly painted, sunny exterior a shiny Necco-wafer pale yellow, much too chipper for the hard business of grief. "I'm picking my mother up at the airport," she said after I introduced her to Henderson, "and we've got a meeting with Father Kelly in an hour about the funeral."

It was unclear whether they meant to invite me to this gathering, but before I had a chance to ask, another voice rang out from inside the house. "Sophy, is that you?"

The voice was identical with Ginny's, but when the door swung open, the woman on the other side was no one I knew. "I should have warned you," Susanna said, and she held open her arms for me. "It's harder to get rid of than a tattoo." This girl who had always been model-thin was now severely plump, buxom as the town tart in an old Western, wearing a blousy Indian wraparound top, loosely tied, that revealed the upper edge of a nursing bra. "Andy says there's more of me to love, but I —" the last words lost or abandoned somewhere in our embrace. She didn't cry, as Ginny had yesterday, but when we separated I saw that her gray-blue eyes, one of the only features she still shared with her twin, and the two of them with their father, were puffy and ringed with red. "Come see the baby. I just fed her." She took my arm, and we had not walked eight feet to the end of the foyer when her husband, Andy, with his mop of curly red hair and lumberjack build, appeared with a bundle swaddled in a flannel blanket with pink polka dots. He leaned down to kiss me, and the baby's sweet scent took me by surprise.

"Isn't she beautiful?" Susanna said. "Say hello to Sophy, little Rose."

There were too many feelings colliding in this room, all the ones you can imagine — the baby I never had, the role this baby had had in my decision to leave my marriage, Susanna's sadness that Will had never seen her — and another, private anguish that I could speak about to no one in the family. I knew that Will had had a raft of reasons for not liking Andy, not trusting him, and not the least was Andy's Svengalian hold on his daughter. Or so Will thought — that Susanna was there on the mountain without a telephone because Andy had brainwashed her, and because she was susceptible to being brainwashed on account of his own failings as a father. Will could go off about Andy: Andy's big ideas about being self-sufficient, living off the land, building a root cellar to store food for the winter, even starting a school for college kids to stay in the summer and learn concepts of interdependence, family farming, appropriate technology. It was, to Will, as if Susanna had sworn allegiance to Dr. Kevorkian.

"Do you want to hold her?" Andy said. He started to hand her to me, but he must have seen something on my face that looked like alarm. It was only an immense sadness. Sadness that Will had misread Andy and Susanna and that they had always felt his disapproval. Sadness that the edges of love are so jagged. Holding the baby would have taken Will's breath away. As Andy reached out to hand her to me, I could feel her about to take mine. "Next week she'll be five months old."

I know I said that Ginny had announced she was leaving to pick up her mother at the airport, so the scene in the foyer I am describing may have lasted only fifteen or twenty seconds, because the next thing I remember hearing was Ginny's voice, sounding as if it were right behind me. "Sophy, I forgot to tell you something." I turned and saw that Ginny had come back into the house, leaving the front door ajar. "I listened to the messages on Daddy's answering machine this morning. One of them was for you. A girl named Vicki."

"What?"

Henderson, who had been dutifully hanging back, and who was more or less unflappable, lurched toward Ginny so boldly, I was afraid he would grab her by the collar. "Today? She called today?"

"I think so. There were an awful lot of messages. I'm —"

"What did she say?" I handed the baby back to Andy in case I dropped her in astonishment.

"She was looking for you. She said she'd heard someone was sick. Something like that."

"Was she here? Did she say she'd call back?"

"I listened to twenty-three messages. I'm not sure."

"Did you erase it?"

"No."

"Did she sound scared?"

"Not particularly."

"Panicked?"

"I don't think so."

"Is the machine here?"

"It's at Daddy's."

"We need to listen to it. She's missing. The police are looking for her."

"Here, call her father," Henderson said, handing me his cell phone, not much bigger than the baby's foot, "and then call the police."

Both Daniel and the detective demanded that I go to the one place I did not want to go, Will's house, and plant myself there in case Vicki called again. In the meantime, the cop would put a tracer on the phone line, and Daniel would close his eyes and sleep for the first time in thirty-six hours.

I handed Henderson back his phone. "How do you think she got your number?" he asked.

"I must still be listed in the Swansea directory."

"What's going on?" Susanna said.

"A friend's child in New York took off. We had no idea what direction she went, but it's a relief that at least she knows I'm here."

"Could she be on the island?" Susanna said.

"That hadn't occurred to me," I said.

"Let's go," Henderson said.

"It's downstairs in the kitchen," Ginny said, about the answering machine, "not upstairs where he died."

Susanna must have seen the dread on my face. "It won't be that bad," she said, though she knew it would be, because she had fled from there that morning.

"Thank you, sweetie," I said.

"At least we'll know where to find you."

My reluctance to go back to the house should come as no surprise. What will surprise you, as it surprised Henderson and me, were some of the voices we heard on Will's answering machine as we waited for Vicki's message.

There was a call from a man named John Watts, who said he had just received Will's letter and was sorry Will did not want to talk to him, even off the record, about some of his experiences in the CIA for the book he was writing, but that if Will ever changed his mind, he should get in touch.

There were two calls from a friend who wanted to know if Will would sail with him in the Around the Island Race on the Fourth of July.

One of our neighbors down the street had invited Will to dinner on a Saturday night that passed a few weeks ago.

But one of the first calls on the tape, which meant that it came close to the day Will died, was from Crystal Sparrow. "Hi, Will, it's Crystal. I just wanted to say that I'm really sorry about what happened the other night. Maybe I'll see you around." Click.

And of course there was the call from Vicki, which we listened to, gaping at the machine, as if it had powers beyond making a record of her voice. "Hi, I'm looking for Sophy. This is, um, Vicki, and I, um, thought you might be there because your husband is very sick but I guess you're not. I hope it's not serious, like AIDS or a coma or anything. That's the main thing I wanted to say but I didn't want to bother you if you're like in a hospital or a nursing home."

Then the machine's electronic voice took over and told us she had called on Saturday at ten twenty-seven A.M. Four hours ago.

"Your husband was sick?" Henderson said.

"Maybe Daniel told her that to explain why I'd left the city in such a hurry. She asked me a few times if I'd ever been married, so she knew there was a husband in my past."

When the phone rang an instant later, both of us sprang back from it, as if it were a sleeping turtle that had suddenly started snapping. I lifted the receiver and said nothing for two or three seconds, hoping to locate the geography in the si-

lence. But there was only stillness and then a woman's voice.
"Is this where I can reach Will?"

"It was."

"Do you have his new number?"

"He doesn't have a new number. He's dead. This is his wife.
Who's calling?"

No answer.

"Is there something I can help you —"

"I'm so sorry. No, never mind," and she hung up, as if
wanting to bolt from the news. Was it Crystal again? It didn't
sound like the woman on the tape. No, this new woman was
older, more businesslike. I remembered the personal ad he'd
started to answer on his laptop. There may have been another
that he had answered.

"Who was it?" Henderson asked.

"She didn't say."

"They turn up, these mystery callers, after people die, if
you're lucky. My friend Claudia was married for ten years, and
when her husband died, she didn't discover one surprising
thing about him. No one from his past showed up. He hadn't
scribbled a revealing line in any of his files or books; hadn't
even saved a love letter. She was terribly disappointed."

"No danger of that with Will. I think we're due for a few
more surprises."

The next one arrived later that afternoon. Henderson had
gone back to the Lighthouse Motel to take a nap and found a
telegram for me. He called and read it over the phone.

SHOCKING NEWS. MY SINCEREST CONDOLENCES TO YOU
AND WILL'S CHILDREN. HE WILL BE MISSED.

ARTHUR GLASS. US EMBASSY. MANILA. THE PHILIPPINES

Will had never mentioned an Arthur Glass but had referred
to an "Arty" he'd known in Vietnam. Nothing strange about

the missing last name: Welcome to the CIA, where name rec-
ognition costs people their lives. Maybe Arthur Glass was Arty
and maybe he wasn't. The mystery was how he had learned of
Will's death when none of the obituaries had yet come out;
how he knew my name and that I was staying at the Lighthouse Motel. The most obvious scenario, I told Henderson,
was that someone at the *Swansea Sentinel* knew Glass and ran
Will's name by him when confronted with the obituary I had
sent there. If Will were alive, he would have spun out two or
three other possibilities, reluctant spy though he was.

But Will was dead, and he did not speak to me that day or
that night, though I sat in his kitchen, beneath the room
where he had died. Nor did I hear from any of the other voices
that sometimes take up residence in my head. I can only think
these rooms were so silent because the people who did speak
to me had such urgent statements to make that there was no
room for anything softer, gentler, more imaginative. And the
house — you're probably wondering what it was like for me
to be in this house that had been mine until a few months before. I had stage fright, which is to say that most of my terror
disappeared once I got there and walked through the first
floor, showing Henderson around. Before long, I even got
used to the changes Will had made since my departure, removing all signs of me, taking down photographs and posters
we had bought together, placing my favorite coffee mugs in
the back of the kitchen cabinets, and a stack of my gardening
books on the floor of the front hall closet, behind his winter
boots. Once Henderson left, I looked through some of those
books as if they were old yearbooks, scrapbooks, souvenirs of
past lives. I kept to the first floor, and when I passed the staircase, I tried not to look at it. When the phone rang, I jumped.
And when Henderson returned at seven o'clock that evening

with a bag of groceries to cook me dinner, I cried, because I
knew it meant that Will was dead, because that is what happens when someone dies: your friends come to your house
with food.

There were five phone calls. One was from Daniel, asking if
Vicki had called again. One was from the detective in New
York, asking the same question. One was from Susanna, telling me they had met with Father Kelly at our Lady of Perpet-
ual Something or Other, and Will's funeral would be Monday
afternoon at one o'clock. If I would like to say a few words or
read a poem, they could schedule that into the program, but I
had to let them know by Sunday noon. I did not ask what
would happen if I let them know Sunday at sunset, because I
was afraid that my anger at being reduced to a slot on the
schedule would flare and combust. Susanna asked whether
the little girl had called again and I needed a place to stay for
the night, and her consideration skimmed away the top layer
of my anger. I said I didn't think so but would let her know.

But it was the last phone call, at nine o'clock, as Henderson
and I were eating dinner, that I least expected. It was Evan,
saying he needed a favor. Urgently. Could he come by in fifteen minutes and explain?

Of course I said yes.

11

The Chicken Coop

THERE WAS a chatty article in the *Times* about the recent celebrity auction on Swansea, held the third Saturday of every August. It raises money for the social service agency where year-rounders go for drug and alcohol counseling, domestic violence awareness classes, and assistance in applying for welfare and food stamps. Once the summer people leave, scores of shops, restaurants, and hotels shut down for eight or nine months, which earns Swansea the unexpected distinction of being the poorest community in the state; hence the need for an agency so at odds with the island's affluent image.

According to the *Times,* the auction raised $150,000, with star-struck summer people paying thousands of dollars for an afternoon sail with a certain movie star, a kayak-and-lunch trip with a famous nature writer, a private ballet lesson with a Russian whose gnarled, arthritic feet have been photographed by Richard Avedon — and lunch at "21" with Evan Lambert, which went for $11,500. The *Times* reporter got someone who would not speak for attribution to say that the scandal Evan and his wife were involved in earlier in the summer may even have increased Evan's auction value. It certainly did not hurt it.

I'd had a taste of Evan and Mavis's troubles the night he removed me from the Winstons' clambake. The story behind the strife was about to become extremely public soon after Evan called me the night I kept vigil at Will's house, hoping Vicki would phone again. Though Evan's and my fortunes were closely linked during those few days, though he was a major player in my life that weekend, I had only a minor and very private role in the dramas that were about to be played out.

Henderson and I were eating the classic island dinner he'd prepared for me when Evan called: grilled swordfish, local corn on the cob, and roasted baby potatoes brushed with olive oil and rosemary, the first full meal I had eaten in three days. It seemed too splendid for the circumstances, but Henderson explained that that was the point: to be reminded that there were also miracles in the world, swordfish and fresh corn on the cob chief among them. The food and its preparation took my mind off images of Will on the floor upstairs, scenarios of what could have happened to him. If he had had a heart attack, was it as he slept, and could it have propelled him off the bed and onto the floor, where Ben found him? Or had he been felled as he crossed the room on his way to the toilet? I could ask Ben which way his body lay, but I shuddered at the thought. A prurient question, ghoulish and irrelevant, something the *National Enquirer* would want to know. And if I asked, Ben might tell me the truth, and the truth might be that he had found Will sprawled on his stomach, arm groping futilely for the phone on the bedside table.

I was on the verge of telling some of this to Henderson, as we ate and waited for Evan to arrive, when the phone rang again.

Like children in a game of Statue, we froze, as we had every time it emitted an electronic bleat. Like adults in crisis and in love, we felt our pulses quicken. Narratives coursed through our veins.

My fingers tingled as I reached for the phone. But it was not Vicki. It was a computer voice selling subscriptions to *The Soap Opera Digest.*

I mention it — I remember it — because it was a moment of comic relief for us, because it inspired the light-hearted turn our conversation took, and we ended up joking about what favor Evan could possibly want from me. "Probably not money," Henderson said, "or the baby-blue polyester curtains in your room at the Lighthouse Motel or your prewar Volkswagen with original upholstery." At that exact moment, like a period at the end of the sentence, the doorbell rang.

Turned out it *was* the car Evan needed, and me to drive it, a sort of getaway job. "I'm about to pick up my brother and his family on the nine-thirty ferry. The young woman I told you about, Jenn —"

"Twenty-five?"

He nodded. "She's also going to be on that boat. I need you to take her to the chicken coop, the place I offered you. She had to leave Boston unexpectedly."

"Can't she get a cab?" Henderson asked. "Sophy ought to be here in case Vicki calls again. I'd offer to drive, but I never learned how."

Evan turned to me, and when he saw that his weighted silence could not persuade me, he said, "I know this is a difficult time for you, and under ordinary circumstances you know I wouldn't —"

"Is she in trouble?" I asked.

After a moment, he said, "We're all in a bit of a jam."

Then there was another silence, with Henderson and me

waiting for an explanation, and Evan mulling over whether he should give us one.

"This is the young woman you used to be . . ." I said driftily, thinking it might loosen his tongue.

"I want her to be seen by as few people as possible. You know what it's like here. I wouldn't impose on you if there were anyone else I could trust with this —" He went silent again and looked at me hard, as if I were a juror he had to bring around, someone stony-faced, unreadable, mute. I was divided, not in two, but in three: I wanted to sit by the phone for Vicki; to help Evan out because he had gone out of his way to help me; and to help him out, not to repay his favors but because I was, after all this time, and in spite of everything, flattered that he needed me, even to be his chauffeur.

Henderson must have seen the way Evan was looking at me, a little needy and off-kilter, the usual suaveness squashed, and he — Henderson — must have done some calculations of his own. "If Vicki calls," he said, "I suppose I can do what's necessary."

It wasn't until Evan and I were outside, standing between our two cars, that he explained. "I didn't want to say much in front of Henderson. I just got word there'll be a nasty story in the *Boston Herald* tomorrow morning. There's a guy with a vendetta against Mavis for her work on the sexual harassment committee at Harvard. When he was investigated for two or three complaints and his contract wasn't renewed, he did enough snooping to learn something about Mavis that's going to force her to resign from the committee. That pile of dirty linen led to another — Jenn and me. A scandal-mongering reporter who's been out to get me for years because he doesn't approve of my clients was handed a sex scandal with my name on it. The whole mess'll be on page one. In the midst of all this, Mavis and I are having a cocktail party tomorrow night for *tout le monde* to honor my law school pal Judge Tucker, who was just nominated to the Second Circuit."

"But what about Jenn? Why is she coming here now?"

"Jesus," Evan said, looking at his watch, "the boat's about to dock. I'll point her out to you and vice versa. She knows a friend of mine will take her to the chicken coop, where she'll hide out for a few days. That's all you need to know. And this." He reached into his back pocket and handed me an index card, filled front and back with his blocky print. "Directions to the house."

"Is she delusional, thinking she can hide here?"

"She's a kid. She panicked. I'll go the back way to the ferry. Follow me." A moment later, Evan's headlights flared, and he was out of the driveway and most of the way down Longfellow by the time I got the Rent-A-Wreck into first gear. He meant "follow me" in a general way — more like "catch me if you can." I caught him at the end of the next block. For a few minutes, the soupy rattle of the old VW engine and the logistics of our route — a series of right turns onto narrow oneway streets, then left into the alley beyond the old Swansea Bank & Trust — obscured the news Evan had handed me. Then the news obscured everything else.

From the parking lot, I could see that the ferry was not in its slip yet. I killed my headlights and looked out to the harbor, in the direction of Chillum's Point. A familiar brushstroke of bright light moved across the darkness. Funny, the things you learn to interpret; from the position of this particular speck, I knew it would be six or seven minutes before the boat would make landfall. I spotted Evan in a growing cluster of people assembled on the landing where passengers without cars would disembark, coming off a ramp that rose to meet a door on the second level of the ferry. Something about trying to keep track of him as he drifted through the crowd gave me the idea that Vicki might turn up on the boat, too; I might find *her* if I looked hard enough. *She's a kid, she panicked.* Hadn't we all, beginning with me and my mad dash from New York, racing here as if Will were on his death bed, Vicki following me, as if I were on mine?

Do you wonder whether I was besieged with thoughts of what might have happened to her, the horrors, the headlines? I was and I wasn't. When the thoughts came to me, they arrived like stones pitched through a window — unexpected, scaring me out of my wits. Without them, I felt a steady thrum of anxiety, my pulse racing, heart working much too hard.

Next time I looked toward the water, I saw the ferry a few hundred feet off shore, its giant garage-like door halfway up, weirdly ajar and about to disgorge fifty cars. My spirits lifted suddenly, incrementally: Hello, Pavlov. My years of living here made the sight of the ferry a tonic. Someone was coming to visit. The possibility of comfort, of company. Or was some part of me energized by Evan and Mavis's undoing, the spectacle of the mighty falling? Of Mavis, the shrill moralist, being unmasked? Was it *schadenfreude* or was it relief at the distraction from my own troubles? All, I'm afraid, of the above. I read the directions to the chicken coop before I got out to join Evan on the receiving line.

From ferry:
West on Ocean Dr. 8.2 mi. R. on Gulley's Creek .6 mi. to stone pillars. L. onto dirt road. Go 1.3 mi. to 3-way fork; take

middle fork .7 mi. to tree on R with 4 signs nailed to it ("Green House" "Randolphs" "Baxters" "Coop"). Take R and go .8 mi to tree on left with sign that says "Coop." Turn left immediately after the tree, even though path looks too narrow for cars. Go 1.7 mi. Yr headlights should be shining directly on coop.

Crawford Cove on your right, 200 paces.

I had been given directions as eccentric as these to plenty of places on Swansea. I loved the poetry in them and dreaded the prose: one wrong turn at one unmarked tree, and you're as lost as Hansel and Gretel. That had happened to me one night coming back alone from a friend's house at Indian Pass, in the heart of the old forest. Round and round I'd gone, a rat in a maze, while my gas gage slipped toward empty. I kept looking for the middle path by the tree that had her name on it, then for someplace wide enough to turn around in, then for any house with lights on, then for any house at all. Just when I'd started to panic, the dirt road gave way to pavement.

At first I didn't notice Francine Cooper in the crowd of people waiting for the boat. I was looking for Evan, who kept disappearing behind a gaggle of tall, rail-thin teenage boys wearing backward baseball caps. Francine's auburn hair was pulled back, and I was used to seeing it down around her shoulders. She was waving to people on the upper deck, though it was so dark up there, I don't know how she could make anyone out. "Francine," I said loudly, and she turned around, searching for the face attached to the voice. I could tell she saw me approach but wasn't sure whom she was looking at. Then she was. She was no friend; she was my divorce lawyer. I'd found her through an article in the island newspaper about unusual custody arrangements. She had recently moved here from

Boston, another overcharged city girl with island fantasies. The day before, when I'd phoned her office, I was told she'd be back to work on Monday.

She did not know Will was dead, and it took her a moment to recall what had become of the separation agreement I'd signed and Fed Exed her earlier in the week. "It was supposed to go to your husband's lawyer so that he could get your husband's signature on it. My secretary typed up a cover letter and left it for me to sign." Seems it had a glaring and most peculiar error, a little too severe to be called a typo: *Enclosed is the signed Separation Disagreement.* Francine had scribbled a correction and assumed the new cover letter would be waiting in her office on Monday.

"What does all this mean?" I asked her.

"Number one, you're still married. Number two, I'm the only one who knows you signed the separation agreement."

"Which means?"

"If he died without a will, as his spouse you're entitled to half his estate."

"Unfortunately, he had a will and left me a dollar."

"You may be able to sue the estate."

"I don't want to sue anyone, Francine."

"If it helps, I think the technical term is 'file a claim against the estate.' Come by and see me Monday."

"The funeral's Monday."

"Then Tuesday."

"Sophy!"

The dock was aswarm with bodies, people cascading into one another, people gleeful, giddy, ecstatic finally to be here, the beautiful island at the start of summer. They carried suitcases, knapsacks, shopping bags from Bread and Circus, babies in corduroy Snugglies pressed to their chests, bicycle helmets, anxieties from the mainland, dreams like the ones Francine and I had acted on, that if you stayed all year long, you would always feel the way you did tonight, invigorated, engorged, in love.

"Sophy!"

I felt a hand on my shoulder and turned to see Evan, his other arm loosely around a young woman so strikingly beautiful, I would have noticed her coming off the boat if I hadn't been talking to Francine. She had short, wavy dark hair, olive skin, eyes large and wide apart, movie-star cheekbones; she belonged on Crete. She was a young Isabella Rossellini, but smaller and very nervous.

When Evan introduced us, we nodded and mumbled weak hellos, uncertain, I think, how gracious the circumstances required us to be.

"You'll be all right getting out there?" Evan asked me. "Jenn'll point you in the right direction."

"Sure," I said, though I didn't sound convincing, even to myself. Evan vanished into the crowd; I grew lightheaded as I led Jenn to the car and tried to make sense of the news from Francine. In the eyes of the law, I was married. I was Will's wife. "My car's this way," I heard myself say. Does that change anything, I wondered, anything at all? Change what I am entitled to feel? To fight for? Could I bring myself to sue my stepdaughters? Take to court the closest thing to children I had in the world to assert a claim on behalf of a person I no longer wanted to be?

"Are you here on vacation?" Jenn asked as I turned the key in the ignition. "Or is this your regular summer place?"

"Evan didn't tell you?"

"He just said you were an old friend and very discreet."

The ferry traffic was moving swiftly down the road that led

to Ocean Drive, though my thoughts ran in circles, spirals —
you could say they ran away with me — and a short time after
we turned the corner and started up the hill, I realized I'd said
nothing in reply, that I had no idea where to begin the story of
what I was doing here and no idea where it would end.

This is not news: women talk. This may not be either: Jenn
and I said little on the long, dark drive to the woods. Once we
were through the town, she asked whether she could smoke. I
said if she opened the window. A few miles later she asked
whether she could turn on the radio. I said it didn't work;
they'd knocked a few dollars off the cost of the rental because
of it. A while later — by this time we were clear on the other
side of the island — she asked whether I wanted to stop somewhere and have a drink. I could have said that we were many
miles from the nearest bar, which was the truth, but it was
more important for me to say "No, thanks," important to decline, though I sounded a little abrupt. I'd been expecting all
day to feel a new craving for the stuff, checking to see whether
the mugger still lurked in the neighborhood. No signs of him
yet, no whispers, no shadows I could not account for. "I'm on
the wagon," I explained. "Otherwise I'd — I don't think a bar
is the best place for me tonight."

"Sure." Her inflection was not a pat on the back; it had a
rough edge. I think it was a euphemism for "whatever."

So we drove in silence, through miles of leafy darkness, past
forests of scrub oak, pitch pine, sassafras, in many places the
trees overhanging the narrow road as tightly as a tunnel, headlights and brake lights our only illumination. She kept a cigarette going and tipped her head to blow smoke out the window. I knew I could easily break the silence and that it would
be the polite thing to do, the decent thing; she was a kid in

trouble, after all; the car was older than she was. But I couldn't talk to her about my circumstances, and I wasn't sure how much I wanted to know about hers. If this was going to become a full-blown scandal, I did not want to know enough to be a source or a witness. I aspired to nothing loftier than chauffeur. That's what I was thinking when Jenn pierced the silence with a dagger: "So did you ever fuck him?" she asked.

I laughed a little. It felt good to laugh. "When I was your age. And he was too."

"What was he like then?"

"Sexy and preoccupied. What's he like now?"

I assumed she would echo my answer, but all I heard was her lighting a cigarette. I could see the burst of flame at the edge of my vision, and an animal, maybe a raccoon, dart across the road. "The thing is," Jenn said, "I've been trying to break it off with him for months, and now this comes up. It's sort of embarrassing, but the best times between us were when I threatened to leave. Suddenly he'd become this real emotional guy. It was hard to resist, you know? I'm supposed to start law school in September, and there's actually someone who wants to marry me. By tomorrow night, Barbara Walters is going to want to interview my mother."

"I know this is cold comfort, but I don't think the details of Evan Lambert's sex life will hold the nation's attention for very long. A hotshot lawyer with a beautiful young woman is more of a dog-bites-man story than —"

"He didn't tell you about Mavis?"

"No specifics."

"*I'm* the specifics."

We had reached the turn in the road where I had to start reading the directions, close eye on the trip odometer, counting off tenths of a mile, and I thought Jenn was about to tell me that she had been Mavis's lover too; maybe that was the other pile of dirty linen that would be aired in the paper tomorrow. I was filled with an overwhelming desire not to know, just as I did not want to know in what position Will's body had been found, or what he had written in his diary, or what had happened to my dog Henry, because by this time I figured none of the news would be good.

That was the end of our intimate conversation. For the rest of the drive, she read me directions, showed me the way, and did not importune me to answer more questions about Evan in the old days or what I thought she should do in the days to come. She thanked me for the ride, and I watched her go into the lovely, freshly shingled cottage that bore no vestige of its past life as a chicken coop. The tiny place glowed as she went through it, turning on lights, and I made a tight three-point turn and headed out.

I did not lose my way going back through the woods. And it surprised me to feel as relieved as I did, maybe even content, on the long drive back to Will's. All I had done was move the prisoner from Point A to Point B; therapeutic, I guess, because it was simple and as distant as Cassiopeia from the chaos of my life. It helped that it was a beautiful night, soft air rushing through the open windows, broad bands of stars I could see through clearings in the trees, the scent of something piney, something sweet, the engine of the old car rattling, the sound strangely soothing the way it might be to hear the clacking of a manual typewriter. The car was the same vintage as Blueberry Parfait, the ancient VW Bug Will had picked me up in hitchhiking twelve years before. At the turn-off for Bell's Cove, I remembered that we were still married, that I was probably entitled to part of his estate; and I realized this might account for some of my implausible calm. I even liked the idea of returning to Will's house, because Henderson was there, because it held the promise of a phone call from Vicki.

When I opened the front door and saw him look up and smile at me from the couch, where he sat with the computer on his lap, I figured the call must have come; it was a rich smile.

"She's okay?"

"No call. But some good news. Come sit down here. It's show-and-tell time."

In the center of the paper-white screen was a box with this inside it:

PASSWORD: •••••••

When Henderson pressed the return key with his pinkie, the screen filled with words, a carpet of black letters against a white page. My eyes fell on phrases: *can't believe she had the fucking nerve to . . . considering the consequences, it hasn't been . . . Connie agreed with me that S. is definitely . . . wants to interview me for a book on the CIA, but he doesn't understand that my regrets are . . .* I jerked my head away, as if from a car accident, and stood up. "How did you figure it out?" I asked but did not really want to know, because there could be no light answer. Henderson would have had to dwell somewhere in Will's brain, and that wasn't a place I wanted to visit now. I didn't even want to wonder how someone who'd never met my husband could have divined his private password.

"I tried thinking like a spy. It was quite delicious, an opportunity that had nothing to do with romantic espionage, spying on a lover. And then I threw in the idea of thinking like a movie buff, because of all that business with the videos you told me about."

"Double-O-Seven? Goldfinger?"

"Think clever."

"Jonathan Pollard?"

"Clever, darling, not pedestrian."

"Smiley?"

"I went upstairs to his bedroom. There are a bunch of videos in the console under the TV. Things he owns."

"Not much, is there? *Chinatown, North by Northwest,* a few of those Civil War things, maybe *Vertigo?*"

"*Citizen Kane* was one of them," Henderson said, prophetically. "I tried 'Rosebud' purely for the hell of it. It opened right up." His gaze returned to the screen, his fingers to the keyboard, and I tried to remember whether Will and I had ever made Rosebud jokes. But all I could think was that Henderson must have read a chunk of the diary and that he was keeping something from me. He looked up, puzzled at my silence. "You're not upset with me, are you, for fooling around with it? You didn't exactly give me permission."

"God, no. I'm speechless at how clever you are. And terrified I have to read the thing, now that I can. Even more terrified that you already did and there's something awful you're not telling me."

"No," he said, seriously. "Since you ask, I did read the last entry, to see if there was anything about suicide, because I didn't want you to have to —"

"Thank you."

"There wasn't. I flipped through the rest to see if I got the whole document — I think I did — and I dipped into the recent stuff. I didn't see anything there either, but I didn't read it thoroughly. You don't have to look at it until you're ready."

"What will I find?"

"A lot of anger and sadness."

"Does that mean I should have stayed?"

"Almost every man I ever cared about is dead, most of them under the age of forty. Friends, lovers, collaborators, and all of their friends, lovers, and collaborators."

"So this must seem paltry to you."

"On the contrary. What I'm trying to say is that people are resilient. I have the names of nine living people in my address book, but I'm okay now. I'm happy to be alive. Some days I'm intensely happy, but I never thought I'd be able to say that when I was going to funerals as often as I went to the dry cleaner. It would have taken some time, Sophy, but Will could have gotten through this — this loss."

I slept that night on the couch in my used-to-be living room, with the portable phone on the floor next to me. Henderson volunteered to sleep in the house, in one of the bedrooms upstairs. I insisted that it wasn't necessary, although I still couldn't go up there and had to ask him to fetch me a pillow and bed linen.

He didn't say, but I got the feeling that he planned to stop off somewhere on his way back to the motel. I knew there was a gay bar in town. What made me think he might go there? I imagined he wanted some relief from the sadness in our midst; or maybe I wanted it for him, wanted to know he would be comforted for his losses, which he did not often talk about. Something else led me to think he was not going straight back to the motel. Before he left Will's, he spent time in the downstairs bathroom and emerged with his hair combed, his shirt freshly tucked in, the lenses of his glasses cleaned to a Windex sheen. And he was too solicitous of me, wanting to be sure I would last the night alone. Maybe because he had doubts that he could. Maybe because he knew that if I called him in a three A.M. panic, I'd discover he wasn't there.

But it was nothing like panic I felt at eleven-thirty when he left — with an extra spring in his step, I couldn't help noticing. I was remarkably subdued, as if the house were a library or a church, a place for contemplation. I checked two or three times that the portable phone worked, that I got a dial tone, and made up the couch while I imagined Vicki calling in a few minutes. While I imagined Henderson striking up a conversation with a kind stranger.

I dozed off with the light on. When the phone rang several hours later, waking me from the deepest sleep, the illuminated living room startled me more than darkness would have. I thought the ringing was the doorbell and that Vicki had finally arrived. It was another ring or two before I got the receiver to my ear.

"Sophy? We've located her." It was Daniel's voice, gravelly with sleep. "I just spoke to her. She's fine."

"Where is she? What happened?"

"It's a long story for another time. But she's perfectly okay. Not a hair out of place. Go back to sleep."

When I woke up a few hours later, the sun cascading through the living room windows, through the filmy white curtains and across my back, I was afraid I had dreamed that call. But when I picked up the phone to dial Daniel and ask if Vicki had been found, it came back to me, everything he had said and the words I had fallen back to sleep saying to myself, words that had lulled me into something faintly resembling tranquility: *The rest will be easy, the rest will be a cinch.*

12

The Humane Society

THE PHONE rang not long after I got up. I'd been standing at Will's kitchen sink, gazing out the back window, taking inventory: the overgrown grass, the wilted, weedy garden, the clear plastic bird feeder that could have been Barbie's Bauhaus Dream House, a squarish, two-level box with a tiny terrace where the birds were supposed to perch and peck for seed in the little holes in the walls. I'd bought it the day I hung the three flags from the front porch. It was part of the same decorating scheme: an announcement that ours was a happy house.

"Sophy, Francine Cooper here." The phone at my ear, my thoughts drifting from the backyard to the front porch, to the moment two years ago after I put up the flags and stepped back to the street to look at the house. But it had been a windless day, and the purple and yellow and bright pink flags hung like flypaper. "I don't have an island number for you, but I thought there was a chance you'd be at your husband's. Got a minute?"

"Sure." The bird feeder was starkly empty, like an abandoned gas station with the pumps still standing. When I got off the phone, I'd look around the basement for the plastic bag of seed.

"I came downstairs to my office to get a phone number, and I remembered what we talked about last night at the ferry. I'm afraid my information wasn't up to date. Looks as if my secretary sent the separation agreement to Will's lawyer Friday morning. While you're at the funeral tomorrow, I'll try to do some damage control. Since the signed agreement is with Will's lawyer now, which says you're on record as walking away from the marriage with nothing but your pajamas, getting you a share of the estate may be a little trickier than I'd thought. It might make sense to sue the estate. Or it might not."

"Damage control?"

"A colleague at my old firm in Boston had a case like this last year — husband died while the divorce was pending. I'm going to talk strategy with him, see how far he thinks we can push the envelope."

"Francine, I'm not interested in pushing any envelopes. And I'm not sure I want to sue my stepdaughters."

"Sophy, you're in the middle of a divorce. This wouldn't be personal, against them. It's a strictly legal, by-the-book —"

"Don't intentions count for anything? The marriage was about to end because I wanted it to."

"I never thought you should have walked away empty-handed. Now that he's dead, you may not have to."

"All I asked you last night was what my marital status is."

"I'm looking through your file. Tell me again your rationale for leaving with nothing."

"He had a government pension and two thousand dollars in the bank."

"The house is half yours. Community property."

"He didn't want the divorce, and I didn't want to drag it out by taking him to court. And I wasn't going to make him sell his house so that he could give me half the proceeds. I think the legal term is 'adding insult to injury.'"

"Hypothetically, if you'd known he was going to drop dead, would you have walked with nothing?" Her bedside manner was beginning to resemble Betsy Schmidt's. Or maybe John Gotti's.

"There's a possibility that he killed himself. He may not have dropped dead, as you put it."

"You didn't tell me that last night."

"Because it's not certain. They're still doing the autopsy."

"That might make a difference. Suicide."

"To whom?"

"The judge."

"But my husband spoke loud and clear in his will."

"Which is why I want to find out about challenging it, because it's out of bounds."

"But you just said that since I signed the separation agreement, and it's with Will's lawyer, I may not have a good case."

"It's not open and shut, but I don't think it's impossible."

"I can't decide this minute, Francine."

"You've got to move quickly."

I started to say that I would come talk to her on Tuesday, but she cut me off. "Was that Evan Lambert I saw you with last night? He a friend of yours?"

"Yeah."

"How's he taking it?"

"The nanny case? He's not exactly a novice, so it's —"

"The girlfriend and the wife case. It's all over the news. Good thing he likes attention; he's getting plenty of it."

"This is the first I've heard." *This* must have been the reason she called me. Of course it was.

"It won't be the last. Seems that two years ago, when his wife —"

"Francine, there's someone at my door. I'll come see you Tuesday."

There was no one at the door, and seconds after I hung up, the phone rang again. It was Ginny, telling me that she and her mother were on their way to the house to pick up some photographs of Will to display at the funeral. "Did the little girl ever call?" she asked.

"Her father called me in the middle of the night. She's fine."

"You must be relieved."

It took me a moment to answer, to know what I felt. Relieved, of course; a little numb, a little adrift, and alone, in a way I hadn't been when Vicki was still missing, still expected to call or show up here. Alone in this house I had fled three months ago because it felt like the tomb it had become. But I couldn't tell any of that to Ginny. Nor that my lawyer wanted me to sue her and her sister. "I certainly am relieved," I said. "Now all I have to get through is your father's funeral."

"Me too."

"Will his body be there?"

"My mother's arranging everything." It was turning out to be Clare's funeral after all, and now that I wasn't consumed with Vicki's disappearance, word of her control angered me anew. "Have you decided whether you'll read anything?" Ginny asked.

"I'll read something," I said, with barely suppressed scorn. It was shorthand for "I'll read something, all right, just you wait and see." His diary, I thought, or the letter he'd sent to the writer who wanted to interview him about the CIA, about the nature of his regrets.

"I'm reading something from Corinthians," Ginny said, "and Susanna has Emily Dickinson."

"Thanks." There were so many ways to say that word, so many intonations, I hoped Ginny was sufficiently numb not to have heard the sarcastic shadings in mine.

"Come over for lunch later," Ginny said. "Is your friend still here? Bring him with you."

Why was her kindness, her decency, such a surprise? Because I imagined that she was as angry with me as I was with her. And her father and mother. It was as if Will was on their team; as if they had the votes, the standing, the history, to declare him theirs. According to the letter of the law, he was my husband. But of course he belonged to no one, to none of us, which is why there was so much to fight over: he was ether, he was air. We could feint and flail forever. We could quarrel over his remains, what remained of them, as if he were Voltaire, whose brain ended up in a jam pot and his heart in the Bibliothèque Nationale.

"My friend's still here," I said, "and we'll come around later, but I'm about to leave the house. I'll be gone by the time you and your mom get here."

"If he killed himself," Ginny said, suddenly intimate, suddenly needy, her voice dropping a few decibels, "how do you think he did it?"

My eyes fell on his computer, sitting on the kitchen table, and I knew I had to read the diary; I couldn't rely on Henderson's skimming. And then I'd give the computer to the girls or leave it in the house for them to find. It wasn't mine to keep. "Why don't we wait until we hear from the coroner? We don't need to torture ourselves."

"Did he ever talk about it with you?"

"Only about how he felt after Jesse died. Nothing more recent." No need to tell her that when we were first together, Will used to say to me, "If anything ever happened to you, I'd kill myself." No need to tell her that back then I was happy to be needed that way. It made me feel important, and, yes, I know it had everything to do with my father's disappearing when I was nine. I figured a man who needed me as badly as Will did would never leave me, and I was right. But two or three years ago, when our life seemed stable and secure, when we were trying to have a baby, Will said on a lovely night as we were going to sleep, "I told you a long time ago that I'd die if something took you away from me, but I don't think I would anymore. I'm feeling sturdier now. Sturdy enough to be a father again." No point passing any of this on to poor Ginny.

"What about you?" I said. "Did your dad ever talk to you about it?"

"Not since Jesse died."

"What does your mother think?"

"She hadn't spoken to him in ages. A year or two."

I hardly knew how to answer. Clare's audacity, taking over the funeral, was breathtaking, but apparently I was the only one who found it objectionable. "Henderson and I will come by later. You'll be in the yellow house all day?"

"As far as I know."

As far as I knew, I would leave Will's immediately, with his laptop, and head to the Lighthouse Motel, where I could read the diary in Henderson's presence, because even though I was determined, even though I knew I had to do this, dread coursed through me and mixed with the feeling of disbelief that filled me since the police first called. He was not dead. He *could* not be dead. Here I was in his house. There were eggs in the refrigerator and a block of cheddar cheese cut at an angle, slices shaved off, and half a container of yogurt and a bottle of Jamaican hot sauce we'd bought a year ago in Boston. He was almost here, wasn't he? Almost home?

I closed the laptop, hoping that the diary would exonerate me. If it didn't, would I hand it over anyway? If it didn't, would I edit it before returning it? I didn't think I had the nerve — or the bad character — to delete or doctor Will's words, even though I could make changes without leaving fingerprints. Maybe I could call that ghost-writing. But if I did, who would I be then? Surely not the same woman who'd bought the bird feeder and the happy flags.

On my way out, I took the flags down from their hooks on the front porch and tossed them into the backseat of my rented car — the nylon sunburst, the rainbow, the engorged purple tulip. How could he have kept them flying after I'd left, when he'd removed every other sign of me from the house? Then I understood. To him the flags might as well have been dish towels, because I had never told him the real reason I had bought them in the first place.

I drove the long way to the motel to avoid going past the yellow gambrel. Another absurdly beautiful morning, the sun blaring with a trumpeter's insistence, the green of every leaf on every tree saturated with color, with light. Roses, snapdragons, and peonies were in full bloom in Karen Griffin's garden on the corner of Pine and Schoolhouse Road, Karen herself in a pale blue sunbonnet bending to cut a few stems and toss them into the wicker basket hanging from the V of her bent elbow. She is the great-great-granddaughter of a whaling captain, and the sixty-year-old daughter of the revered, recently deceased journalist and preservationist who edited the local paper for decades and wrote twenty books, most of them, in one way or another, odes to the fragile natural beauty of the island and its eccentric inhabitants. By whom he did not mean Evan and Mavis. Or Will and me. He meant old-timers like himself, to whom the island is truly home, those who care about the play of sunlight against the leaves, the quality of the shade, the welfare of the fish and the fishermen. I don't mean to say we don't care, only that our caring is somewhat sea-

sonal, contingent, driven a little too strongly by what's in it for
us. Even I, who had been a year-rounder for four years, am a
city dweller at heart, an urbanite who doesn't mind the country as long as there are plenty of people like myself, and the
daily *New York Times,* nearby.

A temporary reprieve. Henderson was not at the motel, and I
had made a deal with myself that I didn't have to read the diary without him. I put the laptop at the foot of the bed I had
not slept in and picked up *This Week on Swansea!* from the
dresser. It was mostly advertisements. Seaplane rides, a store
called Hats in the Belfry, the only movie theater on the island,
sunset sailing trips with wine, hors d'oeuvres, and chamber
music. I lay down on the bed with it and skimmed the calendar of events for the last few days, imagined myself a tourist reading this for the first time, how charmed I'd be, how
impressed with the mix of island quaintness and imported
Boston high culture

A kite-flying competition, pony rides for charity, a straw-
berry-shortcake social on the lawn of the Episcopal church,
the showing of a documentary about Noam Chomsky, a
chamber music concert at Town Hall (Mozart, Sibelius,
Dvorak), a walking tour of nineteenth-century houses, lobster
rolls and clam chowder at the Quaker Meeting House ($7.50,
$3.95, brownies extra), and a recital of songs at the Historic
Society (Schubert, Debussy, Webern, Lili Boulanger). Her
name stood out the way my own would have, tilted me into a
specific moment in my history with a force I had not expected. My abandoned Lili, whom I had first read about in
a music encyclopedia more than a year before, when all of
her heartbreaking might-have-beens had made me painfully
aware of my own.

Thoughts of her fused with thoughts of my abandoned

Will, whom I had left here to die, left because I was dying, left because if I had stayed, it would only have been to make him happy, to be the bright, sunny bulb, the happy flags in his life of fear and regret and secrets. One night not many months before, as I tried to sleep next to him in that room where he died, kept awake by the howling of the winter wind and my own unhappiness, I startled myself with the question that came to me and the answer that followed: *But what about me? If I stay, I will wither away like the plants in my sorry garden, the yellow tomato vines, the drooping irises, the tulips that never open.*

At breakfast the next morning, Will asked how I'd slept. We were at the kitchen table, eating granola and halves of grapefruit, drinking coffee. The wind was still blowing, and it looked like rain. "Fine," I lied. I was making a list of friends to invite the next summer — because even after that awful night, I could not imagine a way out — when Will said something that made me wince. He said he loved me. *I love you.* The basic uniform, no frills. Subject, verb, object. I looked up and tried to smile, although I was close to tears. Then, thinking, perhaps, that I was moved by what he had said, he went on. He said he loved me more than he ever had, and that even though he was depressed about his estrangement from his girls, the granddaughter whom he could not yet go to visit, and of course the death of his son, our love was the bedrock of his life.

He reached for my face to wipe away the tears that had come. There were not many; I was wound very tight. "Thank you," I managed to say, knowing, as he knew, that that was not the proper response.

"Let me make another pot of coffee." That's what I said next, as I stood up. It was in that instant of rising that I understood I was going to leave.

On the knotty chenille bedspread of the Lighthouse Motel, my entire body flinched at the memory of that breakfast, that peculiar, private declaration: *Let me make another pot of coffee.*

Will did not challenge me, did not ask what I meant by "Thank you." He did what people do when confronted with evidence that their love is not returned; he ignored it as long as he could. He drank the fresh pot of coffee and hoped for a better day, more sunshine, less wind. He made plans for spring and for summer and said "we," as he had for the ten years of our marriage.

When I left him a month later, I knew I was not Nora leaving the doll's house, not Nora fleeing a man who had wanted to infantalize and diminish her. A different sort of woman leaving a different sort of man, another time, another place. But I may as well have been Nora: it took everything I had to walk out the door, drive my rented car onto the ferry, and abandon my life and this paradise too.

As I put down the magazine and closed my eyes, I could tell I had been holding my breath. I inhaled. I exhaled. I told myself that the choice had been whether to live his life or mine. I was so still, so intent on stillness, that when the phone rang, I clenched. Then sighed in relief. It's Henderson, I thought. Thank God it's Henderson.

"Is this Sophy Chase?"

"It is."

"Hi, I'm Bree Solomon." It was a breathy, high-voiced girl — I couldn't tell if she was twelve or twenty — who sounded as if she was talking from inside a tunnel. "I'm an intern at the Swansea Humane Society. Someone told me you're looking for your dog?"

I was too stunned to speak. And when I did say yes, I must have whispered.

"Can you hear me? I'm on a cell phone. In a car."

"I can hear you fine." But I could tell that she did not have good news. If she had, she would have given it to me by now. People do. They call and say, *I had a car accident, but don't worry, I'm fine.* "How did you know about my dog?"

"My roommate Danis, Danis Judd, she works at the newspaper? She said you came in yesterday and took out an ad about a missing dog? This one turned up. Danis got me your number."

She stopped talking, which confirmed my suspicions. I considered hanging up before she mustered the nerve to tell me. If I hung up, I could do what everyone else had done: write off the dog as a witness, a clue, a piece of evidence, a piece of my heart.

"He might not be your dog," Bree said. "It's kind of hard to tell. Can you still hear me?"

"Yeah." There was a lot of time between what I said and what she said, like a satellite delay, because she didn't want to come right out and tell me the truth.

"Some people found him on the beach late yesterday. They called us."

"What beach?"

"A private beach on the ocean side of the island."

"You don't mean he was walking down the beach, do you?" He wasn't a beach kind of dog. Short legs, couldn't swim. Will had found him at the island shelter and told me he was persuaded to bring him home because of his droopy hound-dog eyes. *You wanted someone to take care of,* he said, *and this little fellow sure needs a hand.* Will's presumption infuriated me, and his sentimentality, though by that time, a year before, when I had decided to quit trying to get pregnant, I was easily infuriated — but so lonely that I did not do the right thing and return the poor creature to the shelter, where he might have been taken to a more stable home than ours.

"No," Bree said finally. "He was washed up. Beached. That's why it's hard to tell. But from what Danis said — from the photograph she described —"

"You hear about beached whales, but I've never heard of a beached dog. Does that mean he was on a boat and fell overboard?"

"I'm only an intern, only been working for like ten days, and there was this coincidence with my roommate, so I —"

"Where is he now?"

"At the Humane Society on Old Settlers Road. There's this little morgue."

"Jesus."

"Yeah, I know, it's really terrible when your dog dies. I'm like totally sorry."

I smiled when she said that, the way her kind words and college-kid delivery bore so little relation to what was going on. I was totally sorry, too. "Thanks," I said.

"It might help to identify the body, you know, so you can work on closure. And if it's *not* your dog, then it won't be so bad. Someone will be in our office till six o'clock tonight. Tomorrow they'll take him to the mainland to be cremated, unless you want to like bury him in your backyard or something."

"I'll get there before six." But I would have to wait for Henderson; I could not face this on my own.

When I hung up, I tried to call Daniel, who had turned on his answering machine. Then I called my friend Annabelle, whose message said she was in East Hampton for the weekend and gave a phone number so fast that I got only the first three digits. I started to call her machine again when I felt some-

thing swirling beneath my left breast, a sudden, fluttery sensation. Maybe just gas, but when it passed, I understood I had
to see the dog now, without delay, and if Henderson wasn't
back in five minutes, I would go without him. I had to see the
dog's body, because I had not seen my husband's body; and I
had to see the dog's body now, because it might not be Henry
after all, and if it wasn't, I had to keep looking for him.

Had he been left on the beach and tried to swim, gotten
caught at high tide? Had Will given him to someone with a
boat, such an unseaworthy dog, and had he fallen overboard?
Or had Will done something sinister to Henry as a way to
punish me for not taking him to New York?

I flipped on the TV for company, for distraction, and
started to change my clothes. There was a Sunday news show
about the election, an analysis of a candidate's gaffe during the
past week that had cost him a few popularity points with
women and blacks between thirty and forty-five years old.
I idly pressed the channel changer on the remote and saw
a tagline flashing in the corner of the screen — BREAKING
NEWS — and a balding, smartly suited baby boomer at a
Marriott podium, a crop of microphones, like the butt of a
porcupine, jutting into his face: "The main thing my client
wants to convey to the media and the public at this juncture is
that her interests are better served with this change in repre-
sentation."

The next shot was an alabaster-skinned newscaster with a
shoe-polish-black bouffant bobbing her head as she read from
the teleprompter: "That was an impromptu press conference
with attorney Rodney Burns, who has just been hired by
Greta Kohl, the former nanny accused of shaking the Back
Bay Baby to death. Until just a few hours ago, Ms. Kohl's at-
torney was man-about-town Evan Lambert. After revelations

in this morning's *Herald* concerning Lambert's youthful mistress and his wife's alleged affair with this same woman when she was a student at Harvard, Kohl decided she would fare better in court with a lawyer whose private life wasn't as newsworthy. Mr. and Mrs. Lambert, in seclusion at their Swansea summer compound, are not answering questions. And the official word from Harvard on the matter? 'No comment.' We'll be bringing you developments on this story throughout the day. In the meantime, residents of the Boston area are bracing for the arrival of Wanda the Baby Whale at the city's aquarium tomorrow morning. We'll bring you live coverage of the historic convoy leading her into Boston Harbor . . ."

How clever: to juxtapose the Lamberts and Wanda the Whale. Two feel-good stories back to back. We're supposed to feel good that the privileged in their summer compounds can lose their privileges, or at least not enjoy them as much as they used to. And feel good that we can see a wild creature in captivity and forget that it isn't free. Neither, at the moment, were Evan and Mavis. I could picture helicopters circling over their house and TV news trucks competing for parking spaces that didn't exist on the narrow blacktop that led to their property. It hadn't been my choice to leave their house, but as I looked around the motel room for a piece of paper on which to write Henderson a note, I was grateful to be gone from there.

I wrote, "The dog is dead, long live the dog. Should be back by one. Favorite novel with dog as narrator? *The Call of the Wild*," and left it for Henderson at the front desk.

As I made the turn onto Old Settlers Road, I thought of Evan's girlfriend in the chicken coop. Another captive. There was no public sign of her yet, and this pleased me, made me feel a bit triumphant, not because of my role in concealing her, but because it reminded me that not everything that can go wrong does go wrong, as much as my own life, and Evan's and Mavis's, seemed to be steering a hard course in another direction. Vicki, after all, was fine. Henderson had found someone to spend the night with, and much of the morning. The sun was shining, and there, right there on the side of the road, was a flower stand, a homemade wooden table covered with painted tins of lupine and cream-colored roses. For a few minutes on that sun-drenched road, I believed that God might be working her magic. I can't describe it except to say that I experienced an almost physical lifting of the blanket of agony that had been dropped over me three days before. It was a moment of respite, a moment when my mind filled with everything in my life there was to rejoice in.

Then I laid eyes on the dog.

The morgue was a back room in the Humane Society's secluded gray-shingled Colonial, and the woman who walked me back there from the reception desk had the excessively respectful demeanor of an undertaker but the clothes of a middle-aged tourist on her way to the beach: a pink zippered jacket made of terry cloth that fell to the top of her thighs, a pair of partly concealed white short shorts, and platform flip-flops, lime green. "Our intern told me you would be coming," she said with great solemnity.

It was a small bedroom, except that it had an antiseptic hospital smell, and the only furniture was a raised stainless steel table, a truncated gurney. Against the far wall were two sets of windows, the shades pulled down to the sill, flanking a door that led outside. But the inside wall was covered with something like stainless steel, and imbedded in it were three mini-refrigerator doors in a horizontal row, each about three feet by three feet.

"I'm not sure I can do this," I said.

"Everyone finds it difficult."

She led me to the middle door, but did not move to open it. I guess she was waiting for me to give her the go-ahead.

"Maybe I could tell you a birthmark and you could identify him for me. On his stomach there's a brown splotch in the shape of Florida."

She was quiet for a moment. "It might be a good thing for you to see him yourself. If it is him. Closure, you know." Bree had used the word too, probably learned from this woman. "A chance to say farewell."

"Do the trays roll out the way they do in the movies?" She nodded. "Will I see his tail first or his head?"

"His tail, I believe."

"I'd like to stand off to the side so that you can pull the tray out a tiny bit and all I'll see is his tail and back legs. Would you mind? And will his eyes be open or closed?"

She sighed in annoyance, and I wanted to explain my skittishness, my terror, my husband, et cetera, et cetera, but it was more than she needed to know, and I felt a wave of nausea that made me swallow hard and breathe deeply. I must have nodded, even though I did not mean to give her my consent, because she reached for the lever on the door, and I thought, *All right, I can do it.* What she hadn't told me was that the plastic tray with Henry's body on it — it *was* Henry, I could see that immediately — was attached to the door by a spring, so that as the door opened, the tray emerged with it, and before I knew it, all of him, lying stiffly on his side, like a stuffed dog that has fallen over, appeared before me. His signature ears still pointed like a German shepherd's, and his Florida birthmark floated on his pink-tinted belly the way it always had. But he was lopsided, like a beach toy poorly, unevenly inflated, and his eyes — Jesus God — his eyes were open, shiny and moist, not as if he were alive, but as if they'd been shellacked. The nausea must have been building since Bree first called, churning up my stomach, so within two or three seconds of jerking my head away from the sight of Henry's eyes, blank and glassy, dead and alive, but mostly dead, I felt every part of me convulse, and I did not have a chance to ask where the bathroom was before I vomited all over my hands, which had sprung to my mouth, and began to cry.

I signed a form releasing the dog's body to be cremated, and the woman said that under the circumstances, she would not charge me the fee. I thanked her profusely and left wrapped in a fragile calm, aware that it could easily vanish. But it was not until I'd been driving for a while that I acknowledged that part of what was gone with poor Henry was my dream that discovering his whereabouts would lead me to the truth about the end of Will's life, even though everyone thought I was dotty for believing this. Now I had to get on with — with what? With accepting the idea that I would never know what had happened.

I remember wanting to cry out at the injustice.

It was a warm summer day, but I remember shivering.

I remember thinking that I should turn at Harper Creek Road and see if my friends there were home, because I needed company, because I didn't want to dwell on this alone, and on all the injustices, all the other things I would never know: what happened to my father after he disappeared, that old favorite at the top of the list. But I wasn't thinking clearly and missed the turn for their house, missed it and kept going, heading for Cummington. If I stayed on this road, I'd reach the yellow gambrel and my stepdaughters and their mother, and I could not face them in this state. If I went to the motel, Henderson might still be out. I turned into the parking lot of the convenience store at the edge of town to buy a newspaper. Not the Boston paper with the headline BABY-KILLER LAW-YER IN LOVE NEST, but the island weekly that lists meetings on the page with the tide reports and the poem for the week. Open discussion, nonsmoking, St. Catherine's, had started fif-teen minutes ago. The other side of the harbor. By the time I got there, it would be half over, but there wasn't another meet-ing anywhere on the island until seven o'clock, and it would be pushing my luck to wait that long. I don't mean I wanted a drink; I mean I wanted to talk.

But where would I begin?

With the dog today, the poor dog? Or the windswept breakfast in January when Will told me he loved me and I de-cided to leave? Or, if they called on me, should I start my story the moment of that Thursday afternoon in bed with Daniel when the phone rang without ringing, and our fucking and Daniel's coming and Will's being dead all happened in the same instant, fission and fusion, the beginning and the end, the mundane, the marvelous, the unimaginable? Or could I just raise my hand and say whatever came to mind? Was it possible for me to talk without a speech, without a plot, an al-ter ego, without dressing up as Dorothy or Toto or the ghost writer from New York or the widow manqué? Could I just say the truth, not every detail, not the story filtered through someone else's voice, but the core, which must have the same root as *coeur,* and made me think of *cri de coeur.* Not my own this time, but Will's, in the bedroom the night I told him I was going to leave. *You'll change your mind,* he said at first. *You'll see. You'll feel better when spring comes.* . . . But I told him

I could not wait till spring; I'd made up my mind. I said nothing for what seemed a long time, turned away because the dog had done something to catch my attention, and heard whimpering — then something louder, clearer, unavoidable. Will sobbing. A memory I had buried until this moment.

I parked my car a block from the church, in front of a white clapboard house with black shutters and blue gingham curtains sashed with pink ribbons in every window. Could it be the handiwork of another woman trying to manufacture a happy house, or could this one be for real?

Four long unadorned tables had been arranged in a square. People sat around the rectangle and in rows of chairs that fanned out across the room, a meeting hall in a building separate from the church. It was a good-sized group, and I couldn't figure out who was speaking, because I'd walked in and sat near the back during a long burst of laughter. When it quieted down, I heard a woman with a heavy Boston accent, and craned my neck until I could see her at the table. She was pretty and older and blond, the way Joan Rivers might look without the facelifts. "But all kidding aside," she said, "what I've really learned in heah is that if I turn my life ovah to God" — which rhymed with Maude — "theah's no end to the miracles in the univuhse. I can't tell you how grateful I am you're all heah tonight. So thanks for listening."

Ten hands shot up, my own among them.

The woman who had spoken chose someone across the room from me.

"Thanks for calling on me, Grace. I guess I'm still supposed to say," began a woman I couldn't see, whose voice was so flat it was as if she was trying to repress a lifetime of being mad with the world, "that my name is still Crystal and I'm, uh, still an alcoholic. Right?" She gave off a snorty, self-deprecating laugh that no one joined in. There was, instead, a serious, respectful silence, because everyone had a pretty deep understanding of how difficult it had been for her to say what she had just said, and everyone could hear the self-loathing and the shame in her laugh. Warily, because I was afraid of what I would see, I peered around the head of the man in front of me and tried to figure out which one was Crystal. The woman with her head in her hands? She looked up and started talking, pancake flat, plywood flat, hardly any affect, sounding much duller than the gentleness of her face suggested. She had long brown hair with bangs, a denim jacket, the slightly glamorous look of a country-and-western singer, overlaid with depression. "A lot of you know me, better than I know myself. You know I'm in and out of here like a friggin' yoyo, and you welcome me back every time, no questions asked, no judgments offered." She may have been thirty or thirty-five. "There's not a lot I can tell you that you don't already know, but there's probably a lot you can tell me. I haven't been so good at listening lately. I'm trying to do better. I guess that's it. Oh, yeah, I've got twenty-three days. Thanks." Applause went up as if she had won an Oscar — an AA thing, clapping for people counting their early days sober; a kind of three-dimensional slogan — and when it died down, Grace said, "Keep coming back, Crystal."

I'd stopped looking at her by that time. I was doing the math and trying to figure out what to say to her when the meeting was over. After Grace said, "Let's take a ten-minute break," and I saw Crystal head for the door, I leaped up and followed her into the vestibule. "Are you leaving?" I asked.

"Just for a smoke."

"I'm Sophy, by the way."

"Crystal."

By then we were on the brick walkway in the church yard, a dreamy, manicured cloister between the parish house and the church, an outdoor enclosure thick with the scents of jasmine and, now, cigarette smoke. Crystal was taller, rangier than she'd looked sitting down, wore old scuffed cowboy boots, tight jeans, a thick belt with a heavy Native American buckle, not typical island attire, and I thought I might have the wrong Crystal. She held out a rumpled pack of Camels to me, but otherwise was preoccupied. I shook my head. "I think I've been looking for you," I said. "I've been looking for someone named Crystal Sparrow." Her eyes shifted to me when she heard the name, and her soft face hardened in fear; she probably owed people money, or worse. "It's about my husband, Will O'Rourke."

"He said you guys are divorced."

"Separated."

"Guess I got the timing wrong. He's not too happy about it, that's no secret." She was defending herself in case I was about to pounce.

"So you don't know that he's dead." It wasn't a question, or an accusation, either, although she was so startled, it must have sounded that way. Then I remembered her voice on Will's answering machine. What was it she'd said? She was sorry about the other night?

"What do you mean?" she said now. "Since when?"

"No one's quite sure about any of it. The autopsy isn't completed." I was holding back a lot of information, because I was afraid of two things. One, that if I told her Will had died twenty-three or twenty-four days ago and suicide was suspected, she might fear she'd had something to do with it. Two, if she was afraid of that, she would simply turn on the heel of her cowboy boot and take off and do what she always did: pick up a drink. I cared, in a not inconsequential way, that she not do that, but I cared more that she stay with me, tell me what had happened between them, because something must have.

"How do you even know I know him?" she said, her eyes squinting with suspicion.

"I had to go through his mail after he died. He sent you a letter that was returned to him, No Forwarding Address."

"How'd you know to find me here?"

"I didn't. I just heard your name and thought you might be the same Crystal."

"So you didn't come here for me?"

I shook my head. "I came for me. I've been having a hard time since he died."

After that, I didn't need to coax anything out of her until the end. She just started talking, and I listened.

13

In Search of Another Note

I T HAD TO DO with her son, how she met Will.
Define heartbreak: a nine-year-old kid with Crystal for
a mother. That was heavy on my mind as she told me the
story, and so were the echoes of other stories.

It started with a quarrel between Crystal and the boy, Matt,
though she didn't say at first what it was about. But he got awful mad, she said, and stormed out of the house, stormed
three-quarters of a mile down the dirt road to Fresh Meadow
Lane, but she didn't know that until later. She thought he'd
gone to the pond or over to his friends the Lawlers', whose
house was the only other one at their end of the road, about
five hundred feet away through the brambles.

She didn't own any property, so they had to move, like a lot
of islanders in that situation, twice a year. When summer
came, they left the house in the woods so that the owners
could rent it — a tiny two-bedroom nothing, Crystal said —
for fifteen-hundred dollars a week, just because of the pond.
You know, Chester Pond? The usual summer shit, she said,
and then we've got to live in a tent in my sister's backyard
till Labor Day, because she's got every room in her house
rented for the summer to college kids who are waiting tables.
It's hard on the kid, she said, hard on all of us.

I started to feel impatient, with how far the story was straying from the end of Will's life, but I needn't have.

"The next thing I know the day of that humdinger fight Matt and me had" — here she became more animated than I had seen her — "there's this noisy motorcycle roaring down our dirt road, and I look out the kitchen window and it blasts to a stop right next to my car, kicks up a shitload of dust. There's my kid hopping off the back with a fat grin on his face and this guy I'd never seen driving it. 'Course I couldn't see much with the helmet, but they start slapping each other high fives and yukking it up.

"Then I hear this voice through the kitchen window — he says to Matt, 'You wait there, kiddo,' and he starts toward the kitchen door, and I panic. This island isn't the friendliest place in the world. I don't know who the hell this is; he could be a social worker. I've had a few of them at my door over the years. So I stick the bottle of Jim Beam in the cabinet with the cereal and the peanut butter and tell myself to remember to move it before Matt sees it, because he'll dump it down the drain.

"'Is anyone home?' That's the first thing I hear, then a knock on the edge of the screen door.

"'Who is it?' I'm still at the sink, and the door's about eight feet away, and all I can see is half the man's body through the screen.

"'My name is Will O'Rourke. I wanted you to know your son was hitchhiking on Fresh Meadow Lane. I almost didn't see him coming around the turn. Scared the hell out of me. I stopped as soon as I could and went back to make sure he was all right. And to tell him to hitch farther down the road, on the straightaway.'

"I was at the screen door, saying thank you. I must have said it three or four times. He interrupts, real serious, 'Could I talk to you for a minute?'

"'We're talking now.' But that wasn't how he meant it. I'd stuffed a few pieces of gum in my mouth and grabbed a Diet Coke, so I didn't look like the drunk I was — that's what Matt and I'd fought about, the bottle of whiskey. We'd had a tug of war with it; I won. And he ran away.

"'Would you mind opening the door?'

"I opened it and stood there, kind of suspicious, chomp-chomp-chomp on the Juicy Fruit. 'Course he'd taken off his helmet by now, and I could see Matt out of the corner of my eye, circling Will's motorcycle, touching it, stroking it, in hog heaven. Will looked familiar. A salty-looking guy like someone you'd see around the shipyards. I was hoping Matt hadn't told him what we'd fought about. Hoping that's not what he wanted to talk to me about."

She was silent. The meeting had reconvened, and we were outside by ourselves. A few cigarettes had come and gone, and I was in a state of rapt amazement, as if a home movie of Will had turned up. He hadn't been so alive to me since the moment I'd learned he was dead. "Will said, 'I don't mean to be nosy, but when I asked your boy where he was going, where he wanted a ride to, he started crying. He said you hated him. He said you lived down here. I put him on the bike and gave him a ride. I thought you should know.'

"'You don't believe that, do you, that I hate my kid?'

"''Course not. I've got kids of my own. I know how they —'

"'Thanks. That's real nice of you to bring him back. Appreciate it.' I thought that would be the end of it, but he didn't go away.

"He said, 'Is there anything I can do to help?'

"I got real itchy. 'You work for the county, for social services?'

"''No.'

"'The state?'

"'No. Nowhere anymore. I'm retired.'

"'We're fine, the boy and me.'

"I could tell he wasn't convinced, but what could he do? I think he said something like 'That's good, glad to hear it.' Then there was about a minute — or it *felt* like it; it was probably six seconds — when we stood there, both of us wanting to say something. It wasn't a sexual thing, what we couldn't say, it was a truth thing. It was like how much are we going to let on that we know about me, about why my kid is hitchhiking and crying and telling strangers I hate him? Not much.

"The last thing Will said to me was, 'He's a good kid.' Then he walked back to the bike, horsed around with Matt for a few minutes, couldn't have been nicer. Broke my heart, you know, because it's just me and him, no particular men, and no nice ones when there are, and we had to pack up and leave that pretty spot of ours a week later, because it was almost June and the owners had a big plumbing job to do so they could jack up the rent for summer." She took a long time sighing — smoke went in and out of her lungs — and I thought that might be the end of it. She said, "You want to sit down on that bench?" and started to walk that way, about thirty steps to the middle of the church yard, but when I asked, "Is that it? Is that the story?" she stopped and turned to face me.

"Don't I wish."

It *was* the end of Will's visit, and she and her son moved, on schedule, a week later, to her sister's house on the outskirts of Cummington, five or six blocks from Will's house. The college kids hadn't shown up yet, so there were empty bedrooms for them, and the cousins all got along, played Nintendo till their eyes crossed, planned a treasure hunt, and had a funeral in the backyard for a dead hamster. Crystal didn't say and I didn't ask, but it all sounded too idyllic for the fractured, boozy life she'd described. There must have been a lot she wasn't saying, a lot of truth going by the boards.

She lit a wooden match against the zipper of her jeans and held it to the tip of a Camel. "I ran into him at Millie's Place the third night we were living in town." Her face was cloaked in smoke until the whorls rose and broke apart. "He recognized me at the bar and said he'd mailed me a letter a few days before. How'd you know where I live? I was there, he said. Well, I'm gone for the summer from there, maybe the post office'll forward it. What'd your letter say? Give me a call sometime, that's what it said. He asked about my kid. And the usual island stuff. Where you from, what do you do. At first it's like he's coming on to me, until he starts talking about you. A lot. Don't worry, I won't tell you what he said. And you don't want to know either. But what do you expect? You ditched him. He saw you in New York the day before on the street with some guy. You're entitled, right? People don't own each other. And he's entitled to be pissed off. I was pissed off about something or other that night, what else is new? My landlord, my sister, my kid's father, but that's a whole other story. We had enough in common to get loaded. I don't remember a whole hell of a lot of the stuff later, at his house. I didn't spend the night. That's about it. Hard to believe he's dead. They think it was a heart attack?"

But that couldn't have been the end of the story. She had ended too abruptly; I could hear it in the rhythm of her speech, the sudden rushing, the summary. Did she think I wouldn't want to know they'd slept together? Did she think I'd care? Or was she hiding something? Then I remembered: "Why did you call him and apologize?"

"When?"

"A few weeks ago. You left a message on his answering machine apologizing for 'the other night.' What else happened?"

"I thought you don't live there anymore."

"I don't. After he died, I had to listen to the messages. There were some for me."

"When did you hear mine?"

"Yesterday."

"When did he die?"

"A few weeks ago. What else happened that night?"

"I don't remember all the details."

"You remembered enough to apologize a few days later."

"Now I get it." Her voice changed; it got lower and sharper, like an animal growling. "You think he killed himself and you're looking for someone besides yourself to blame. Yeah? Well, fuck you. I've got enough guilt about all the dead people in my life, I don't need yours too." She sprang up from the bench, and I lurched in her direction, reaching for her elbow, her arm, but I missed. I got air. She was moving across the church yard, away from the meeting room toward the church itself.

"Crystal, no, that's not it." But it was, sort of. I ran after her, not knowing what I'd say or do.

She stopped at a set of three stairs leading up to a double door and lit a cigarette. "I don't know why I started talking to you to begin with. I must've felt sorry for you for a minute, or sorry for Will." Smoke poured from her mouth as she spoke, no shape, no direction, just those witchy tendrils. She shot me a look. "How the hell did you know I know him? I don't believe this whole thing is a coincidence. You've been following me or you've gotten someone else to, haven't you?"

Her hysteria calmed me, as did her misinterpretation of the evidence, because it was so far off, because I had been telling the truth. "I told you, I had to go through his mail after he died. He'd written you a letter that got returned." I plunged my hand into my shoulder bag and groped for it. "I've been carrying it around for days, but I may have left it at the motel." I did find it, though, and let her see it. She calmed down; she believed me and softened up. And when she did, I felt terrible for her, getting ensnared in this. "No one knows if he killed himself. If he did, it wasn't in any obvious way. He might've swallowed something, but they can't tell yet. The thing is" — we were standing at the foot of those three stairs, talking almost comfortably — "I hadn't seen him in three months, since I left. You saw him three weeks ago. I thought maybe you had some — some impressions. That's all. I didn't have anything in mind to ask when I found you. I'd given up thinking I would." I was leaving aside her apologetic phone call, unsure what to say about it. But something I said must have touched her.

"He wanted to fuck me," she said quietly, her eyes down. "Or he thought he did. But he couldn't. That's the story." And she added something that surprised me even more: "But not the whole story. The whole story is" — another long pause, and I could almost feel the words straining to come out of her — "I wasn't too nice about it." Said so softly, I almost asked her to repeat it. "I was kind of a shit. I get mean. A lot of times I don't remember stuff I say and do. People tell me. But I remember that. How much more do you want to know?"

"That's why you called to apologize?"

"Yeah."

"He was upset."

"Yeah. He was as drunk as I was. You know how it gets." No pronouns: how it gets. Disavow responsibility. *He cried, I made him cry.* That's what she wasn't saying. How do I know that? I don't. But why else would she have remembered it, and what else would she have had to apologize for? I couldn't bear to ask. I'd already put her through too much, and it wasn't her fault that I'd left him or that he died, or that he killed himself, if he had.

"I left in the middle of the night. Walked back to my sister's. Only a few blocks. The morning after — or the afternoon after — I got my ass back here. I won't bore you with the details, like my sister and my kid about to divorce me for the three-hundredth time. After a few days on the wagon I called to apologize. I was hoping he wouldn't be home. I wanted to leave the message and get it over with. You know, making a few amends like they say you should. But I guess I was too late with that one, because you're telling me he was dead by then." I nodded. "But no one knows how he died? How does that happen?"

I told her how it happened in Will's case, and about the conversation I'd had with the coroner, and the one I was to have later in the week. Just as I was getting to the end, the double door to the church flew open, released by a tall young man in a tux. He was handsome in an attenuated, Jimmy Stewart–*Philadelphia Story* way, and professed to be delighted to see us there. He fiddled with rings on the hydraulic hinges to keep the doors from closing, and explained that a wedding ceremony was about to begin, and it was such a beautiful day, everyone wanted the doors wide open. Behind him the pews were beginning to fill, and there was a decorous bustle and hum and a number of long-limbed, blond-haired women in lavender dresses.

We drifted back to the meeting house on the other side of the yard, and I saw Crystal smile for the first time.

"Before and after," she said. "Should we go back and tell

them you start in the church in your tux, and you end up in
the meeting room with a cup of coffee and an Oreo?"

"Let's let them find out on their own."

"You remember the last time you wanted all the doors open
so the sun could shine on your life? I sure don't."

As we walked down the vestibule toward the meeting room,
it was too quiet. Everyone had gone. The coffeepots and bags
of cookies had been put away. So had the folding chairs.
"Shit," Crystal said with great vehemence, "I'm late." She
must have seen the clock on the far wall. "I've got to run. I just
started a new job." She turned to say something more than
goodbye, but I could see she was frantic.

"Go. I'll find you again. And thanks." I made to shoo her
away; I didn't want her to feel I'd get schmaltzy or twelve-
steppy and try to hug her. "Thanks for talking to me. For telling me what you did." I watched her bolt from the building,
and I stood for a while in the empty room. What had happened between us made me feel that we were almost friends:
the eerie conjunction of our lives around Will's death, my
finding her here today, the moments she had suspected me of
spying, the story she had not wanted to tell, the story she had
told.

But then I remembered that I hadn't asked her about the
dog. She was at Will's house three weeks ago and might know
whether the dog was there. I ran out the door, as she had, and
jogged back to my car as if I could catch up with her or knew
where to find her, but looking at the intersection fifty feet
ahead, I realized I didn't know her sister's name or where she
worked. And I admitted to myself that she, drunk as she'd
been, wouldn't have noticed the dog even if he had been there.

All the things I still didn't know were lining up like the
Rockettes or more like suspects in a police line-up, raggedy,

unruly, unreliable. I had found the dog and the dog was dead, had found Crystal and she was half-broken herself. And had found Will, in Crystal's story, more alone, more bruised than when I'd left him.

The only thing for me to do was read his diary, yet now I hoped that when I got back to the motel, Henderson would still be out. I wanted to read it alone; it was something private, between the two of us. I didn't want anyone else, even Henderson, to know the depth of Will's pain. Or of my own.

But Henderson was in my room, waiting for me on one of the beds, sections of the Sunday *Times* arrayed around him like autumn leaves. He apologized for his absence that morning and said that Ginny, who answered when he'd called Will's house looking for me, had passed on the good news about Vicki.

"I forgive you everything if you're in love," I said lightly and flopped down on the other bed, exhausted, depleted, and relieved to see him, even though I couldn't yet talk about what had happened in the last few hours.

"Love? What are you talking about?"

"All right, lust."

"I went out for the paper and a bagel at the crack of dawn, and who should be at Swansea Bagels & Buns, but — Oh, yeah, I got your note. What happened to the dog?" The poor dog was everyone's afterthought, in death as he'd been in life.

"I'm not ready to talk about him. Didn't you spend the night out?"

"In my dreams, Sophy."

"Really?"

"Of course. I told you, I went out for a bagel, and you'll never guess who recognized me in the line for cream cheese."

"Do I know him?"

"No."

"That narrows it down."

"Major house on the bluffs overlooking Chillum's Point."

"Claude Perry."

"How'd you know?"

"He's the only one up there. But he's married. He plays tennis with his wife in public and holds her hand on the ferry. There's a rumor going around that they sleep together."

"I told you, it has nothing to do with love. Or lust. He wants to syndicate my show. *He* came up to me in the bagel store and said he's been watching the show for years. He has a houseful of guests in the TV biz. Execs. CEOs. He *invited* me on the spot to breakfast. I'd barely brushed my teeth. I was there all morning. I don't have a contract, but I have three days of meetings next week with these guys. I called you at Will's to let you know where I was, but you'd already left, and when I called here, you were gone. You must tell me where you've been; you look deeply burdened. But before I forget, your stepdaughter invited us to dinner tonight. Said she and her sister want to talk to you about the funeral."

"What could that mean?"

"It means they're contemplating something horrid and they want to prepare you for it."

"What could be worse than a Catholic funeral for an atheist? What do you think I should read tomorrow? Are there any funeral favorites besides Corinthians?"

"Sure, depending on the themes you want to highlight. Miss Manners would not approve, but under the circumstances, you might get away with reading 'Dover Beach' because of the seaside setting. 'Let us be true to one another, for the world, which seems to lie before us like a land of dreams something something something hath really neither joy, nor

love, nor light, nor certitude, nor peace, nor help for pain,
And we are here as on —"

The phone ringing interrupted him briefly " — a darkling
plain." He picked up the receiver, because it was closer to him.
"My dear," I heard him say tenderly, "you had all of us, but especially Sophy, apoplectic with worry. She's right here, I'll put
her on. What? No, honey, I don't think she's mad at you."

"I'm not" were my first words to her.

"Are you sure?" Vicki asked.

"I'm sure I want to know what happened."

"My dad says I have to apologize. I have to say, 'I'm sorry
for causing so much trouble.'"

"I accept your apology. Did you try to come to Swansea?"

"No, I read about it on the Internet. It was too far away."

"Where did you go?"

"Nowhere."

"What?"

When she was silent, I thought she may not have heard me.
At last she said, "I didn't leave New York. I was at my friend
Bettina's. She was hiding me upstairs like Anne Frank in the
attic. She has a house like ours. There's a whole floor where no
one ever goes, because her sister died and her brother is a summer intern in France. She's in kind of a lot of trouble. I am
too. My dad and her parents had this meeting today."

"My heavens. I can see why." I thought of the detectives flying to Swansea and showing up at Evan's door, of the stake-out
at Will's house last night, of the pints of adrenaline all of us
had secreted. It was enough to make me mad, but I stopped
myself. What I had to admit was that my anger was about how
we felt, we grown-ups. To Vicki, it was something entirely different. To her, it was about getting our attention; it was a *cri de
coeur*, blood-curdling in its way.

"My dad wants to talk to you."

Before he said hello, I heard him tell Vicki to go downstairs with the other kids. "I'll be down soon. Sophy?"

"What a story," I said.

"I think she has a great future as a novelist or a mastermind criminal. An honorary member of the Lavender Hill Mob. My parents would have shipped me off to boarding school for that. They shipped me off for less than that."

It occurred to me that Vicki's disappearance, for which I had quietly been blamed, had turned out to be something of a practical joke. I was no longer the villainous girlfriend whose silence had led the child into realms of unspeakable danger. I was nice again. Trustworthy again. Kind to small children again. Maybe he would care for me again. But I didn't know in what way I could care for him. That woman I'd been three days ago, the funny one who pretended to be Dorothy and Toto, the sexy one who pretended not to care that her lover's only term of endearment for her was Ducks — that woman had lost her voice. Daniel was speaking now to someone else.

"How are you managing?" he said. "I know it's been absolute hell for you. And I know this business with Vicki was the last thing you needed. Have you found out anything about Will's death? Have you settled on a date for the funeral?"

I gestured to Henderson that I needed some privacy, and he scurried off the bed, carrying his shoes and an armful of the *Times* to the connecting room. Yet once he closed the door behind him, I didn't know what to say to Daniel, except to recount some of what I had discovered. It was not nothing, and it took a while to cover the territory, but it was hardly intimate. I could have been telling the story to anyone.

He listened patiently, asked questions, and was in every way attentive, considerate, well-mannered. He said finally, "When do you think you'll be home?" but the very idea of home was haunted, and I didn't know what to answer. My home wasn't here on the island. But was it there, on the outskirts of his life, in the suburbs of his affections?

"Maybe the end of the week," I said casually. "I should be finished with what I need to do here. If I can figure out what that is."

"The children will be happy to see you. And I shall, too."

"That's all?"

"I can't think of anything else. Can you?" When I didn't reply, he added, "If you want to talk between now and then, ring me. I'll be here."

Clearly he hadn't understood my question, and I wasn't up to saying, *I mean, that's all you feel? All you're willing to say? To offer?* I wasn't about to write the script for him. The other day, when he'd called me "darling," that was an accident, a slip, something I wasn't likely to hear again soon. "And I'll be *here,"* I said.

"Good enough."

"Not quite."

"Sorry?"

"Nothing," I said, and I'm sure I hung up with him in a state of mild befuddlement. But it would pass and he would slide back to the state of profound befuddlement in which he ordinarily resided.

Within a minute, the phone rang again, and I let it go for four or five rings before answering. There was no one I wanted to speak to except Will. The last phone call he'd made was at ten o'clock four Wednesday nights before. I figured now that he'd gone out afterward to Millie's Place and spent the rest of the night with Crystal. And died after she left. But died how? A heart attack? A seizure? A handful of pills?

The phone call was from someone who had never called me

on Sunday: the Eighth Deadly Sin. "How did you find me here?"

"You left a number on your answering machine."

"Are you serious?" I had no recollection of doing so, but with his prompting I remembered that late last night, I called my machine in New York and changed the message moments before falling asleep on Will's couch.

"I'm in my car on the L.I.E., heading back to the city," the Eighth Deadly said, "and I've got a book I want you to ghost. I just had brunch with her at the Maidstone Arms. Are you ready for this?"

"Ready as I'll ever be."

"The nanny who takes care of Bill and Melinda Gates's kids wants to quit and write a book. Tell the whole story. She's been on vacation in East Hampton for the last week."

"Don't people like that sign a contract that says they'll never write a book or sell the story to the *National Enquirer*?"

"Obviously there'll be a few details to work out. I put in a call to our lawyer. In the meantime, this woman has a story you wouldn't believe."

"You'd be surprised what I'd believe these days."

"You having a good time up there? Everyone talking about Evan Lambert and the Harvard girl who *schtupped* the wife and then him? That's a helluva story, but I'm not sure how long its legs are."

I hadn't said in my answering machine message why I'd gone to Swansea; I'd just given the phone number of the motel. But I still hoped for something closer to a condolence call than this.

"You're the first writer I thought of when I heard the nanny pitch her story."

"Why's that?"

"You're used to rubbing elbows with the celebrity genius types up on Swansea. I wouldn't think of you for Andre Agassi's life story, you know? Can you have lunch with me in the next few days?"

I told him then that I couldn't, and why, and I know the phone call was longer than he'd intended it to be, but by the end, I had an idea for a book of my own, though I wasn't ready to discuss it with the Eighth Deadly. Henderson came back to my room and remarked on the change in my demeanor — "You're almost smiling" — even before I began to explain.

When I finished, he said, matter-of-factly, as if he were my lawyer, "So you'll write both. You'll negotiate a two-book contract and be set for years. First you'll deliver the nanny, which will be a walk in the park, and then you'll write your story, which won't be. Isn't that what you're thinking?"

But I wasn't yet thinking that clearly, and I didn't want to be. I wanted to lie back on the chenille bedspread and not make any decisions. I'd been running for hours, for days, chasing phantoms, leads, lost dogs, my history, my hysteria, which derives from the Greek word for *womb*, and my husband, whose death might turn out to be another riddle wrapped in a mystery inside an enigma, but whose life was a more ordinary mix of contradictions, good intentions, bold gestures, compromises, and mistakes that it was too late to do anything about. When I used to compare him with Evan, there had been so many ways he came up short: Evan's ambition, Evan's confidence, Evan's authority in the world, never mind the moral center, or amoral center, at the heart of it. Say what you will about Evan, he never stops believing in what he does, and succeeds in convincing a lot of other people — jurors and judges, for starters — that he's right. Will's authority was more hit-or-miss; and in the decades he was a spy and a

CIA functionary, the line on the graph that mapped the conjunction of his convictions and those of the CIA split off sharply around 1968 and never met up again. But when he was at the helm of a sailboat, even the dinky runabout he could barely afford to keep running and moored, he was magnificent — as fine and sure of himself as Evan was when the NYPD showed up at his house and he improvised from start to finish. Will could do that on the water. He could do it in five or six languages in countries where he was not at all sure the United States ought to be mucking about. But closer to home — and at home — he often seemed lost, unmoored. He watched a lot of videos, ogled expensive sailboats on the Internet, got in touch with other sailors who needed crew to deliver yachts to Ibiza or Corfu, and occasionally went with them and came back feeling good about himself for three or four weeks.

"Why don't I come back a little later?" Henderson said, "and we'll go see your stepkids. They said we could come by any time, but thought they'd have an early dinner."

"I guess I'm a little distracted."

"Of course."

But that was better than what I'd been for the last twenty-four hours. The Eighth Deadly's phone call had been a kind of blessing, not only because it sparked the idea for my own book, but because it had reminded me that I had choices, more choices than almost everyone I'd encountered in the last few days. I was not trapped in a chicken coop, a celebrity love nest, a fake marriage, a lonely marriage, an affair with a man who did not love me, a coma, an aquarium, a coffin.

And later that day, something else lifted my spirits. You see, my stepdaughters wanted to talk to me about matters other than their father's funeral. One thing led to another, and they ended up telling me far more than they meant to.

14

The Night Before

I HAD MET CLARE only three times, so I did not expect her to do what she did when she opened the door of the yellow gambrel at six that evening: embrace me as if we were sisters, crumple into sobs in my arms. I had gone somewhat apprehensively to the house with Henderson. It wasn't only that I anticipated a hostile gesture, some new twist in the funeral plans — *oh, by the way, we're making Daddy a Muslim before we bury him* — but that I had finally read the last six months of Will's diary and found a few things Henderson had missed, furry animals camouflaged in the woods. Clare's tears moved me and almost brought on some of my own, but when she pulled herself together, I felt the old coldness toward her: the bully, the drama queen. Henderson and I exchanged a split-second look: *What a piece of work.*

I was on my guard, though no one else seemed to be. There was a feast on the dining room table — platters of smoked bluefish, gravlax, potato salad with bits of bacon, green salad with bright yellow tomatoes — and a lavish display of concern and affection that pulsed in every direction. Susanna's baby, Rose, slept in a wicker basket in the corner of the living room, swaddled in flannel and a flannel sleeping hat. Around the table the rest of us talked as if we were in an art museum

— soft voices, respectful gazes. But I was nervous, picking at a plate of salad, waiting silently for the museum fire alarm to sound or the guard in the corner to herd us out. I tried to keep my eyes on whoever was speaking, but I found myself staring at a large painting over the dining room sideboard, a Winslow Homer-y seascape that reminded me of Will's semiserious instructions for the end of his life, always said playfully, wistfully, never wanting to believe there would be such an hour, such a day: *When the time comes, put me on a rickety old sailboat with a case of Scotch and a carton of cigarettes and push.*

"Sophy, any news about the dog?" Susanna said.

"It seems he died, though no one's quite sure how."

"That's starting to sound like a familiar story," Ginny said.

"Poor Will," Clare said, and reached for the salad bowl. "So many things left unsaid. Sophy, have pasta with your salad. This is not the time to diet."

Clare's tears at the front door had made me forget briefly what a dictator she was. This command brought it back, though she did not look the part. She was fifty-six or -seven, fit, youthful, with the accessories and air of a woman who sells high-end real estate. The smoothness of her skin may have indicated a nip and a tuck, or those injections of fat some women get, or plain good luck. Her lightweight knit blouse, salmon-colored, and off-white linen skirt hung on a tall, trim frame. Her hair, blond with frosted highlights, looked as if it were done every three weeks; she wore a gold necklace and heavy, ridged gold earrings that clung to her lobes like fists. Perhaps she was another reason Susanna lived in the mountains with no telephone.

"Mom, leave her alone," Ginny said, "for God's sake."

"Mourning requires calories," replied Clare, "and carbohydrates."

"It does not require people telling each other what to eat," Ginny answered.

"Speaking of eating," Henderson said brightly, "did you know I was on my way to a Swiss fat farm two days ago, where I was going to consume nothing but water for ten days? Last year I went and lost twenty-three pounds. It was a perfectly gruesome experience."

"What happened?" Andy asked. "Why didn't you go this time?" While Henderson told the funny story of his aborted plane trip, I stared at Clare and wondered at the spell I'd allowed her to cast on me. Why had I let her take charge of the funeral? Why hadn't I insisted, resisted, done something other than roll over and play dead? Because of my bacchanal with Daniel. Because I'd felt guilty about leaving Will. And was shy, maybe even ashamed, because the only religion I could offer up on this solemn occasion was the shadowy church-basement one, with cigarettes and coffee instead of communion wafers, and the only god a fuzzy, personal, invent-me-as-you-go-along sort.

"Where do I sign up for this fat farm?" Susanna said, "and can I bring the baby?"

"You'll lose the weight eventually," Clare said. "It's only been four months, honey."

"You didn't say what happened to the dog," Ginny said. "Poor Henry."

And I didn't say that I'd found buried in Will's diary a chilling comment amidst the general sorrow and specific anger toward me, written on his last birthday, in May: *Would this be a better or worse day than any other? No, too unfair to the girls.* Did he keep a bottle of pills in the safe deposit box? Or were his remarks just a diarist's ruminations? I asked myself: Would I rather learn that he had killed himself and died painlessly than that he had had a heart attack and struggled in terror across the bedroom floor?

Of course I didn't tell Ginny and Susanna about Crystal, whose dark story of what may have been Will's last night swooped into my thoughts like a crow into a cornfield.

I told them about the dog. About the ad I'd taken out in the *Sentinel* and the phone call from Bree Solomon, but as I started to describe my drive to the Humane Society, the baby began to wail. Our rhythms got rearranged. Susanna leaped up, and I was surprised all over again by how heavy she was, especially next to her rangy sister and svelte mother. She returned with a quiet Rose in her arms, and asked again about Henry, but his likeness to the baby, I mean a small creature who can't reliably get far on its own, made me too sad to speak, and I think the others realized that. Clare, in mind of her own losses, her son and now his father, reverted to heavy tears, and her display of emotion made me get a grip on my own: like her daughters, my reflex was to keep my distance from her.

"This is too unbearable," she said softly, and at that instant she seemed as old as she was, and more broken down than at first glance. I could see how difficult it would be, if you were a daughter, to hate her for any length of time. She may have been a drama queen, but her grief was convincing. These were not crocodile tears.

Ginny went to her, leaning down, folding her arms around Clare's shuddering shoulders, and I remembered once again that we were here because Will was dead — a most unimaginable circumstance, like lightning striking your house, or the boy Icarus falling out of the sky.

Henderson began to clear the table. Clare shook her hands and her head, her territory invaded, and said, "Don't do that."

"Don't be silly," Henderson said and kept clearing. "You've got more than enough to worry about."

"As always," she mumbled, and I could hear a faint, collective sigh of exasperation in response to her self-pity, self-pity that she wore like those heavy gold earrings, garish, Clare-ish, *de trop*. I knew I'd given in to her funeral plans as much because of my skittishness and guilt as because she turned every encounter into "Queen for a Day" and was determined to win each round.

"Henderson told me you wanted to talk about the funeral," I said, looking from Ginny to Susanna. My annoyance with mercurial Clare had peaked, and I was prepared to endure whatever new indignity they might foist on me.

"Not actually about the funeral," Susanna said, the baby sleeping against her bosom.

"But you are reading something, aren't you?" Clare asked. "We have you slotted between Will's friends Diane and Ben Gibbs."

"Between?"

"Is there somewhere else you'd rather be?"

This was not what I had in mind, to be "slotted," one of several people in Will's life saying a few words. I wanted to be last; I wanted the last word — but I said nothing for the time being.

"What are you going to read?" Ginny asked.

"A poem by an Irish writer about the birth of his daughter. It's very celebratory." Henderson's friend in New York had faxed it shortly before we'd left the Lighthouse Motel.

At that Susanna pulled Rose tighter against her and started to tear up. "Thank you, Sophy." Her sweetness made me remember another line from Will's diary, about his wanting to go to California to see Rose but putting it off until *I feel better than this*. When I read it, it made me think he had not killed himself, that he would not have chosen to die before seeing his granddaughter.

"What we wanted to talk to you about," Ginny said, "is Daddy's house."

"We're trying to figure out what to do with it," Susanna said. "Neither of us can be here for the summer, except for a few weeks. Mommy thinks we should rent it out for gazillions of dollars, but we don't want to right away."

"I didn't say you had to," Clare said. "I merely said that financially, it makes sense to —"

"We can't bear to go through Daddy's things now and try to make the house all nice for summer rental. So we wondered if you'd house-sit until Labor Day. In September we'll get a renter for the winter."

It was a touching gift, but it couldn't have been more complicated. I don't imagine the girls had thought it through: the house stored the memories of everything I had yearned for and loved and abandoned. It was a branch of my psyche, and I didn't know how long I could stand being there.

Then I was puzzled. Did they know the depth of their father's anguish, or was that clear only to those of us who'd read the diary? Would they change their minds about the house if they knew how deeply I had hurt him? "Thank you," I said softly. "I don't exactly know how to —"

Susanna must have been reading my mind or the bemusement on my face. "We thought it was awful that he left you a dollar in his will."

"On the other hand," Clare said, "*you* wanted the divorce."

"Mother," Ginny said, "was that necessary?"

"I only meant that's why he was hostile." When the rest of us greeted her explanation with stony silence, she went on: "I'm sure I'm not the only one here who has experienced Will's spitefulness."

"Ginny and I didn't come here to bash Daddy," Susanna said.

"I didn't either," I said, taking shelter in the lee of the girls' criticism and still smarting from Clare's jab at me.

Her face darkened. Did she always say whatever came into her head? Or was there a coherent pattern to her personality that I was missing? Within seconds, she pasted on a thin smile and said cheerily, "How about some dessert?" She leaped out of her seat and moved toward the kitchen. I could see her daughters roll their eyes at each other as she pushed open the swinging door. "I picked up a splendid apple pie at the bakery on Main Street. And I'll make a pot of decaf for us."

Once Clare was out of the room, Ginny turned to Henderson and me. "I can't believe the things that come out of her mouth." Two days before, Ginny had been keen on her mother's arrival, but she was being reminded that Clare did not wear well, though she had enough money to make a splashy entrance and enough *chutzpah* to promise she could part the sea.

"There are people who hate to miss a funeral," Henderson said. "It's one of great stages for drama, the pageant of death. When my lover Ricardo died, I felt like the star of my favorite opera, *La Traviata*. And my favorite soap opera, 'General Hospital.' But all of that was nothing compared with what happened when Ricardo's mother arrived: Hello, Mommy Dearest."

"I'm thinking about your offer," I said. It was easier to speak with Clare out of the room. "I'm touched, but I'm not sure if spending the summer there would be the way to get on with my life or to avoid getting on with it." I tried to picture Daniel and his children there, and to imagine a life without any of them. Could I douse every last spark that flew between him and me? Crush out of existence my tender feelings for the children? But when I considered my idea for a book about all of these lives and deaths, I thought Will's house might be a

fertile place to start writing it. Maybe the best place. Certainly
the riskiest. The eye of the storm. But painful as it would be,
wouldn't I rather be there than inside the mind of Bill and
Melinda Gates's nanny?

I looked from Ginny, whose face was soft and focused on
mine, to Susanna, who had wandered deep into her own
thoughts. Then she looked up at me, somberly, and at everyone around the table, except Andy, who had taken the baby to
the couch. "I hadn't seen him in two years, not since Andy and
I got married and he came to the wedding. The last time I
talked to him was a few days after Sophy left. He cried. I sent
him pictures of the baby and kept telling him to visit us. He
promised he would, but I stopped believing it when he said he
had to help someone deliver a sailboat to the Virgin Islands."

Her hand on the table was close enough for me to touch. I
wrapped my palm around it and saw her eyes glass over with
tears. Should I tell her what I had read in the diary: his children frightened him; real life was terrifying; and sailing was
the best way he knew to dull the terror. "He wanted to," I said
softly. "I know he wanted to. He was just so . . . fragile." So
fragile, and I had left him. Should I have stayed? If I had,
would he be alive now? Did his daughters need to know that
these questions pressed on me like the March wind?

"But he wasn't always fragile," Ginny said. "He used to be
full of energy. Always planning adventures for us, wanting us
to sail and rock-climb and learn Chinese. Remember the summer we were ten and he took us down the Wye River on a
barge? And afterward we went to Bath, and he hired a horse
and buggy to take us around the city center? We went about
five times, like a merry-go-round we didn't want to get off.
And the summer we both did Outward Bound and Daddy
couldn't stop telling everyone? Do you know what we found,

Sophy, when Mom and I were at his house this morning? His old passports. There was one from the 1960s, and every single inch of every page was stamped. Hong Kong, Saigon, Taipei, Manila, hundreds of trips. God only knows what creepy spy things he was doing, but he wasn't moping around feeling sorry for himself. That wasn't always Daddy's life. We have to remember that."

"He was different after Jesse died," Susanna said.

"We all were."

"Daddy was more different," Susanna said. "I read a story in the paper a few years ago about a hunter who accidentally shot his son. As soon as he saw what he'd done, he shot himself dead. That's how Daddy must have felt after Jesse died, like a man who wanted to turn the gun on himself."

"But he didn't do that," I said. "We don't know he killed himself. He didn't in any obvious way, so until we hear otherwise, we —"

"Daddy was ingenious," Susanna said. "Maybe he thought that if he killed himself, we wouldn't get the insurance money, so he found a way that didn't seem like suicide."

"There aren't too many of those," Henderson said. "But if he did, it'll turn up in the autopsy."

Did I need to remind them that there was a chance it wouldn't? Did I need to tell them everything I knew, felt, and feared? Isn't it a parent's prerogative, to withhold information? Isn't it everyone's?

"How was he the last time you saw him?" Susanna asked Ginny, who was arranging a slice of salmon on a piece of bread. I hoped she would not ask me that question.

"I was here for Christmas," Ginny said quietly, "just before I met Mark." The new boyfriend in Maine who was expected on Swansea later that night, on the last ferry. "I didn't know there was anything wrong between Daddy and Sophy. They seemed the same to me. But it was wicked gloomy here, the way it is in winter. I never understood how you could take it."

"I couldn't very well," I said. "Your dad didn't mind the isolation the way I did."

"After you guys split up, I called him every few weeks from the TV station. He didn't say a lot. I didn't either. He wasn't the easiest person to talk to if you were related to him. I spoke to him a few weeks ago about my coming here next month with Mark. I guess I knew he was having a hard time, but he'd had them before and always pulled through."

Then she looked at me. I understood it was my turn, and I remembered the famous short story by Shirley Jackson, about the quaint New England village where every year there'd be a town lottery on the village green, and the loser would be stoned to death. But that was a parable, wasn't it?

The next voice we heard, an exuberant waitress's trill, was Clare's, calling from the cracked-open kitchen door. "Does everyone want decaf?"

I should have been relieved by her interruption, but it was the screechy off-note she often struck. Almost everyone nodded. She planted herself at the door and counted us with her forefinger, like the teacher on "Romper Room." When she retreated, I still didn't know how much of the story, of all of the stories I knew about Will's last days, I was going to tell.

"The last time I saw him was the day I left the island in March. We were in the driveway, my rented car was packed, the wind was blowing hard. Will looked like a dog who knew it was going to be left. I'd known for weeks that I was going, but I wasn't sure I'd be able to do it when the time came. He walked me to the car, and when I opened the door, a map flew out and blew across the yard. He ran after it, reflexively, and then was very sheepish when he handed it to me. The map was the evidence that I was leaving, that I was really going away without him. He closed his eyes, because he was starting to cry."

To his daughters, I said, "I hope you don't think it was easy for me to leave."

"We don't," one of them answered, though I didn't know who, because I'd closed my eyes the way Will had. "We knew it wasn't," the voice said softly, whoever was speaking in the royal we, as twins often do, certain each speaks for the other.

"The last time we talked was a few days before he died. He owed me some money from our health insurance. That's what we talked about. He didn't want to give it to me because he was mad about the divorce. It wasn't exactly a fight." It was less wrenching to talk about the money, or wrenching in a different way: how I wish those had not been our last words. "At the end of the call, he agreed to send me the money. When it didn't come, I called and left messages on the answering machine. I thought he'd changed his mind."

"I saw an envelope addressed to you on Daddy's desk," Susanna said. "That must have been what it was. There was nothing inside. I checked."

"It was awful every time I spoke to him. I didn't know what to say, how to be decent and concerned without making him think that I wanted to get back together."

"He hoped you'd change your mind after the divorce," Susanna said. "He told me that once."

"He told me that, too," Ginny said.

"But we didn't think you would," Susanna said, "even though we were sad for him and wished you'd wanted to stay."

I could see that the power of what she'd said was a surprise even to her, like a mouse darting into the room. That was what it came down to, what it always comes down to, a choice as stark as death, even when you dress it up with psychology

and history and evolutionary biology: you want to stay or you
don't. And what I mean about the mouse was that the three of
us went silent and our eyes teared up almost in unison, because Susanna had spoken so plainly — about all of us. We
had retreated from Will, had kept our distance, had taken for
granted that there would be time another time to apologize or
reminisce or be friendly and maybe even be friends.

"There's another time," I said. "It wasn't the last time I saw
Will, but it was the last time he saw me." I could see bewilder-
ment on everyone's face except Henderson's, who merely
looked surprised that I had begun down this path. I knew I
didn't have to tell this story, but there were so many things I'd
kept to myself, I had to make a clean breast of this, to err on
the side of the truth this time. I didn't need to introduce Crystal here, but I believed I owed them a little more of myself.

"After he died," I began, "his friend Diane told me that he
had gone to New York at the end of May to see me. He had
told me on the phone that he wanted to come, and I'd dis-
couraged him. It seems he came anyway, a day or two after we
talked about the money he owed me, and he saw me on the
street with a man I know. I didn't see him. Apparently he left
the city right after he saw me and drove his motorcycle to
Cambridge to tell Diane what he'd seen. He came back to
Swansea the next day. Probably died a day or two after that."

When neither of them said anything, I feared I had made
the wrong decision, said too much. "Was the man your boyfriend?" Susanna said finally. "The father of the little girl who
was missing?"

"How did you know?"

"I heard her message on the answering machine," Ginny
said. "I didn't realize it at first, but when you called the police
and her father from here, we guessed."

"I didn't think you'd want to know."

"It wasn't the biggest surprise in the world," Ginny said, though I was sure I heard their disapproval in the silence that followed, the sting of betrayal, picking up where their father left off. But when I looked from one to the other, I saw them trading a look I'd call a shrugging of the eyes: *Well, why not?* "We talked to Daddy's lawyer this morning," Susanna said in a serious tone, with an air of confession about it. "He knew Daddy hadn't signed the final separation agreement, which means you're still married. He told us that means you can file a claim against the estate. And you'd probably get something."

"What did the lawyer advise you to do?" I asked my step-daughters. If they were as old as I, they would have known not to answer; they would have known not to mention any of this, not to reveal their hand. But now their nonchalance about my love life made more sense. They couldn't afford to be openly outraged, even if what I'd done had led to Will's death, because they didn't want to alienate me, not if they believed I could make a claim on the estate.

"He advised us to give you a gift."

"Like the house for the summer?" So it was a bribe, not a present, letting me spend the summer in the house in which my husband had died, maybe killed himself.

"That was Mom's idea. She thought two months on Swansea would be enough of a gift to —" Ginny paused, maybe coming up against a word she did not want to admit, or not knowing the word.

"Placate me?"

"Would someone give me a hand here?" Clare called out, pushing her shoulder into the swinging door, bringing forth a wooden tray of filled coffee cups and a pie whose crusty top was seared with a Zorro-like Z.

"Here's Mom and apple pie," Ginny said and stood to take the tray from her and place it on the table.

"*Warmed* apple pie," Clare boasted. "That's what I've been doing in there: stoking the fire. Why was I so sure this house came with a microwave? I could've sworn the rental agent told me it did. Just as well. I couldn't have used it with the aluminum pie tin." Now I saw all her manipulations through the most piercing lens, including her collapsing in my arms at the door and putting on this lavish spread.

Henderson, I was certain, did, too. "Clare, you've gone to such trouble to heat it up," he said. "The least I can do is run to the deli down the street and get some vanilla ice cream. It'll be three minutes. You all start. Just save me a piece."

"It's not necessary," Clare said. "I'd hate to —"

"In my family it's sacrilege to eat naked apple pie. Besides, I'm going on a serious diet as soon as I finish this meal, and I want to go out with a bang." And he was gone from the room and through the foyer, leaving me to ride these rough seas alone. I heard the front door click shut. Andy returned to the table, Susanna held out her arms to her child, and the rest of us poured milk and sugar into our coffee. Clare, the mother superior, was the only one who didn't know which confidences had been breached.

"Sophy, will you wait for ice cream or —"

"I'll have a piece now," I said.

"Me too," Ginny said, coming to an awkward full stop, aware that she and her sister might have said too much.

"I'll wait," Susanna said, with that same nervous full stop after her order.

"I'll have a piece now and a piece with ice cream," affable Andy said, and pasted on a showy smile for Clare.

"Sophy, while the pie was heating up," Clare said, cutting seven neat pieces, "I was remembering the first time I met Will, and I wondered what your first memory of him was."

"Honeysuckle Road, out on the West End of the island. In

Blueberry Parfait. I was hitchhiking, and he picked me up in the old Bug. What's yours?"

"Mom, we told Sophy what Daddy's lawyer said this morning," Ginny said, "that we should give her a gift. That you came up with the idea about the house."

All we heard for a while was two or three people sipping coffee, noisily rearranging spoons on saucers. I could have made the silence vanish by telling them what my lawyer had told me — that my winning wasn't certain — or even that I was not inclined to file a claim, but I enjoyed seeing Clare squirm. Her smile had turned to stone, her nostalgia to dust, and her apple pie had been ruined by unsavory revelations. Worst of all, her daughters were wavering in their loyalty. Or so it must have seemed. She gaped at Ginny and would not meet my eye. I figured Ginny was getting back at Clare for her earlier rudeness. Maybe Ginny and Susanna really did want to lay everything on the table and do what was right by me. Or maybe they wanted to do everything they could to avoid a struggle over the estate.

"Mom, don't make a production out of it," Ginny said. "We're not fighting over the future of Microsoft."

But the gravity of the next silence made it feel as if we were.

"Maybe the best thing," Andy said finally, Andy who cared nothing for money and things, who had no use for phones or electricity, whose love of nature wasn't a matter of seasonal good taste, a vase of wildflowers on the dining room table, and a copy of Thoreau's *Cape Cod* in the bathroom, Andy, who had said almost nothing for the last two days and now piped up at the most awkward moment. "Maybe the best thing would be to ask Sophy what she thinks is fair, instead of playing some fucked-up chess game with her that she doesn't even know she's playing. She was the one still married to him."

The fucked-up chess game was a particularly nice touch; I

wished Henderson was there to hear it and to see Clare wince, her lips pucker as if she'd sucked a lemon. But I hoped she wouldn't ask me right away, because I had no idea what would be fair.

"For God's sake, Mom, lighten up," said Ginny, herself not always as light as meringue.

"Maybe Sophy hasn't thought about the legal stuff yet," Susanna said. "Have you, Soph?" Dear, sweet, guileless Susanna, who lived like Goldilocks in the woods without a microwave or a modem.

"I'm in the middle of a divorce," I said, but not unkindly, "and some of this has crossed my mind. And my lawyer's mind." Clare was staring at me as if I held a dagger in my hand, instead of a forkful of apple pie. "She's doing some research, and I'll talk to her in the next few days."

"That makes a world of sense to me," Clare said. I knew she didn't mean it; I knew she'd rather hear that I was as naïve as Susanna and content with no more than the house for the summer.

"To me too," I said.

All of us were still, so when we heard the front door open and Henderson call out, "The Good Humor Man is back," the dining room filled with relief, with oxygen, with another subject than this. "They were all out of vanilla," Henderson said at the entranceway, "so I ended up with Chunky Monkey and Wavy Gravy."

"I'm afraid I've lost my appetite," Clare announced and got up from the table with a sigh, a baroque display of regret, Clinton rising from the table at which Barak and Arafat had failed to make peace, and brushed past Henderson toward the foyer. We said nothing as we listened to hear where she was going next. Up the stairs, down the hallway. A door clicked shut somewhere.

"What did I miss?" Henderson said.

"We sent her to her room for some 'time out,'" Andy said, and we laughed and then tried to stifle our laughter and then quit trying. It was a great relief to give in to it, after days of pent-up grief and guilt and reasonably good behavior. It felt delicious, this sudden chorus of hilarity, laughing before long at our laughing. I was afraid the raucousness would bring Clare downstairs and we would have to explain what was so funny.

But she did not appear. We settled down and ate most of the pie and all the ice cream, and I told the girls what I had not wanted to say in front of Clare. "I'd like to stay in the house."

"Good."

"The more difficult subject —" I stopped and began again, properly this time. "You'd have no way of knowing this, but I agreed to leave the marriage with nothing, because I didn't want to make the separation any more painful for your father than it already was. But I never imagined we'd end up in permanent legal limbo, almost married and almost divorced. I'm not eager to file a claim against the estate, but I can't walk away from this with my dollar and" — I started to say "let bygones be bygones" — when Ginny interrupted.

"We didn't know any of this," she said, "but we were planning to give you some of the insurance money when it comes. Mommy wanted us to start with the house for the summer and see how you felt about that."

I was too surprised to say anything, surprised by the stand I'd taken, by the rush of words that had come out of my mouth on my behalf. And surprised that my stepdaughters were going to defy their father's will — and probably their mother's — and give me a share of their inheritance.

This was not exactly a happy ending, but it soothed me as

nothing had before. Not the money, mind you — I didn't care how much it was — but the thought. The thought that I hadn't been dismissed, discarded, nullified by all of them.

I said thank you too many times, but only because I didn't want to say more and end up sounding sappy, too *Tuesday Mornings with Morrie,* because I knew their good will and their consideration would help me get through tomorrow. I would need everything I could summon of myself to wake up tomorrow and go to Will's funeral, and, when it was over, to my lawyer, and later in the week, to see Daniel and his children without the comfort of my old costumes. Then I knew I had to sit down and write the story I have just told you, and I was growing more certain that the best place to begin it, and the only place it made sense for me to dwell right now, was the house I had fled three months before.

That night, when Henderson and I returned to the Lighthouse Motel and adjourned to our adjoining rooms, I sat at the Formica table and turned on Will's tangerine laptop, a simple gesture, though it felt like opening a coffin lid. The diary contained no suicide plan. I knew I didn't need to fear finding that. Then why subject myself to more of it? Because I intended to give the computer to his daughters the following day and had to decide how candid to be about the diary; I was the one who knew the password, after all. I wanted to know what else was there before I let them have it; whether he had written anything upsetting about the two of them.

The file opened to a one-sentence entry dated December 8, when Will and I were still together, when he had no idea of the depth of my unhappiness. I don't know why the file opened to that entry, but I had not seen it before, and I turned my head the instant I finished reading it: *I would have killed myself ten years ago if it had not been for Sophy's love.*

THE GARDEN

August is one of the quietest months in the garden, matched in some ways only by the deepest winter months. But whereas in those months Nature seems bound in a deep sleep, in August she appears to be merely in a daydream, or perhaps a gentle doze.

— Joe Eck and Wayne Winterrowd,
*A Year at North Hill: Four Seasons
in a Vermont Garden*

15

A Happy Ending

I T IS NOT a manicured English garden nor the rambunc-
tious, wild place in *The Secret Garden* that meant so much
to Vicki. It is a garden that purists would frown on, because I did not plant it myself. I did not design it. What I like
to do best is look at it, either from the kitchen, through the
sliding glass doors, or in the yard, where the children and I
spent much of the last week, or from the nursery upstairs — I
still think of it as the nursery — where I set up my desk with
a view of it, and where I write now. The bee balm, the asters,
the marigolds. The heirloom roses and snapdragons. A garden
at last.

With Ginny and Susanna's blessing, and a bit of the money
they gave me from the life insurance, I hired an imaginative
landscaper from Island Design to do everything. Since it was
late in the summer by the time he started, mid-July, I had him
plant flowers already in bloom. I know that is cheating at a
very high level. It may as well be a stage set, a shopping mall,
my own Potemkin Village. Why didn't I just stick plastic
flowers into the ground like birthday candles on a cake, you're
probably wondering, and plan instead for next year? I thought
about it.

But next year is a long way off, and since Will died, I have
been afflicted with that common response to death, *carpe
diem*. Until it happens to you, you have no idea what form it
will take, which days you'll want to seize and which you'd
rather do without. And of course it's a metaphor; you can't
clutch a day the way you can an umbrella, a steering wheel, a
book. The saying implores you to seize your pleasure, seize the
pleasures of the world while they are still available to you.

In this spirit, this effort to live in the moment, not the spi-
ral of the past or the maze of the purely speculative, I recently
gave up thinking it is essential to have all the answers: How
precisely did Will die? How did the dog end up the way he
did? And why did I get a telegram from a man Will had
known in Manila even before the obituaries were published? I
wrote to the man, Arthur Glass, to thank him for his condolences and ask how he had found out before everyone else. I
don't expect an answer from him — he's a spy, after all — but
when I wrote two months ago, I still felt that if I didn't learn
the answer, if it existed somewhere in the world and I could
not seize it, know it, pull it from the sky like a helium balloon
on a string, I would never have a moment's peace. Some days,
speaking of days, it's touch and go, but other days I think I
might.

The day the coroner's report came back, two weeks after the
funeral, was not a good day. *Cause of Death: Inconclusive*. It's
funny how that's being the last word doesn't mean you stop
thinking about it. It means only that you're one of the few left
thinking about it.

Today, six weeks later, one of the last days of August, is a
much better day. First thing after breakfast, Vicki and Cam
watered the garden. Tran and Van bicycled up and down the
street. We went grocery shopping and to the beach for many

hours. When we got home, Daniel phoned, as he has done every day, from London, and the children lined up to speak to him. They all reported that they were still having a good time, after five days here, and three out of four asked why they can't live on Swansea, because there are more things for kids to do here than in New York. Then we had a cookout, as we've had every night since they arrived, with toasted marshmallows on sticks for dessert. Putting them to sleep after so much sunshine is a cinch; they long for the bed, they collapse onto it like actors doing pratfalls. Boom, down, and they're out.

Tonight moths hurl themselves against the screens. Maple leaves and oak and sycamore on long branches sway and rustle like distant waves crashing against the shore. The night is thick and lovely, the children are asleep upstairs, the wind is warm, and I am at the kitchen table with the early pages of the story I have just told you, when I hear a soft skittering noise. A squirrel on the roof? I go back to my pages, so when I hear Vicki's voice across the room, at the foot of the stairs, I start. Her eyes are the color of ebony and as bright as a cat's. "I had a bad dream" is all she says.

When I open my arms, she comes to me. Her hair smells of baby shampoo and her skin faintly of salt, of long days in ocean water. She's wearing Lion King theme pajamas, the summer model, with all the beasts of the jungle emblazoned on her narrow chest. "What happened in your dream?" She folds herself onto my lap, and to me, her bad dream, her needing me, the feel of her hair against my cheek, the pulse of her heartbeat against my palm, are bliss.

"When I got to my house, there was no one there. And everything was gone. I opened the front door, and there were no rooms, no floors, no ceiling, only air and the sky on top of it."

"Where was everyone?"

"I think they were in Haiti with Toinette."

In real life, Toinette, their housekeeper-nanny, is in Haiti; that's why the children are with me in Will's house. Daniel had a business trip to London planned for some time when Toinette's mother died suddenly and she had to go back to the island. There aren't many people you can ask to take care of your four young children for five days. You are desperate. You ask your former lover. You ask *me,* the woman one of your kids pretended to run away to. I did not hesitate for an instant before I said yes. He made me an offer I couldn't refuse, and I made him one: the children could spend the last week of August on Swansea. Tomorrow morning he'll fly into Boston from London and take an Island Air flight here to pick them up.

It has been two months since Will was found dead. Two days after the funeral, I returned briefly to New York to collect some belongings, pay my bills, and tell Daniel I could not keep doing what we had done before. I was surprised at his surprise. "But you always seemed to enjoy yourself," he said.

"It was starting to feel a little thin."

"How so?"

"Watery."

His brow furrowed in puzzlement.

"Lacking nourishment."

"I'm not sure I understand what you're getting at."

"I want to be with someone who loves me."

"I didn't imagine that would be important so soon after your separation. I assumed you'd want to sow a few wild oats. I never could understand why you chose someone in my position."

Sitting now with Vicki on my lap, I shudder to think of how oblivious he was; how thoroughly he had misread me; and how thin his feelings for me had been. I shudder on my behalf and also on his children's. When they tell him they have bad dreams, does he have any idea what they mean? Does he know they *have* meaning? Is he aware that they matter?

I say to Vicki, "Would you like to be in Haiti with Toinette?" She shakes her head against my neck. "How about London with your dad?"

"Maybe a little."

"Vietnam?"

She takes a long time to answer and sounds grown-up when she does. "I'll wait until I'm older."

"Will you be sad to leave Swansea tomorrow?"

There is a distinct nod, different from a shake of the head, against my shoulder, but no words.

"Everyone is sad when they have to leave here," I say. "People write books about Swansea, because it's so beautiful."

"Is that what your book is about?"

"That's some of it."

"Will it have pictures?"

"It's not that kind of book."

"What kind of book is it?"

Her head leans tenderly on my shoulder. We are speaking softly, like lovers; my arms encircle her arms, like lovers'; and I am uncertain about how to explain it to a child, even this child, who knows so much, who has lost two mothers, a father in Vietnam, God knows how many biological siblings, her country, her language, the date and year of her birth, her entire history. When I don't answer right away, she slings another question at me: "Just tell me this: is it going to have a happy ending?"

The predictable ending I've been considering is Will's funeral. So, no, not particularly happy. But as funerals go, Will's
was dull, much duller than the man himself, presided over by
a doddering, pious Boston Irishman. I don't mean to sound
flippant, but it did have the flavor of a parody, of the wrong
man's funeral. The coffin — I call it Clare's coffin, since she
picked it out and paid five thousand dollars for it — was a
piece of Mafia-rococo furniture, a bronze finish with silver
buckles and miniature marble caryatids in which I knew Will
would not want to spend eternity. But there he was on the cat-
afalque, in Clare's Cadillac, about to be buried next to his son
in an old island cemetery. I sat between Henderson and our
neighbor Ben in the second row, behind my stepdaughters
and their mother, and cried quietly, except when the priest
was actually talking about Will, because everything he said
had an "as told to" quality. It didn't feel like Will distilled; it
felt like Will watered down, a dim Xerox of the man. He was
hardly there.

When it was my turn, I read two poems, the Emily Dickinson that begins, *That it will never come again/is what makes life
so sweet,* and Henderson's gift of Paul Muldoon's "The Birth,"
about his daughter's first moments in the world. When I
spoke for a few minutes after I read, about Will's love of
Swansea, about our meeting on Honeysuckle Road, about
how game he always was, I found myself looking over the audience for Crystal and was disappointed not to see her, although there was no reason to expect I would. Our encounter
the day before had brought something to a close for me, and I
entertained a brief fantasy that it had for her, too. But for her,
it was probably more bad news about her own life: no relief,
no illumination. She had caused someone in bad shape a lot of
pain; that's all. Chances are she was trying to forget about it. I

didn't have that luxury. What I had was that haunting line from Will's diary, which I had shared only with Henderson, and I went back and forth on how to interpret it, like someone pulling the petals of a daisy. He loves me, he loves me not. I saved him, I let him go, I saved him, I killed him, I loved him, I should have loved him longer, I left him, I shouldn't have, if I hadn't he'd be alive, but then again he might not be. *Cause of Death: Inconclusive.* The answer is that there will be no answer, ever. My love may be what kept him alive ten years ago, but would my devotion have done as much for the next ten years? Crystal had no reason to come to his funeral, but in front of me were forty or forty-five people who had cared about him. They were here because of his decency, good humor, and adventurousness. The sadness and fragility were not what he showed the world.

"Well," Vicki says again, this time more sharply, "will it or won't it have a happy ending?"

In lieu of the funeral, I've considered ending the book with my phone call to the Eighth Deadly when I returned to New York for those few days after the funeral. I told him I wouldn't write the autobiography of Bill and Melinda Gates's nanny. I told him it was time for me to quit being a ghost writer, and told myself I had to quit being second-in-command, the interpreter and inheritor of other people's lives, the second wife, the stepmother, the mimic. I had to tell my own story, not everyone else's. I wanted to dwell in my own ragged, insolvent, unkempt life, and I wanted to seize all the days I could.

That is too complicated to explain to a child, even one as precocious as Vicki, but I start in anyway. I stop talking halfway through the first sentence, when I see I am being as oblivious of her needs as Daniel was of mine. She had a bad dream, and all she wants to know — all any of us want to know — is that there will be a happy ending, despite all the evidence to the contrary.

"Of course there will be," I tell her. "No question about it."

And who's to say that the two of us, entwined on a wooden armchair in this house that used to be mine on this beautiful late summer night, this child who has lost as much as she has, and I — you know my story — who's to say that this is not it?